BLOOD UNDER THE BRIDGE

BLOOD
UNDER
THE
BRIDGE

Bruce Zimmerman

1817

Harper & Row, Publishers, New York

Cambridge, Philadelphia, San Francisco

London, Mexico City, São Paulo, Singapore, Sydney

FIRST EDITION

Designed by Karen Savary

Library of Congress Cataloging-in-Publication Data

Zimmerman, Bruce.
  Blood under the bridge.

  I. Title.
PS3576.I48B5   1989   813'.54   88-43005
ISBN 0-06-016087-X

---

89 90 91 92 93 AC/RRD 10 9 8 7 6 5 4 3 2 1

For my mother and father

My mother killed me,
My father ated me,
My sister pickit my banes
And laid me atween twa marble stanes—
And noo I've grown intae a little white dove
To fly ower the fields of Airlie.

—CHILDREN'S RHYME FROM DUNDEE

1

I N ANY OTHER CITY it would've been called rain. It was wet and cold and it came down from the sky in drops and if you collected enough of it you could brew coffee. But the announcer on the car radio had already assured me otherwise. What was streaming down the windshield of my van and dripping from the street signs and making old ladies dash for cover was, in his deep, calm, comforting voice, "heavy fog."

I caught the red light at Van Ness and Vallejo and sat drumming my fingers on the steering wheel as the wipers went thump-thump-thump and the defrost huffed and puffed to maintain visibility.

Heavy fog . . .

I took a deep breath and let it go. This wasn't the morning to get irritated with San Francisco's compulsive need to be characteristic. My ribs were hurting, and soon I would be having breakfast with the woman who could yet be *the* woman, and if the beleaguered Bay Area population inching to work in overpriced cars from overpriced condos to the land of No Free Parking needed a little embellishment or two, well then . . . yes, Virginia, there *is* a city where rain is fog, where Porsches are imperative, and where a big earthquake will never topple all the glistening toys into the Pacific Ocean one fine, bright day.

My ribs hurt because of a defect in my personality; a defect that insists keeping in shape should be more dramatic than twenty push-ups, twenty sit-ups, and a few sweaty miles down some forlorn jogging path. This defect led me to Newman's, a boxing gym in the heart of the Tenderloin where young, tough, hungry fighters feed on a diet of white, thirtyish dabblers like me.

The light changed and I continued up Van Ness, poking a cautious finger between this rib and that to see if maybe something was broken. Goddamn Roscoe. I'd sparred with him before and he'd always gone easy with me, practicing against my superior height and hand speed, letting me tag him now and then and only throwing an occasional patty-cake punch in return. But this morning he'd forgotten himself. Suddenly he'd just made an awfully uncomfortable boat trip from Africa and I was the blond, smiling, blue-eyed demon who'd auctioned off his frightened wife and kids to a jeering, lecherous crowd and *wham!*—the shred of inherited memory had turned his fists to granite and his eyes red-black furious and he'd stretched me out on the canvas with one bone-crushing hook to the ribs.

It would make a decent over-breakfast story. Sonia would laugh, Hank and Carol would shake their heads at such foolishness, and then—if the heavy fog would quit pouring from the skies—we'd all drive out to Stinson

Beach as planned for some salt air and sandy sandwiches.

I swung right onto Union Street and found a parking space directly in front of my apartment building. Home is 1464A Union Street, top floor, the "A" distinguishing it from the "B," "C," and "D" that make up the rest of the building. A restored Victorian, full of turrets and carvings and bay windows, blue and white and fresh as a sea breeze. A little heavy on the quaint, but there was nothing I could do about that.

You have to work to get to my apartment. Six steps up from the sidewalk, key in the door, and then you're looking at another set of stairs, thirty-six if you bother to count, that stretch up and away from the first-time visitor like some heavy-handed symbol of endlessness in a foreign film. Tackle the thirty-six and it's still not over. A small landing, turn 180 degrees, go up another dozen steps, and you're there. With two sacks of groceries it's not fun, but once you're up, you're up. With the fire banked and the curtains drawn, the crowded, jangled city is light years away. You could be anywhere. In frictionless space, drifting slowly toward the moon.

I went straight to the kitchen, poured a large glass of orange juice, and killed it while straddling the end chair of the dining table. I was trying to figure out what had shocked me more: Roscoe's left hook or my finding a parking space right in front of the building. I weighed the issue for several anxious moments and then decided on the parking space.

The dining room occupies the northwest corner of the building, and what you can see from the window is what doubles the rent—the Golden Gate Bridge, Marin Headlands, a long sweep of the bay, Angel Island, and, if you stand in the corner and crane, Alcatraz.

I gave the window a couple of minutes and then headed

down the hallway. My four-bedroom apartment forms a kind of inverted L as it faces the street. Bedrooms one and two form the base of the L, both with windows overlooking Union Street. The long stem of the L holds bedrooms three and four, the bathroom, and the living room.

Six months ago I converted bedroom two into the world headquarters of Amalgamated Tropical Enterprises, Inc., of which I am the founder, president, chief executive officer, and—when the trash basket is full—janitor. My telephone answering machine showed two calls. The first, as I expected, was from Andrew Baxley.

"Quinn. This is Andrew Baxley. About that thing we talked about. I've been thinking it over and maybe we should hold off awhile. I . . . well, let me know what you think."

The second call, as I also suspected, was from Andrew Baxley.

"Jesus, Quinn. I don't know what the hell to do." Nervous laughter. "Is this normal? Maybe we don't call it off. I'm going around in circles."

The machine clicked off. I stared up at Oscar the parrot, sitting in his cage in full early-morning plumage, looking good and knowing it. Oscar was a scarlet macaw I'd brought back from Guatemala ten years ago, and there was a decent chance he'd outlive me. When Quinn Parker's dust is resting in a box somewhere, Oscar will still be spreading his wings in the San Francisco sunshine. It made me think of him differently than I would a goldfish.

"Poor Mr. Baxley," I said to Oscar. "How vain and vile a passion is fear."

Oscar hates it when I quote Ben Jonson. He turned around and showed his backside and I decided to get on with the breakfast. Andrew Baxley wasn't the only one with hesitation on his mind. I had a vain and vile passion of my own. She was standing—or sleeping—about five miles away. I grabbed my Windbreaker and headed down the stairs.

Hank and Carol live on Woodland Avenue, out behind the University Medical Center, so I swung by there first. Hank was waiting outside the house, huddled against the rain, listening with pained expression as an intense young man spoke and gestured at the sidewalk with a bony, fanatical finger.

I gave the horn a blast. Hank looked up, focused, then broke into a run across the street.

"Thanks a lot," he said, settling in and slapping the rain from his jacket. "You really pick your times to be late."

"Where's Carol?"

"Can't come. Matty's got a fever and she took him to the doctor."

I nodded my head at the guy on the sidewalk. "Who's your friend?"

"Shocking news." Hank pursed his lips and looked gravely at the dashboard. "Shocking, shocking news. I doubt you know this. Only ten minutes ago I didn't either, but Kennedy's brain . . . it's alive and throbbing and the Russians have kidnapped it."

"No kidding?"

Hank nodded grimly. "They smuggled it out of the hospital in Dallas and transplanted it into another person. Now it's full of truth serum and babbling all our nuclear secrets."

"How come I'm not shocked?"

"Because you worship false gods. I asked if the brain was

sticking to the nuclear stuff, or whether the Russians were getting any juicy details about Marilyn Monroe."

"And?"

"He didn't know." Hank raised a portentous finger. "But the possibility concerned him very, very much."

Hank Wilkie was, chronologically, my oldest friend in life. He stood about five foot eight and gave the impression of frailty until you saw him up close. Then you could see how solid he was. His light brown hair didn't have a trace of curl, and the first hints of a receding hairline were making inroads. He had a strong jaw, soft blue eyes, and might've been called handsome but for the judgmental scowl that too often settled on his face. Hank's goal in life was to be a stand-up comedian. In the old days it was up to me to be sure he had shelter, clothing, food, and a library card, but now he was married and the father of two little boys. Champion of the underdog, closet cultural anthropologist, and a 95-percent shooter from the free-throw line, Hank was currently having his problems reconciling the economic uncertainties of comedy with the nuts-and-bolts responsibilities of fatherhood.

I got going west on Geary, made an illegal left on Nineteenth Avenue, and passed through Golden Gate Park. Empty and rainy and green. Traffic plugged up as the commuter crowd eased along slickened streets, headlights flickering in the morning gloom.

"Hell of a day for the beach," Hank said.

"So we find a bargain matinee."

Hank nodded and kept his eyes closed. He was a night person, a shutter-downer of bars, a watcher of late-late movies. Eight-thirty in the morning was strange and uncharted territory for him, and despite the alarming news of JFK's kidnapped brain, Hank's mouth slowly came open and his head lolled to one side and and he was back in the land of leaping sheep.

The traffic was bad. Corporate up-and-comers driving bank-owned Mercedes leaned on their horns and geared up for another anxiety-ridden day of keeping it in the black.

I knew the feeling well. Five years of my own life had been spent with nose to the financial district grindstone, but no more. One sunny Saturday morning several Aprils ago while helping a friend repair a roof down in Redwood City, the brand-new power drill I was fiddling with blew up in my hands. Nothing serious—some ligament damage in my left hand that prevented me from making a particular kind of fist, and a metal fragment that caught my right eye and temporarily added another zero to my twenty-twenty.

But the company that manufactured the power drill had just been getting up a head of steam, making money, elbowing competitors aside, buying Super Bowl airtime, watching all the little lines on all the little graphs in all the little regional headquarters going up, up, up. They were also figuring ways to cut corners, and I was a victim of one of those cuts. So we settled out of court for what lawyers like to call "the low six figures." A stockbroker friend suggested I sink as much as I could into a struggling young firm in Menlo Park—a tiny, futuristic laboratory with an unpronounceable name where men in white smocks and the dream of social biology in their eyes tinkered around trying to reproduce certain rare chemicals of the body in large quanties. Genetic engineering, my friend had called it. Couldn't miss. I sank the money in. I don't commute anymore.

In a few minutes I was through the Golden Gate jam-up and swinging right on Ortega Street, down the long, gradual asphalt slope leading to the Pacific Ocean. The movement woke Hank up. He snorted, sat up straight, rubbed his face awake.

"So how was last night with Sonia?" he said. "You didn't get all sweaty and Biblical, did you?"

"We ate popcorn and drank a bottle of wine and watched a Fred Astaire movie on her new VCR. Is that wild enough for you?"

"Popcorn and wine?" he said, making a face.

"That's right."

"And Fred Astaire?"

"You got it."

Hank groaned and hugged himself against the innate wonderfulness of the image. He was a New Yorker and had what could politely be called a "troubled" relationship with California. Popcorn, wine, and Fred Astaire had that studied, West Coast feel of a Spontaneous Good Time.

"Let me guess," he went on. "The popcorn wasn't a brand name, was it?"

"No idea."

"I'll ask Sonia. Five bucks says it came from a micro-biotic commune of moon pilgrims."

"It was awfully good popcorn."

"And the wine . . . had to be red."

"Had to be."

Hank tapped his finger to his nose. "Probably from a small vineyard . . . Sonoma County rather than Napa . . . an obscure-enough label and odd-enough variety so you could kind of feel like the wine was your own special discovery. How am I doing?"

"Touché," I said. "The relentless Wilkie eye once again

exposes the phony underbelly of the San Francisco good life."

"That's why the Fathers sent me out here." He yawned. "Just make sure you behave yourself with Sonia. She cried on my shoulder three weeks the last time you guys broke up."

I couldn't blame Hank for his suspicions. I'd met Sonia Lucia about a year ago at a party in Berkeley. How I came to be there I've long since forgotten, but the party was held at the apartment of a Scandinavian studies major. Pale people with pink lips sat in little groups, jabbering Finnish at one another. Dreadful Swedish folk music scree-scrawed out of the stereo, and I spent most of the evening wandering around with a Dixie cup of authentic Danish punch, looking at maps of Nordic countries tacked to the walls, and wondering why I was spending one of the twenty-five thousand or so nights we have allocated on earth doing this.

I was in the middle of calculating that I had roughly ten thousand down, fifteen thousand to go, when a young woman appeared at my side. She was medium height, olive-skinned, with full lips, dreamy dark eyes, and a Medusa-like avalanche of thick black hair that cascaded to the middle of her back. She looked out of place amidst all the paleness—a smoldering poster girl for "Visit Brazil."

We chatted awkwardly for a while. She was, in fact, from Rio de Janeiro but had lived in the United States most of her life. After a particularly deadening silence, she brushed back her hair and said, "I checked the back door. It's unlocked."

"Is that good or bad?" I'd said.

"Do you have a getaway car?"

"Full tank and the engine's idling."

She smiled and looked up at me with frank, confident eyes. "Then it's good, wouldn't you say?"

So it was that Sonia Lucia entered my life. We ditched the midnight sun motif and headed back into San Francisco for ribs at Leon's and an après-barbecue bottle of wine down at the Marina. Dangled legs over the wharf, told each other our life stories, filled and refilled the paper cups, concluded we had nothing in common and no future together, and bought another bottle of wine.

A year ago. Three-hundred sixty-five more nights had since clicked off the nocturnal timer. The first half of them had been shared with Sonia. The second half wondering why the first half had fizzled out.

Wondering why . . .

I didn't have to wonder that hard. "You must accept me as I am," Sonia had said on more than one occasion. Reasonable enough, except that "as she was" stretched the known boundaries of heedlessness with each passing week. She operated entirely on impulse: drinking, loving, disappearing for days at a time. A trailblazing pilgrim on the frontiers of unreliability, and, alas, eventually Sonia Lucia wore me down. Once a philosopher, twice a pervert, though if twice became thrice . . . *c'est la vie.*

So, at the six-month mark I'd said good-bye. Gathered up my ethical knickknacks, put them in my bag, and retreated to the migraine-making world of problematic monogamy, dos and don'ts, little square pegs of moral propriety that I insisted on trying to hammer through small round holes that were getting smaller all the time.

We had remained friends, as per the era. Got together now and then to do this and that, and I watched Sonia from a distance. And the more I watched, the more I wondered if I hadn't blown it. In a world of timidity and bet-hedging, Sonia had tremendous appeal, excessive as she was. And so it had stayed until last night. Last night had hinted at a change in the order of things. . . .

The rain had slackened off a bit by the time we reached Sonia's building on Ortega and Twenty-third. I rang the buzzer to her apartment. Waited. Hank leaned up against the wall, arms folded.

"How late did Mr. Astaire keep the two of you up?"

"One-thirty."

Hank made a face. "You stayed up till one-thirty and still went boxing this morning?"

"Creature of habit."

"Creature of bad habit."

I rang the bell again. Waited again. Hank refolded his arms across his chest and sighed. "How often have you known Sonia to stay up past one and even be semiconscious to answer a doorbell at eight-thirty the next morning?"

I shrugged. "First time for everything."

"No. For some things there is never a first time. Let's go up."

I let us in with the key that had been given me in honor of my role as Feeder of the Cat whenever Sonia was away. We climbed the stairs to the second-floor apartment, and Hank went into the kitchen to get some coffee going while I headed down the hall to wake up Sonia. The door was cracked a few inches. Her bare foot was outside the sheet on the edge of the bed.

I was reluctant to push open the door and barge in. The thought of a nude Sonia, sprawling in the warm vulnerability of slumber, was not an image I wanted to confuse my virtuous self with just now. I went back out to the kitchen.

"She up?" Hank said.

"No."

We silently watched the coils turn molten red beneath the coffeepot.

"Are you going to wake her up," Hank said, "or do we hang around here till noon waiting?"

"I can't just stroll into her bedroom."

"You can't?"

"No."

Hank hesitated. Together we watched the coils get redder. "Why not?"

"I'm not her husband, for Christ's sake."

"Her 'husband'?" Hank said. "You didn't let that distinction get in your way about a year ago."

"It's in my way now."

"Okay," Hank said. "I pronounce you man and wife for the next ten minutes. Wait. Make that thirty seconds." Hank scooped the coffee beans from the plastic container. In his haste a dozen little brown beans spilled and slid across the drainboard and down the crack behind the stove, off to Never-Never Land, food for ants. "Goddamn coffee! Now get in there and wake her up!"

Thirty-second marriage or not, it was too intimate, too real. The kiss she had given me at the door last night was merely an overture, not a blank check to rustle her naked body out of bed whenever the feeling came over me. I'd have to . . . make an entrance. Yes, that was it. I'd be Fred Astaire, kicking open the door and singing the morning in, twirling her toward the bathroom and imploring her in a melodic way to brush her teeth and get her butt in gear. I got down on the kitchen floor and started going through the bottom cupboards.

"What are you doing?" Hank said.

"Have you seen a serving tray?"

"A what?"

"Never mind. Here it is." I pulled out the floral-patterned breakfast tray and set it on the drainboard.

Hank shut his eyes and shook his head. "I have a bad feeling about this."

"Coffee ready?"

"If I didn't have to grind the stupid . . . !"

I went into the living room and got Sonia's miniature tape player and rummaged around through her mountain of cassettes till a suitable Fred Astaire soundtrack presented itself. Then I plucked a flower from her planter box and went back into the kitchen. Hank grimaced. His worst fears had been confirmed.

"I should have stuck with Kennedy's brain."

I set the flower on the tray and began fast-forwarding the cassette to get it ready on the right song. "Isn't the coffee ready yet?"

"Would you knock it off about the coffee!" he said, throwing his hands in the air. "If I didn't have to practically go down to goddamn South America and pick the frigging beans myself we'd be drinking it right now! Shovel, grind, filter, refrigerate, clean. . . . Whatever happened to instant coffee? Open the jar, stick in the spoon . . ."

I located the song, "Night and Day," put the tape player on the tray next to the flower, and poured a cup of Hank's hard-wrought coffee. Then I added a spoon, bowl of sugar, and small serving pitcher of cream.

"Back in a second," I said, balancing the tray on my right hand. "Check the paper and see about movies."

Hank gave up his coffee speech and, mumbling under his breath, disappeared into the living room. The coffee cup was too full for me to do the half-skip into the bedroom I'd intended. A glide would have to suffice. I went down the hall and nudged the door open with my knee and peeked in. Sonia's foot was where I'd left it. I turned on the tape, adjusted the volume, and waited while the orchestra scratchily led up to Fred and Ginger's entrance. Then I kicked the door open and breezed into the room.

I slammed against the wall, and the tray crashed to the floor. All around me the room roared, and when the roaring stopped there was no sound on earth but Fred and Ginger twirling each other through a sparkling world of gardens and gazebos and harmless, happy people. . . .

And at my feet the flower I had plucked rested gently afloat a pool of dark, arterial blood.

2

S OMETIMES THE SHOCK absorbers work too well. By anybody's mental yardstick, the scene in Sonia's bedroom should have launched me well into a life of gentle and complacent crayon-chewing. But my brain had already shaken off the blow and resumed its job of identifying *that* as a leg, *that* as a head, *this* as a shallow lake of cool, thick blood. It isn't right that we cope so well. We bend too far without breaking.

What used to be Sonia was in bed, on her back, nude. Her head had been severed and rearranged on her torso so that the face was buried in the pillow. On backwards. A ghastly human doll yanked apart and reassembled by a madman.

But it was the blood that overwhelmed me. It decimated the senses. I found myself instinctively looking for another body, thinking it impossible that one person could ever have held so much blood. The physics just didn't work out.

When I felt I could safely attempt to walk, I ventured away from the wall and called the police on the bedroom phone. Then I went back down the hall, leaving faint bloody shoeprints on the carpet. Hank was stretched out on the living room couch, hands cupped over a chalk-gray face.

"You all right?" I said.

"No."

"I called the police."

He neither answered nor moved. Hank, for all his hard-boiled New Yorkisms, had had the sanest reaction to the scene. Hearing the breakfast tray crash to the floor, he'd come into the room only to be propelled back out, careening down the hallway like the Phantom of the Opera with a faceful of acid, bouncing off the walls until crumpling in the foyer, where he vomited everything that was in his stomach, and more.

I walked back into the bedroom, and the sight hit me again, sharp, like a physical blow. I took a deep breath and looked away. Then I turned and forced myself to look at the chunks of meat before me.

The room showed no signs of a struggle. Nothing out of order. Nothing to indicate that Sonia hadn't willingly offered up her body to the surgical slaughter. Then something flashed across my mind. Something missing. Lola, Sonia's cat.

I called her with Sonia's usual whistle, the opening notes to Beethoven's Fifth Symphony. Hard to whistle. No moisture in the throat. Then something scurried in the opened closet. I moved closer and peered in. There she was, way in the back, burrowed in among shoes, slippers, and fallen clothes. Her eyes were wild and searching.

"It's okay, girl." I knelt at the closet, surprised at the

shakiness of my own voice. "Come on, Lola. Come to Quinn. It's okay."

She wouldn't move. I reached in and she bolted but I caught her in midair and held her close to my chest.

"What happened, Lola?" I whispered, stroking her white fur, resting my lips on the trembling head. "What did you see? What in God's name did those eyes see?"

The sound of the door buzzer jarred me. I went back to the foyer and pushed the intercom button. The police. Hank righted himself on the couch. He looked God-awful.

In a moment there was a knock at the door and I opened it to two blue-uniformed San Francisco city cops. They took a second to size me up. The Screwball Assessment. One was older and wore his hat at a slight angle. The other was younger and had the scrubbed-clean look of those eager soldiers who smile out at you from army recruiting posters. Tough-as-nails veteran and fresh-faced, vulnerable rookie, just like on television.

"Are you Quinn Parker?" the veteran asked.

"Yes."

"I'm Captain Denham, this is Patrolman Tanner. You reported the discovery of a body?"

"Yes."

The veteran, Captain Denham, took a deep breath. Irritated, as though this was going to be the first of the daily dozen false alarms. He stared disapprovingly at the cat in my arms.

"May we come in?"

"Sure."

They crossed the threshold, and Captain Denham looked around.

"What's that smell?" he asked.

"My friend . . ."—I pointed at the vomit in the foyer corner—"he threw up."

The trap door fell out from Captain Denham's condescending smirk. He looked at the vomit, then at Hank, then at me, and a new seriousness had settled in his eyes.

"Where is it?" he said.

"Down the hall. Last door on the left."

We went down the hall, and I pointed to the room and waited outside while Captain Denham walked in. He reemerged in ten seconds, jaw steeled in place, struggling with his eyes to make them stay steady. He brushed past me and had a few quiet words with his partner. The partner nodded and left the apartment. Captain Denham took off his cap and looked me straight in the eyes.

"Patrolman Tanner's contacting homicide," he said.

I nodded.

"At what time did you discover the deceased?" Denham asked. His voice was thinner than when he'd marched in the door.

"About eight-thirty."

Captain Denham walked around the living room with his cap in his hand. He cleared his throat and informed us in the phony polysyllabic language they all memorize that until homicide arrived we were requested to remain where we were.

"Remain where we were!" Hank said later, throwing his hands in the air. "Like I was going to pop out for a bite to eat! Like I was going to check the oil in the car!"

Fifteen minutes later they came. Men in uniform and men out of uniform swarmed through the apartment. Cameras snapped and officials snooped around, brushing furniture and filling little vials with blood and leftover wine and even a sample of Hank's vomit. The entire apartment building was cordoned off with a bright, festive yellow ribbon, and below the living room window the rubberneckers had begun to congregate on Ortega Street.

The head of the investigation was Lt. Mannion. He was a ruddy-faced, slightly overweight Irishman with slate-gray eyes and a habit of tucking in a shirt that was already tucked in. It was hard to tell how old he was —maybe forty, maybe fifty. Too much drinking had confused his age lines. He had Hank and me fingerprinted, gave us the short-form version of an interrogation, then left us alone.

Two hours later everyone but Mannion and Captain Denham had cleared out. The photographers, the men with their vials and blood samples, the guys lugging out the heavy black plastic bags containing the debris that used to be Sonia.

Lt. Mannion came back out of the bedroom, tucking in his tucked-in shirt. He looked at Captain Denham and shook his head. "Well," he said. "I guess we can rule out suicide."

Mannion and Denham exchanged tight, grim smiles, then Mannion turned and saw me sitting right there, within earshot. The smiles evaporated. Mannion said something to Captain Denham in a quieter voice and Denham nodded and left. Then Mannion took a deep breath, looked in my direction, and signaled for me to come with him. We walked together down the hallway toward Sonia's bedroom.

"What time did you say you left last night?" Mannion said.

"Around one-thirty."

"I don't suppose anybody saw you leave?"

I shook my head.

"Yeah, well . . ." Mannion rubbed his fingers deep into his neck. "Don't sweat it. I want you to take another look at the bedroom, if you don't mind. See if anything strikes you different. It's cleaned up in there and you might be able to concentrate better."

"Fine."

"Want to leave that cat in the other room?"

"I'd rather hold her. She's a little spooked."

Mannion shrugged and led me back into the room. The bed was stripped and the bare mattress sagged in the middle from the dark, absorbed weight of Sonia's blood. At the end of the boxspring, as if to mock the gravity of what had happened, was the ubiquitous factory-guarantee slip that sternly warns the sleeping public not to remove under penalty of law. The room smelled of chemicals. Lola's soft body clenched.

I took a deep breath. "What am I looking for?"

"Anything." Mannion swept his hand across the room. "Anything at all that looks the slightest bit out of kilter since you last saw the deceased."

Sonia was not Sonia anymore. She was "the deceased." I let my eyes roam the room. As far as I could tell, everything was as it had always been. Except . . . except for the poster of Bob Marley that usually hung over her bed. Odd. It was now hung on the far wall, and a framed eight-by-ten photograph of Sonia stretching seductively in a meadow of wildflowers took the spot above the bed.

"The poster and the photograph," I said. "They've been switched. They weren't like that when I left last night."

Mannion nodded and chewed the eraser end of his pencil, unconcerned. "What else?" he said.

"Nothing. At least nothing obvious."

"Okay, let me ask you this," Mannion suggested. "Do you know whether or not the deceased wore a nightgown to bed? I hate to make it so personal, but it would be helpful if we knew."

"When I knew her she slept in the nude. Sometimes a T-shirt."

"Did she ever wear a nightgown?"

"I never saw her in one, no."

Lt. Mannion nodded and scratched the information into his notebook.

A pale lavender nightgown was draped across the bed-side armchair. I tried to trace the thread of logic that made it significant, but Mannion finished off scribbling and told me to take a walk around the room.

"After the movie you didn't watch any more television?" he said.

"No, that was it. She just bought the VCR yesterday and we were trying it out."

I moved toward the television and picked up the rented cassette, *Top Hat,* and turned it this way and that. It felt strange to the touch. Lt. Mannion anticipated my question.

"Graphite dust," he said. "For fingerprints."

I nodded and set it down and began to look away when something caught my eye, something out of place, unsettling. My eyes retraced their path, over the television and the VCR, scanning the peripheral area. Then I saw it. The flesh prickled on the backs of my hands.

"Something wrong?" Mannion said.

"Maybe."

"What is it?"

"The numbers on the VCR . . . they're off."

"What do you mean, off?

"Last night . . . I cleared it. Right here." I pointed to the tape counter on the side of the VCR. "Last night I zeroed it out before I left. Now there are numbers. Nine, nine, six, three."

Mannion looked disappointed. "That's it?"

Yes, that was it. I stood mulling over what it all meant, and Mannion took that as the cue to tell us we could leave. But we were to stay available for further questioning in the next few days.

Lola buried her face in my flannel shirt and closed her eyes. She was badly in need of sleep.

I suppose there are more mature ways of dealing with incomprehensible tragedy than by getting drunk, but neither Hank nor I could come up with one. So we drove back to the apartment on Union Street and I built a makeshift, pillowy home for Lola in the guest bedroom and then we both walked through the late-morning drizzle to the Bus Stop, our standard watering hole, on the corner of Union and Laguna. Hank decided to wait on calling Carol. It would keep for a few more hours.

"It really happened, didn't it?" Hank said, chancing the question with alcohol safely in hand.

"Yes. It did."

He killed his Scotch in a single gulp and stared down at the empty glass. "That's one."

"Go easy, Hank."

"You know what Sonia's problem was? She wasn't smart about people. She couldn't weed out the good from the bad. That guy blabbering about Kennedy's brain . . . Sonia'd have him sitting in her goddamn kitchen eating doughnuts."

"Doughnuts for the brain character was also what made Sonia special," I said.

"That kind of special she could have done without."

"She was young, Hank."

"No excuse. The world's too strange to be 'young' in. You can't just open your heart and apartment door to everybody." Hank scrunched his forehead and looked across at the bar mirror. "What was her drink, anyway?"

"Take your pick."

"No. I mean the pretentious drink she always ordered. Sounded like the name of a romance novelist."

"Brandy Alexander?"

"That's it!" Hank signaled for Roger, the bartender. "How about two Brandy Alexanders down here?"

Roger strolled over, a bemused smile on his lips. Trim, fit, deeply tanned, Roger had a blond, streamlined handsomeness that Hank never tired of ridiculing. "Two *whats?*"

"Brandy Alexanders. And make them memorable or I'll take my business to another saloon."

"But you just ordered another Scotch."

"So I'll take both. What's the problem?"

Roger shrugged and walked off to the other end of the bar.

"I saw Sonia Monday morning," Hank said. "She came over to the house all upset because this modeling agency hadn't hired her. A summer job, between semesters. Said she was too exotic. Too sexy. Something." He paused, smiled. "We had great plans. She was going to make me her private secretary and we were going to fly around the world together being glamorous and obnoxious and intolerant of people less fortunate than we."

"Carol was all for this, I suppose?"

"We didn't exactly come out and tell Carol." Hank smiled. "But I would have explained it. Outlined the economic advantages." Pause. "Sonia felt so bad telling me my globe-trotting career had gone down the tubes, you know what she did?"

"What?"

"Took me to Mel's for breakfast."

"Doughnuts?"

Hank looked at me sideways and smiled. "Right. Doughnuts. Christ, you know . . . that was the last time I saw her." His knuckles whitened around his empty Scotch glass and he nodded his head as if to verify the fact. "That was it. That was the last time."

Roger was suddenly before us, plunking down the Brandy Alexanders. "Two frou-frou drinks for the boys at the end of the bar. What's the special occasion?"

Hank looked away. Roger was smiling.

"A friend of ours was just murdered," I said.

Roger put down his bar towel. "Jesus . . ."

"Don't mean to be blunt, but that's the only way I know how to say it."

Roger leaned over the bar for a minute, staring off into space, assimilating the information. "Good God . . . was it anybody I know?"

Hank smiled. "Knowing you, and knowing Sonia, it's entirely possible, Roger. Entirely possible." Hank then took a deep breath and raised his glass in a toast. "To all those Sonia touched, and to those who touched Sonia, though they be legion, lucky shits. *Requiescat.*"

And with that he downed his entire Brandy Alexander in one gulp. "Good God!" he coughed. "How could she drink these things? How *could* she?"

It was dark by the time we stumbled home to Union Street. Hank gave me a maudlin slap on the back and stumbled into the guest bedroom. I called Carol and told her what had happened, and that I'd put Hank in a cab in the morning. She stammered an okay through no-vocained lips and hung up without saying good-bye.

I somehow had the wherewithal to fix a nightcap and

build a fire, though building a fire in San Francisco means unwrapping the five-buck chemical log you bought at Safeway and setting a match to it. While I was kneeling at the fireplace a white head appeared tentatively at the edge of the hallway. Lola. I gave her a muted Beethoven and she came to me.

I pulled up a chair and sat in the flickering dark with my feet on the coffee table, Lola snug in my lap. I thought of Hank and his last breakfast with Sonia, and I began thinking of lasts myself. Lasts . . . and firsts.

It occurred to me, suddenly, that Sonia was the first woman I'd ever made love to who was no longer living. The fact sat leadenly in my head like the answer to a trivia question. When had been the last time? The very last time? Must've been Big Sur. Yes, that was it. In Stewart's cabin way up Palo Colorado Canyon. We'd gone down for the weekend and had made love the morning before coming back to San Francisco. There'd been a fight of some kind the previous night and we had slept coldly back-to-back till morning, when Sonia pulled me close and our bodies locked and we coaxed physical apologies out of each other. I didn't know it then, but it was Sonia's way of saying good-bye. We returned to San Francisco and went our separate ways.

"I love the things people can do to other people's bodies," Sonia had murmured that last morning in Big Sur. It was vintage Sonia. Vintage young, fiery, Girl from Ipanema—fun, vapid, embarrassing, sexy, unthinking, and true, all at the same time. Then she had laughed and kissed me, and I held her sideways on the large oak bed, trailing a finger slowly down the length of her spine and feeling her terribly alive body arch into mine at the touch.

I stared at the fireplace, imagined those half-shut eyes,

the interested lips and humid voice—all of it snuffed out, cold as refrigerated lunch meat, lying on a slab in some morgue with a couple of ID tags fastened on to keep the pieces straight. The five-buck log hissed and popped into grotesque chemical flames of green and purple and pink before subsiding into the "authentic" colors promised on the wrapper. Sonia portioned out, and firewood manufactured on the assembly line. I clenched my eyes against the day's impossibilities. The world was out of synch.

I wandered into the bedroom and stood at the window, nursing my drink and holding Lola. On the corner of Union and Van Ness, occasional midnight cars hurried home or hurried away from home. Menace was in the air. Nobody was up to any good.

Somewhere out there in this whiter-than-white city by the bay was a madman. And, if my guess about the VCR was right, there was also in this city a small, black cassette on which the final, horrifying moments in the life of Sonia Lucia were etched in videotape, in bright, bloody color.

"The things people can do to other people's bodies . . . ," she'd said that warm morning in the fog-filled canyons of Big Sur. I downed the rest of my drink and climbed into bed, satisfied that I had bludgeoned myself with enough alcohol to be spared both the nightmares of sleeplessness and the nightmares of sleep.

3

H ANK WAS ALREADY UP when I dragged myself out
of bed the next morning. He was sitting at
the kitchen table, bleary-eyed, hair rumpled, reading an
article in the *Chronicle*. At his right elbow, several hundred neglected Rice Krispies were floating facedown in a
bowl of milk.

"Hung over?" he asked without taking his eyes from
the paper.

"Fresh as a daisy."

"I took the liberty of opening a can of the Cure." He
gestured toward the counter. "You're next."

I winced, but there was no getting around it.

The Cure was first given to me years ago on a beach
south of Puerto Escondido, way down the coast of Mexico,
after a particularly debauched camp-by-the-ocean night
of mescal drinking and ranchero love songs and women of
weak moral fiber. I'd woken to hot, salty daylight, sand in

my face, and a headache that lent me a new perspective on pain. That's when he appeared. An old man, bent under the weight of a bag slung over his shoulder. He walked past me, backed up, asked in Spanish if I had *cruda*—a hangover. I nodded and he reached into his bag and removed a small can of La Cumbre Chilis Jalapeños and a drugstore can opener. He opened the can and pushed it under my nose and held up three fingers.

Hardly *Journey to Ixtlan,* but it worked, and as the years have gone by I've often thought of that ragged old man hobbling down the Mexican beach, bag slung over his shoulder, a supermarket mystic for all those who don't know when to quit.

There's only one way to take the Cure. Quickly. One, two, three, and then hold on to something. I faced it like a man and suffered a few silent minutes in the corner.

"What are you reading?" I managed at last. "Sonia?"

"No. Dolphins committing mass suicide in Florida. They beach themselves and marine biologists haul them back to sea and they beach themselves again. The apocalypse is at hand."

"Is there anything about Sonia?"

Hank nodded at the coffeepot. "On the drainboard. Page five."

I opened to page five and the small photo at the top of the right-hand column stung me. I'd taken it myself, the previous winter on a ski trip to Lake Tahoe. She was smiling, a strand of hair blown across her cheek.

I read the article. Victim nude, age twenty-four. Evidence of sexual assault. Graduate student at San Francisco State. A recap of two recent murders of the same general pattern and a drooling journalistic aside of how this could be another Zodiac Killer.

"I wonder if they know something we don't," Hank said.

"Who?"

"The dolphins."

"Forget the damn dolphins," I said. "Did you read this?"

"Of course I did."

"And?"

Hank set down the dolphin article and tentatively poked the cereal with his spoon. "Wilkie say: nothing like psychopath to boost honorable newspaper circulation."

Forget it. Over the course of many years I had come to recognize certain tendencies in Hank, and one was to tack up a curtain of feigned disinterest and hide behind it in times of emotional distress. Last night he'd forgotten himself for a while. He'd had a lot to drink and had mourned Sonia openly and had even given me a sentimental, heartfelt slap on the back before going to bed. But now he was back in control. I headed down the hall to take a shower.

Once upon a time a tenant had wallpapered my entire bathroom—walls, ceilings, fixtures, everything—with engravings of splendorous Rubenesque nudes prancing around like wood nymphs who'd gotten into the food locker. They were all boobs and behinds and improbable rolls of come-hither flesh, but sensuous in an engulfing sort of way. They ran and danced and high-hurdled sunflowers, and, after initial resentment, I'd grown quite fond of them all. Over the months I'd given them names. Trixie, Dottie, Hermione, Bubbles, Vixen.

It was a quick, somber shower. I scraped the razor across my face a couple of times and called it a shave. Trixie watched from the far wall, peeking over my shoulder. Trixie was the flower-sniffer, frozen forever in naked wonderment of a dandelion. I looked at her in the mirror and she looked at me. Neither of us seemed inclined to break the ice, so I kept my mouth shut and finished up the shave.

The law offices, such as they are, of Erik J. Paige occupy two drafty little rooms on the fifth floor of a dark, musty, Market Street building. I was on my way to see Erik for several reasons. Inasmuch as Sonia ever had an attorney, he was Sonia's attorney. Having been a trial lawyer, he had tentacles that could still grope into the deepest nooks and crannies of the police department and City Hall. And he was a friend. Someone I could trust.

Once upon a time Erik had been among the brightest of the bright young comets streaking across San Francisco's legal skies. That's when I'd met him. He was fair, intelligent, well liked, and preposterously competent. The only real question in anybody's mind was how high he would go before he peaked . . . state legislature . . . congressman . . . senator.

Then one day he quit. Resigned his post, packed up, and headed off to a small village in the south of Ireland to "sort things out." Former associates were stunned. They tsk-tsked over martinis and talked about Erik as you'd talk about the most popular kid in high school who'd gone off to war and came back a shell-shocked introvert, living with his mother and filling his days with television game shows.

"I grew to hate the face I was seeing in the mirror every morning," Erik told me shortly after returning. "So I got out. Simple as that."

I parked the van in the Union Square garage and walked over to Erik's building on Fourth and Market.

He, of course, had been wrong. It wasn't "simple as that." Erik had underestimated the value we the people attach to relentless ambition, and the penalty we the people impose on those who would threaten the rat-race superstructure by sauntering away from it all.

So when Erik Paige returned from Ireland he gathered up his files, his plaques, his parchment collection from Stanford and Yale, and resumed his career on a scaled-down level. Took inexpensive office space in an inexpensive building and handled whatever cases drifted his way—primarily the affairs of friends or aliens with immigration problems who couldn't find any other lawyer.

Ludmila wasn't at her reception desk, so I tapped on the smoked-glass door. There was no answer, but the light was on inside so I nudged the door open.

He was standing at the far wall, facing the street, his back to me, gazing out the window.

"Erik?"

He didn't respond. He just stood and stared, stroking his chin in the yellowed sunshine. I cleared my throat with more force than necessary and he jerked and turned.

"Quinn!"

"Ludmila wasn't at her desk, so I . . ."

He crossed in front of his desk and gave me first a handshake, and then, after a moment's hesitation, an embrace.

"God, Quinn," he said. "What a terrible thing. You okay?"

"I don't know what I am."

He took me by the elbow. "Sit down."

Erik went back behind his desk and I pulled up a chair. Erik stands five-eleven, with an oval face, soft eyes, and very fine blondish brown hair. His office was strewn with copies of *Sports Illustrated* and empty glasses and stray chessmen . . . the unmistakeable feel of not much money being made, or sought, or cared about.

"I heard about it last night," he said. "Was going to call you, but it was late and . . . I didn't know how you were doing."

"It's okay. Hank and I spent most of yesterday getting drunk."

"Drunk." Erik contemplated the word. "There are worse responses. You don't look too bad."

I patted my stomach. "The Cure."

Erik managed a smile. "How's Hank taking it?"

"About what you'd expect." I took a deep breath and looked at the door leading to the reception room. "Where's Ludmila?"

"Took the day off. She and Sonia got to be pretty good friends, you know."

"No, I didn't."

Erik lit a cigarette and nodded vigorously at the first puff. "Just in the last couple months. Sonia'd come by and they'd go out to lunch together. That sort of thing."

I nodded and Erik nodded and a very serious silence filled the room.

"Tell me what happened," he finally said.

I leaned back and gave my version of the last twelve hours or so in the life of Sonia Lucia. As I spoke he shook his head and rubbed his face and concentrated intensely on the end of the burning cigarette, as though the crime were being reenacted in the middle of the red glow, and if he only stared hard enough he might catch a glimpse of the murderer's face. When I got to the part about the numbers on the VCR Erik's attention sharpened.

"Hold it," he said. "Run that by me again."

I counted off the steps on my fingers. "I took the Fred Astaire cassette out of the machine the night before, after rewinding it completely. Then I cleared out the tape counter to zero. Then I turned the machine off. Next morning the tape counter reads nine, nine, six, three."

"You sure you cleared the tape counter?"

"Absolutely. It's one of those quirky things I always do. Always."

Erik scratched his chin. "This is pretty damn far-fetched, Quinn."

"Then you tell me how the numbers changed like that."

"There must be a dozen ways."

"I'm waiting."

"Maybe Sonia . . . maybe after you left she watched or recorded something else."

"No good. If she did that, the tape counter would be zero one hundred, zero two hundred, something like that. Not nine, nine, six, three. There are only two ways to get to ninety-nine sixty-three. Fast-forward several minutes, or rewind a few seconds. The rewinding seems a lot likelier. Besides, she didn't have any other tapes. The machine was brand new. The tape we watched was the only one in the house."

Erik stood and went to the window. "And all this makes you think what?"

"That the killer videotaped the murder. He put the cassette with the murder into Sonia's VCR, rewound it a little, watched some of it to make sure he'd gotten it. Then he took the cassette and left. Everything's where it was when I left, only the tape counter is thrown off."

Erik pursed his lips. "How does somebody murder a woman *and* tape it at the same time? Are you saying there are two killers?"

"No. He could have brought a tripod. Or killed her first and then started taping."

Erik was silent for a moment. He stood at the window,

jingling the change in his pockets. He wasn't in the mood to buy my video theory. Then he finally shook his head and sighed. "The business with the pictures . . . you're positive about that?"

"Almost positive."

Erik came back and sat on the edge of the desk. He seemed much more bothered about the switched pictures than the video element. "Who's handling the case?"

"Lieutenant Mannion. You know him?"

Erik nodded. "We worked together a lot before my fall from grace."

"What's he like?"

"He's like most of them. Competent. Shrewd. *Deceptively* shrewd. Attentive to details. Ambitious to at least make captain so he can retire on a decent pension." Pause. "You told him about the VCR?"

"Yes."

"And?"

"He was underwhelmed by the disclosure."

Erik nodded. "That makes sense. What's he supposed to do? Confiscate every videocassette in the greater Bay Area?"

I chewed on my thumb. Resented the effectiveness of Erik's argument. "Read the *Chronicle* this morning?" I said.

"Yes."

"They mentioned two other murders that could be related."

Erik made a face. "Wishful thinking. You get reporters who want to be in on the ground floor of something big, then they write a book about it and go on all the talk shows."

"You don't buy it, then?"

"It's not for me to buy or not buy. I'm out of all that now. But my instincts say no."

"I'm the kind of guy who needs reasons, Erik."

"Then I'll give you one. There isn't the slightest connection between Sonia's death and the others. None."

"You sound pretty sure of yourself."

"I am. If I may invoke the hallowed names of Stanford and Yale—"

"You may not."

"I will anyway. Look, Quinn. Serial killers have MO's. They write their signature on every crime they commit, and someone with a trained eye can spot it in a second."

"Suppose a serial killer has the audacity not to follow the rules?"

There was an exasperated pause. Erik was an astronaut and I was a charter member of the Flat Earth Society. "Criminology is now a very, very sophisticated science," he said. "There are people out there who are experts in nothing *but* multiple murders. Take my word for it. There are rules."

I leaned back in the chair and gave Erik's ceiling a few frustrated seconds. "Just for the sake of humoring me," I said, "what were the other murders?"

The phone rang before Erik could reply. It was a short conversation, and when Erik hung up he told me that I wouldn't have to speculate about Lt. Mannion any longer.

"That was Hank. Mannion just called and wants to talk with you in his office right away, if convenient. Hank got the impression that it had better damn well be convenient."

4

C OFFEE?" Lt. Mannion gestured with an open palm toward a wooden chair.

"Thanks," I said.

He didn't ask if I wanted cream or sugar. Mannion's office was in the Hall of Justice building on Bryant Street. It had all the size and atmosphere of a large walk-in closet. Predictable arcane clutter filled the office from floor to ceiling, and dusty rays of light slanted in through yellowed windows. Mannion retucked his tucked-in shirt and pushed the intercom button on his desk and asked "Irma" to bring in a cup of coffee for "Mr. Parker." Then he sat down in a creaking swivel chair behind his desk and steepled his fingers beneath a blotchy drinker's face.

"You didn't return my call," he said.

"What call?"

"I called yesterday afternoon and got your answering machine. I asked you to get in touch."

"I didn't listen to it last night," I said.

"Why not?"

"I have trouble sticking to routine when friends have their heads removed."

Mannion unsteepled his fingers and pointed one of them straight in my face. "Don't be a wise-ass. I know you're shook up about this, but I have a job to do and get nervous when principals can't be reached and don't return phone calls. Do we understand each other?"

There was a little rat-a-tat-tat on the door. It creaked open and a middle-aged woman wearing a pink polyester pants suit came tiptoeing in with the coffee, smiling a saccharine "aww" smile as if she were watching puppies at play. Had to be Irma.

"Heeeeere we go," she whispered, setting the coffee on the desk in front of me. It was a deferential whisper, as though somehow by speaking softly her intrusion would be less annoying to her boss. Irma was an anachronism. One of those women untouched by the social upheaval of the past three decades, a secretary proud of the coffee she brewed, proud of her sixty words per minute, proud of the trivial scurrying she did every day for her boss. She gave me a corny little wink and tiptoed out of the office.

Irma had taken some of the punch out of Mannion's chew-out session. He closed a pair of long-suffering eyes, cleared his throat, and moved on to the business at hand.

For fifteen minutes we reviewed the events at 2314 Ortega Street. Mannion asked me questions from a shielded folder—times, dates, names—by and large the same questions he'd asked in Sonia's living room yesterday. See if Monday answers jell with Sunday answers.

No, I didn't know Sonia's current boyfriend, or whether she even had one.

"Sounds like just a regular college girl," Mannion said.

I shrugged. "Pretty much. That's not to say she didn't travel in wild circles now and then."

"Wild circles?"

"Sonia was twenty-four. Away from home, in college. She was also full of life and curious and experimental. Maybe in Omaha those qualities won't get you into much trouble, but in San Francisco you're a twenty-minute bus ride from everything under the sun."

I had Mannion's attention now. "What was she twenty minutes away from, for instance?"

"For instance, the Folsom Street crowd."

Mannion wrinkled his forehead. "Folsom Street? You mean the S&M bars?"

"She liked to dance there. Said it was more fun than the slick disco places downtown. I went with her once. She was right."

"What else?"

I took a deep breath. The interview was going sour. "Lieutenant, I think I'm giving you the wrong impression."

"What's the right impression?"

"Sonia had a lot of . . . passion for life. That's all."

Mannion's steel-gray eyes rested on me for a moment. "I talked to her folks in Oregon last night," he said. "They made her sound like Pollyanna."

"Does that surprise you?"

Mannion just sat and looked at me. I began to suspect that I'd said too much. Sonia Lucia had suddenly fallen into a file labeled Stoned and Promiscuous, and the gears of relentless justice were winding down. This wasn't really "crime." Not like a purse-snatching. Not like the murder of a doctor's wife or a kidnapped Pacific Heights businessman. This was something else. A casualty of the burgeoning drug culture and all its immediate-gratification spinoffs.

"What's the matter?" Mannion said.

"Nothing."

"I'd rather you didn't bullshit me. What's the matter?"

"Maybe some of the zeal goes out of a murder investigation when the victim dances on Folsom Street."

Mannion laughed a little. His face changed when he laughed. The eyes lit up. He looked like someone who'd be fun to have a few drinks with.

"Mr. Parker, a woman was brutally murdered. Believe me, we take this case as seriously as any other." Pause. "There was one thing, though, I wanted to ask you about. We found a deck of cards under Miss Lucia's body."

"Cards?"

"Tarot cards. Under the torso. About half the deck. Spread out, face down. You know anything about that at all?"

I took a moment to think. "She fooled around with it a little. Tarot. The *I Ching*. But if you mean was she really into it, I'd say no. It was more like fun to her. Like reading your horoscope in the papers."

Mannion nodded as if it wasn't real important anyway. He looked over at me. "You were down at Erik Paige's?"

"That's right."

"Any particular reason?"

"We're friends."

"From school, or . . . ?"

"He helped me out of a legal jam a few years ago. We go to ball games together once in a while. That's all."

"I used to see a lot of him myself," Mannion said. "More than I do now, anyway. We worked together now and then before he junked it and headed off to wherever."

"Ireland."

"Right," Mannion nodded. "Ireland. Everybody around here thought he was nuts, but I was saying, who the hell doesn't want to bag it and head off someplace. Half a chance I'd do the same thing. I admire what he did. I really do. Takes guts to turn your back on everything and shake up your life." Mannion paused to play with a pencil sitting on his desk. "What were you doing over at Paige's?"

"He was Sonia's lawyer."

"What's a twenty-four-year-old college girl need a lawyer for?"

"He gave her advice now and then. Some legal, some personal. Why don't you ask him yourself?"

"I will. What line of work are you in, by the way, Mr. Parker?"

I reached into my wallet and gave him one of my cards. Amalgamated Tropical Enterprises, Inc., at the top; Quinn Parker, Consultant, my address and phone number on the bottom. Oscar the parrot in full plumage bordered the left; to the right, a coconut palm tree leaned toward Oscar. The color was so bright you could almost hear the monkeys screeching. Mannion fingered the card, admiring the graphics.

"Let me guess," he said. "Import, export?"

"Just export. I arrange trips for people." Talking about it now suddenly reminded me of Andrew Baxley and his back-to-back phone calls. It seemed like years ago.

". . . agent?" Mannion said.

"What?"

"Are you a travel agent?" he repeated.

"I suppose you could call it that."

"What else could I call it?"

"Outdoor psychology. If somebody's afraid of flying, I take them flying. Scared of heights, we go mountain climbing. That sort of thing."

"Seriously?"

"Seriously."

Mannion nodded, kept looking at the card. "Good money in that?

"Not enough to afford a four-bedroom apartment on Russian Hill, if that's what you're getting at."

Mannion looked up without moving his head. Just eyes. A smile tugged gently at the corners of his mouth. "Did cross my mind. Got a sister-in-law in your neighborhood, just moved out from Denver, and I know what she pays for a lousy little studio."

"A few years ago I had an accident with a piece of equipment. The company that manufactured the equipment settled with me. Thanks to a friend, I invested wisely."

Mannion asked the name of the company and I gave it to him and he made a big display of how he was writing it down.

"This is your home address, right?"

"I work out of my apartment."

"But the phone's different."

"I have two phones. One private, one business. Both have answering machines."

Mannion nodded and examined the card some more. I thought of what Erik had told me of his "deceptive" shrewdness.

"Mind if I keep the card?" he said.

"It's yours. Next time you want to take a vacation, call me."

He chuckled and tucked it away in a side drawer. "What'll you make me do? Wrestle alligators and dive for sunken treasure?"

"Depends. Are you afraid of wrestling alligators?"

"Listen, most dangerous thing I pack on vacation are the golf clubs. And the wife, forget it. She likes the creature comforts. A cruise. That's all the hell she can talk about now. It's those damn 'Love Boat' reruns on television. I try to tell her it isn't like that, with all the adventure and intrigue, how it's just a bunch of Hollywood writers sitting around hyping it up, but she doesn't care. Me, I got enough of boats in the service. Sitting around a pool in the middle of the ocean doesn't do it."

He stood up, and I took the cue and stood with him and we began walking to the door.

"A lot of cruises have golf tie-ins," I said. "Clinics, guest instructors. Even driving ranges."

"You're kidding!"

"Cross my heart."

Mannion's eyes got a faraway look. "How do I find out about these?"

"Any good travel agent would know."

"Yeah, yeah. Good, thanks a lot. Geez, I never knew they had that sort of thing."

We stood at the door a second while Mannion further considered his prospects for a happier vacation.

"Then I'm not a suspect?" I said at last.

"What? Oh, no. Killers generally don't call the police, and they're usually too preoccupied with keeping all the lies stitched together to notice something like a couple of posters turned around."

I looked Mannion in the face. *"You* switched them?"

"While you were in the living room. Wanted to make sure you knew the room like you said you did. It's what they do out in Vegas when the house thinks somebody's counting cards. You know those mirrored ceilings above the blackjack tables?"

I nodded.

"Two-way. Guys walk around up there looking down on everything. When they see a guy they think's card counting, what they do is drop a dime on the ceiling and let it rattle to a stop. If you're playing straight you look up to see what the hell's going on. But not a card counter. He doesn't do anything. His mind's somewhere else, all full of arithmetic. Let's just say that at Miss Lucia's apartment I dropped a dime and you noticed it."

"And Hank?"

Mannion shook his head. "Not a guy who throws up. But I'll tell you one thing that happened once. Not here. Over in Sacramento. This guy, he murders his wife and then drinks a half-gallon of salt water and throws up all over the floor. While everybody was patting the poor sucker on the back, one of the paramedics thought the puke looked a little strange." Mannion chuckled and shook his head at the wacky world of homicide. "They tested the puke down at the lab and that was that. Since then we automatically check vomit to make sure it wasn't self-induced. Your friend's vomit was legit, don't worry. He's in the clear."

It was a strange drive back to my apartment. I was thinking of legitimate vomit, phony fireplace logs, and why the interview with Mannion had switched so dramatically in midstream. One minute he was all furrowed brows and pursed lips, the next he was strolling down Memory Lane, smiling at personal anecdotes from Vegas to Sacramento.

I caught the red light at Third and Market and sat chewing my knuckle, thinking that maybe I'd blown it. In my eagerness to hand Mannion a host of suspects, I'd made Sonia sound borderline herself. The pencil had stopped, the eyebrows had arched. Despite what Mannion'd said, the message had come through. When nuts kill other nuts it's not such a big deal. Subcultures take care of their own.

Hank was still at the apartment when I returned, watching television. "How did it go?" he said.

"Lousy."

He didn't pursue it, but nodded down the hall. "Carol's here. In the office."

I took off my coat and went into the office. Carol was sitting at the desk, staring blankly at the framed photographs on the wall. She was up there, along with Hank. Sonia. Roscoe. Erik. Others. I like to have all my friends in one room.

When I came in she simply looked up at me with reddened eyes and smiled a weak smile. "Hello, Quinn."

"Hello, Carol."

I moved to the desk, and she reached up and hugged me, and the tears began to come. Thirty seconds passed. I'd known Carol for a long time. Had introduced her to Hank, watched her get married, have her children, rear her family. She was honest-to-goodness San Francisco Italian stock, with North Beach roots that went back about fifty generations. Jet-black hair, dark complexion, close-set eyes, gorgeous smile, and teeth kidnapped from the set of a toothpaste commercial. She was all energy and movement. Handcuffed, she'd be incapable of uttering a word. But now she was drained. Emptied of the usual vitality and humor.

"I have to go," she sniffled at last. "But I needed to stop by."

"I'm glad you did."

"This is killing Hank, you know."

I nodded. "I know."

"He doesn't act like it, but . . ."

"I know."

Then, decisively, Carol stood and wiped the grief from her face and assumed a brave, tackle-the-world posture. "There! I really have to go. But I didn't want to miss you. Life or death, it doesn't matter to the day-care center."

"Give the boys a tweak on the butt from Uncle Quinn."

"I will." Carol picked up her coat and glanced back down the hall. "Watch Hank for me, okay? Don't let him drink too much."

"I won't."

Carol nodded and tightened her lips. Then she leaned up and kissed me on the cheek and hurried out and down the stairs. I took a deep breath and went back out into the living room. Hank was still camped in front of the television.

"What was lousy about it?" Hank asked.

"About what?"

"The meeting with Mannion. You said it went lousy."

"I'll tell you on the way to Sausalito," I said.

"What's in Sausalito?"

"Ludmila Rolko."

Hank turned off the television. "Who's she?"

"The woman who works for Erik. She and Sonia were friends. Maybe she knows something about Sonia's private life we don't."

I stood at the large, windowed corner by the dining table and looked out at the misty panorama of the Golden

Gate Bridge, the Marin Headlands, and the bay, pale green and flecked with whitecaps.

"Carol's worried that you'll hit the bottle over this," I said. "So please don't."

"I'm not an alcoholic."

"Nobody said you were. I think she'd just rather you steered whatever you're going through right now in her direction rather than Johnnie Walker's."

Hank was silent for a moment. Then he nodded his head. "Fair enough."

I gave the bay another ten seconds, then dug through my wallet for Lt. Mannion's number, went to the phone, and dialed. Irma answered.

"I'd like to speak to Lieutenant Mannion, please."

"Who may I ask is calling?"

"Quinn Parker." I didn't like her tone. A touch of arrogance. The Good Secretary, screening her important boss from the teeming rabble who would want to swarm over her desk and invade his important world. "I was there about an hour ago, remember?"

"Lieutenant Mannion isn't in his office at the moment," she said. "May I take a message?"

"When do you think he'll be back?"

"I have no idea, Mr. Parker. The lieutenant is a very, very busy man. May I take a message?"

May I Take A Message sat there like the Berlin Wall. No getting past it. I started to hang up, then changed my mind.

"Sure, Irma," I said. "Got a pencil?"

Pause. "Pardon me?

"Here's the message."

"How did you know my name?"

"Better start writing. I'm only going to say this once

and Lieutenant Mannion won't be happy if he doesn't get it right."

I could hear scrambling on the other end.

"Dear Lieutenant Mannion," I said in a slow, even voice. "You asked about the 'right' impression of Sonia Lucia, and I've decided to give it to you. She also liked ballet, French restaurants, tennis, and was fresh and buoyant in lovemaking. If you have any further questions, you know where to contact me. Quinn Parker."

I waited a moment. Irma's pen was scratching like crazy.

"Fresh and what?" she finally said.

"Fresh and buoyant. Buoyant."

"How do you spell that?"

"B . . . u . . ."

"Is that *b* as in *boy,* or *d* as in *dog?*"

"Forget it."

I hung up and turned around to see Hank leaning against the fireplace, grinning.

"She didn't know how to spell *buoyant,*" I said.

"Hard word to spell. But I like it. I like it."

"Praise me on the way to Sausalito." I put the number back in my wallet. "Let's go."

5

W<small>E DROVE ACROSS</small> the Golden Gate Bridge and down the twisting two-lane road above Fort Baker till it leveled out at the waterfront among houseboats, restaurants on stilts, and expensive gift shops.

"Ludmila Rolko . . . ," Hank said, pulling at his lower lip and letting it snap back. "Have I ever met her?"

"I doubt it."

"The name's familiar . . . "

We inched through Sausalito, catching every red light the way you do in all tourist towns. Electronic speed bumps, rigged by the chamber of commerce so you don't go sailing through without having the chance to do some impulsive consuming.

It was a bad day for tourists and merchants alike. Ragged gray overcast, wind blowing like hell, the bay to our right green and choppy and sick-looking. An older couple with midwestern faces stood forlornly on the sidewalk, hunched against the cold, cameras dangling use-lessly from their necks—uncomprehending victims of a cruel hoax perpetrated by bright blue travel posters back home in Kansas City.

"Sure I did!" Hank said, snapping his fingers. "Ludmila the secretary. Tall. Curly dark hair. Banned-in-Boston body and real thick accent."

"The accent's not so thick anymore, but you've got her."

Hank leaned back, satisfied. "She was at Erik's Super Bowl party last year. I *knew* I'd met her before."

I made a left on Napa Street and climbed a gradually steepening hill to Ludmila's apartment building on the right. Eight units, four on top, four below, all with a terrace offering a somewhat obstructed view of the bay. Ludmila's was the top unit closest to the street. Before I even had time to cut the engine she was dashing out to meet me.

"Oh, Quinn!" She threw her arms around me and buried her face in my shoulder. "Terrible! It's so terrible!"

Hank got out of the van and stood at a polite distance. I held Ludmila tightly and felt her tears on my neck and whispered into her hair the hollow reassurances people are reduced to in such situations.

"It's all right," I said. "Let's go inside."

She nodded and followed as I led her by the elbow back up the sidewalk to her apartment.

We settled into her small living room and I reac-quainted Ludmila with Hank. They nodded awkwardly at each other and Ludmila sat down on the ottoman next to me, clasping long, delicate fingers over her knees. She was from Czechoslovakia and had a lovely, broad face, high cheekbones, and an ephemeral sense of style that we in America are fond of associating with Europeans.

She had long lashes and pale green eyes and a slender, elegant body. Ludmila did not fare well when strolling past construction workers.

"Erik told me you and Sonia had gotten to be friends," I said.

"Yes, good friends. It was just starting, you know. Sonia was so sweet, so funny and happy. We could talk about things easily, like we knew each other forever."

I took a deep breath. "Ludmila . . . this must be hard for you. It's hard for me, too. But I need to know. Was Sonia seeing anybody at the end? Anybody special?"

"You are talking about men?"

"Yes."

"She was with several men," Ludmila said. "Sonia was not an exclusive woman. She preferred variety."

The words clawed at me. A hook of jealousy still snagging from the grave.

"But did she mention anybody in particular?" I said.

"Yes. Recently she began an affair with a man from the university. Sonia was very excited about him. A professor."

"Professor?"

Ludmila nodded. "There was great secrecy in their affair. Sonia told me her new man would be in trouble if the university discovered their affair. He would lose his job. The intrigue of it was appealing to Sonia. She would get so excited talking about—" Ludmila broke off as the emotion surged unexpectedly and caught in her throat.

"What was his name?" I said.

Ludmila shook her head, gathered herself. "I don't know. Sonia always called him 'the professor.' You know, such as—'I am going to see the professor tonight.' No, wait. Sometimes she called him Ron. Yes, she sometimes called him Ron."

"Ron what?"

"Only Ron. Ron, or 'the professor.' "

"Who else was she seeing?"

"Oh, let me think." Ludmila closed her eyes and put a finger to her temple, just like a cartoon character. "A boy named Rick, also from the university. A student."

I knew Rick. Had met him a couple of times at Sonia's. Clean-cut, athletic, studying to be an oceanographer. Not the slicing-and-dicing type. Then Ludmila's eyes suddenly opened wide and her finger dropped from her temple.

"My God! Of course! There was another man who was bothering her. Sonia was very upset by this. He called her on the phone all night, he followed her around, and one time even tried to grab her and hit her at a dance. Sonia told me that if it continued she was going to call the police!"

"How did she know this guy?"

"Sonia volunteered at a clinic for drug problems. She knew him from there and he liked her. But Sonia had no interest for him. No romantic interest. This was the problem."

Hank leaned forward in his chair. "Did he have a name?"

"His name is Jeff," Ludmila said. "Only Jeff."

The conversation tapered off, slowed to a trickle, then dried up completely. The three of us walked to the sliding glass door leading to the terrace. Ludmila had been notified the week before that they were converting her apartment complex into condominiums. It meant finding a new place to rent within sixty days, and rents were so much higher now. She would never be able to afford Sausalito. She was thinking about moving back to San Francisco, but it wasn't much cheaper there, either. We all stood at the sliding-glass door and looked out at the wedge of bay view that someone would soon be paying hundreds of thousands of dollars for and nodded at the unfairness of condo-conversions.

Then Ludmila walked us both to the van, huddled against the windy gray, and gave me a kiss on the cheek. I climbed in and started the engine.

"You're positive Sonia never used a last name for this Jeff character?" I said, leaning out the window.

"I'm sure." The wind pushed Ludmila's billowy dark hair flat against her face and brought out the red on her pale cheeks. "But I think maybe he stopped bothering her because Sonia didn't talk about him very much in the last few weeks. She was much more interested in her affair with the professor. She said he was special. Very special."

"Sonia thought every man was very special," Hank said as we headed back across the Golden Gate. "For God's sake, she even thought you were very special for a while."

"What's your point?"

"My point is there must be two million men in the Bay Area, and we're looking for Ron, Rick, and Jeff."

"I know who Rick is, and there aren't two million professors at San Francisco State named Ron."

"Sounds to me like Jeff is our problem, not Ron."

"What was the drug clinic Sonia worked for?" I said.

"Can't remember," Hank said listlessly. "Somewhere in the Haight."

"Maybe they'd have records."

Hank shrugged. "Maybe."

We drove in silence for a while. "What's your objection to all this?" I said at last.

Hank looked away, out the window. "I guess I think people ought to bury their dead and get on with life, that's all."

"And the guy who killed Sonia, what about him? What if his idea of 'getting on with life' is to give the rest of us more dead to bury?"

"That's why we have the police," Hank said flatly. "That's why the taxpayers keep somebody like Lieutenant Mannion around."

"You wouldn't say that if you'd been in Mannion's office this morning. He's hardly what you'd call straining at the leash."

Hank folded his arms and watched the scenery roll past the window. End of subject.

The campus was dreary. Lawns wet and abandoned, political booths boarded up. Students strode back and forth along the Quad with grim purpose, collars up and eyes to the sidewalk.

Hank begged off immediately and headed for the library. I went to the transcripts and records window in the Administration Building and asked a young guy with an orange Mohawk and acne for a copy of Sonia Lucia's class schedule. He said in an adenoidal voice that regulations prohibited him from providing that kind of information. I said I was a friend, and that it was important. He said that didn't make any difference. I wondered out loud whether fifty bucks might cause him to make an innocent mistake, and he climbed off the stool and reappeared in thirty seconds, mistake in hand.

It was right there, staring me in the face on page one. Schedule of classes for spring semester: Ronald L. Hemming, professor of English. A quick scan turned up no other professors named Ron. I gave the file back to the Mohawk character and headed off.

The English department was housed in a depressing building at the north end of campus, near the baseball and soccer fields. It was a two-story shoebox, the color of unwashed bedsheets, all the warmth and coziness of a correctional facility.

Ronald Hemming's office was on the second floor, at the end of an institutional-green hallway. His door was locked, and taped to the glass was an index card outlining his classes and office hours. At eight-thirty he had a Medieval Literature class. At eleven, a graduate course titled "Literary Trends, Historical Consequences." Then nothing till two, when he had office hours. I glanced at my watch. Quarter to one.

I killed time wandering around the Student Union and got back to Hemming's office at the stroke of two. The door was still locked. Five minutes passed, then ten, and I was just about to go looking for him when a tall, handsome fellow in a natty vest and tie came loping down the hall. He had a stack of folders in one hand and was fiddling with an oversized key ring with the other. A girl hustled along beside him, books clutched to her breast, talking earnestly. He nodded his head in a distracted fashion, listening but not listening, and was on top of me just like that. My presence startled him.

"Ronald Hemming?"

"Yes?"

"My name's Quinn Parker. I'd like to talk to you."

"Regarding?"

"It's personal."

He paused, squinted up at me as though he didn't understand the language. "What?"

"I need to talk to you about Sonia Lucia."

He quit fiddling with his key ring. The hallway got a little quieter. Professor Hemming looked at me, then his eyes shifted to the girl waiting at his side. "Susan," he said. "I'm sorry, but could we reschedule this for next week?"

Susan was crestfallen. She gave me a dirty look, clutched the books tighter to her chest. "But I only have a few—"

"Susan. Please."

She turned and walked away, and Hemming watched her go. Then he unlocked the door to his office and motioned me in.

"Sit down, please," Hemming said, motioning to a chair on the other side of his cluttered desk. It was a tiny office, and unnaturally warm.

"Thanks."

Hemming sat, took off his glasses, and pinched the bridge of his nose. "You didn't announce the fact, so I assume you're not from the police."

"No."

Hemming put his glasses back on and fumbled around his vest for a pack of cigarettes. "Smoke?"

"No."

"Mind if I indulge?"

"It's your office."

Professors come in two general categories—unapproachable academicians and "good guys." Ronald Hemming was a "good guy." Talk straight, offer cigarettes. He had short brown hair, brown eyes, strong features. He wore tortoiseshell glasses, and they tended to enhance his looks rather than detract. The professor's five o'clock shadow got underway at two-thirty, but even that was acceptable. It made him look dedicated, interested, committed to his occupation—the way presidents are fond of being photographed looking slightly haggard after all-night crisis sessions. I could see why Sonia had been drawn to him. There was an inherent confidence in Hemming you don't see much anymore. Secure, understated, masculine.

"So who are you?" he said.

"Just a friend."

Hemming relaxed a bit, shook his head. "A horrible thing," he murmured. "She was in my eight-thirty group. Medieval Literature. We spent a good part of this morning's class talking about Sonia. About the proliferation of violence in general, historical precedents." He paused, fiddled with his cigarette, and gave me another sidelong glance. "So why did you want to talk to me, Quinn?"

"Isn't it obvious?"

"Obvious?"

"Let's not play games, Professor. Sonia was a little bit more to you than just another student handing in homework."

Hemming paused. "She told you this?"

"Yes."

"And you believed her?"

"Why shouldn't I?"

Hemming put out his half-smoked cigarette. He leaned forward and put his hands on the desk as if now he was going to set me straight about a few of the world's tougher truths.

"Quinn, . . . men in my profession have a problem. An enviable problem, maybe, but a problem nevertheless. We stand up every day in front of a lot of impressionable young girls and pontificate about worldly things as if we know what the hell we're talking about. Inevitably, some of these impressionable young girls see their professors as romantic figures. There's no way around it. Same thing with doctors or athletes or . . . disc jockeys, for Christ's sake. We're public and we're vulnerable. I can't tell you how many girls have"—he made quotation marks in the air with his fingers—"fallen in love with me over the years. Susan? The girl in the hallway? A perfect example." He pushed his swivel chair back from the desk. "I don't know what Sonia told you, but with her it might have been, I don't know, a question of projection. Fantasy projection."

It was a smooth little speech, but I didn't buy it. If there was one woman in the world who didn't need to fantasy-project, it was Sonia.

"You were having an affair with Sonia. I know it. So do others."

Hemming exaggerated a nod and leaned back in his chair. "Oh?"

"Right," I said. "I should quit wasting your time and talk to the Board of Trustees. I'm sure they'd be interested in your extracurricular activities."

"Top floor, Room four twenty-seven." His eyes had turned hard. We weren't friends anymore. "Woman you want to talk to is Mrs. Leonard."

"Thanks." I got up and headed for the door. I hate bluffs that take me halfway out of an office, but that's how far I got before Hemming's clipped voice told me to sit the hell back down.

"I don't need the trouble you could cause, so this is it. My involvement with Sonia was a three-week thing. No more. In fact, I'd broken it off only a few nights before . . . before she was killed."

Hemming paused, reached for another cigarette, then thought better of it. "Look, Quinn," he said. "I'm not in very good shape this afternoon. It hasn't . . ."

Hemming stood and exhaled deeply and walked to the window.

I was getting tired of this. "Was she having a problem with a boyfriend? Ex-lover?"

Hemming wasn't completely with me. When he turned back from the window his eyes had that running-for-cover look. Then he snapped to. "Actually, there *was* someone. Christ, you hate to point a finger when murder's involved . . ."

"Go ahead and point."

"This guy I'm thinking of was a Grade Z oddball, and he had it in for Sonia. Called her up at two in the morning, pushed her apartment buzzer and yelled obscenities. Name is Jeff Miller. Sonia knew him from some drug rehab thing. He even came here once, right into this office, and threatened me. That's when I knew it was time to wrap things up."

"Jeff Miller. I don't suppose you know where he lives?"

"No. Sonia said he always hung around the Gingerbread House. It's a bar out in the Haight. Maybe they'd know."

The interview was over. At the door Hemming grabbed my elbow. I looked down at his hand and he loosened his grip.

"Why did you come here?" he said.

"Have the police been here?"

"No."

"That's why I came here."

That stopped Hemming for a moment. He thought it over, then his voice dropped low and conspiratorial. Man to man.

"I've sacrificed a lot to reach this spot. Next year I come up for tenure. A thing like this with Sonia . . . police questioning me . . . my name in the papers . . . personal life, career, everything. Do you understand what I'm saying?"

He paused to watch the effect of his plea. I looked in at the office Hemming was so proud of. A monument to himself, lined with books and diplomas, with a chair pulled up to the desk so a constantly rotating crop of book-clutching Susans could sit and be mesmerized. And, flesh being what it is, sometimes the almost-tenured man will set aside his lectures and dip into the coed porridge to have a taste, except that if the coed happens to turn up murdered he spits it back out and wipes his mouth and puts on the innocent face and even works the still-warm corpse into a class discussion. The proliferation of violence in general, historical precedents. Look at how Professor Hemming handles human tragedy! Somehow he grapples with it and molds it into the raw material of which memorable English classes are made. A mind never at rest, relentlessly seeking out truth, justice, beauty. And a guaranteed salary.

"Sonia cared about you," I said.

"Sonia was a caring girl."

"She said you were very special."

"Listen," Hemming said. "I don't expect you to like me or respect me. But I expect you to return a favor. I told you about Jeff Miller, you keep my name out of it."

"Don't worry." I scanned his dreary little office. "It isn't often that you find a man exactly where he belongs. Thanks for the talk."

I headed off down the hall, and with each step I could feel Hemming's presence behind me receding in the distance.

Well done, Parker. Hard guy. Mean ass. Took the professor and put him firmly in his place. It had nothing to do with the fact that he and Sonia had been lovers. Of course not. This was noble investigatory zeal. A response to Lt. Mannion's sluggishness. It had nothing to do with the fact that my mind insisted on picturing Hemming and Sonia in bed together, had seen the graphic, rhythmic flesh tone against flesh tone. Had seen her parted mouth breathlessly urging him on, and had almost heard the words she had whispered.

Thank God it had nothing to do with that.

6

I WAS FAMILIAR WITH the Gingerbread House. It was
one of those small nightspots out in the avenues
where folk singers still sang about the plight of striking
coal workers. A smoke-filled time capsule you could crawl
into when you needed a breather from the present.

I got there at eight and sat down like just another
customer off the street and ordered a Dos Equis from a
waitress who looked like she'd gone straight from heroin
to wheat germ with no stop in between for fries and a
cheeseburger. When my harmlessness had been firmly
established, I off-handedly asked her if she'd ever heard
of Jeff Miller. She hadn't. She looked as if she hadn't
heard of anybody for an awfully long time.

The place began to fill up. According to the chalkboard
next to the stage a man called Rommentrance was supposed to read from his recently published collection of
poems—*Chants for the World Beneath the Rubble*. Then a

group from San Jose who did letter-perfect Kingston Trio. Only at the Gingerbread House would such a billing pack 'em in.

I gave up on the waitress and walked over to what the Gingerbread House called a bar. It was a counter with a coffee machine and two refrigerators full of wine and beer. No mixed drinks. The "bartender" was a thick-set man of about forty, bald on top, bushy light hair on the sides, a confrontational way of moving his body. A large earring dangled from one ear, and there was something of the deckhand buccaneer about him. The first to pull out his cutlass in battle, and the first to die.

"No counter service," he said without looking up.

"I don't want a drink. I'm looking for a friend."

"Don't need no more friends." He smiled at his own joke. "I'm all full up."

"I'm trying to find Jeff Miller."

He snatched four wine glasses from an overhead rack and began sloshing them full of white wine.

"Jeff who?"

"Jeff Miller."

He shoved the jug of wine back in the refrigerator and looked me straight in the face for the first time. His eyes were pavement-gray, and about as soft.

"You and him friends?"

"That's right."

"No you're not."

"We're not?"

"Nope." He went back to toweling off the spilled wine.

"Then why don't you tell me what we are?"

"I'll tell you this, sport. Take your questions and ram them ten inches up someplace I'm too cultured to mention. I don't mess around with that shit, no matter what you heard, so bug off."

"I don't care what you mess around with. How do I find Jeff Miller?"

The bartender tossed his towel to the side and stared me straight in the eyes. "Look, buddy. Do yourself a favor and beat it pronto before I get mad and start messing with you. I'm busy."

The waitress was back with an order. He hit a button on the coffee machine, yanked down more glasses. A strange guy to be pouring Chablis and making cappuccino.

"I'm not leaving till I have an address," I said, leaning away from a couple of customers who were listening in.

The bartender coughed out a short, dry laugh. "Man, you're about to get your ass airmailed out the door."

Time for the litmus test. I took a twenty-dollar bill out of my wallet and set it next to the jug of wine.

"Waitress forgot your tip," I said.

He looked at the bill. "That's the problem with the food and beverage business. Cheap customers."

I pulled out four more twenty-dollar bills and tossed them onto the counter next to the wine.

"You're getting warm," he said.

"Wrong," I said. "You're paid in full. Now let's have it."

"Anybody throws a hundred bucks on a table in ten seconds has got to have a little more tucked away somewhere."

"Is that so?"

"I wanna go to medical school." He smiled a tight, ugly smile. "Make something of myself. Heal the sick. My instinct figures Jeff Miller information runs about two-fifty."

I leaned close. "My instinct figures that if you don't give me Jeff Miller's address right now, your earring's coming off the hard way."

The smile went flat. His eyes clouded and grew so thick with murderous intent I could barely see his pupils. The customers who'd been eavesdropping moved away. I held my stare.

The gears were turning. He was positive he could snap me in half like a piece of peanut brittle, but somewhere wedged in the back of his mind was a sliver of doubt. I'm not small. Six-two, hundred and ninety pounds, and my boxing routine, hopeless as it is against a professional like Roscoe, had hardened my muscles and strengthened my gaze in the face of potential physical calamity.

"He lives on Irving," the bartender mumbled. "Above a vacuum place. I don't know the number."

"Irving's a big street. For a hundred bucks I'd prefer you know the number."

"Don't push your luck, sport."

"What's the cross street?"

"Seventh, eighth, ninth. Somewhere in there. Dyke bar across the street."

"Thanks," I said. "It's been a pleasure."

He gathered up the twenty-dollar bills, crushed them in his fist like they were so much Quinn Parker vertebrae dust, and shoved them in his pocket. "The pleasure was all mine, buddy. All mine."

I turned and walked out of the club, jostling past those still trying to squeeze in. A smattering of applause started up, and a wispy, Bolshevik clone I could only assume was Rommentrance got up onto the stage as the lights dimmed.

I reached the door and stepped out onto the sidewalk, breathing the night air, letting my heart return to normal, apologizing to my face for the danger I had exposed it to. The fog was wet and gusty and Rommentrance had begun to read his poetry inside. I could see his mouth moving silently beyond the window. Square head, square glasses, a face still waiting to experience its first smile.

He didn't seem like a very nice man, Rommentrance. Perhaps he sensed the crowd was staking out spots for the Kingston Trio group to follow. He clutched his scathing manifesto and looked out at all the wine sippers while he read, as if secretly deciding who among them would live, and who among them would have to die, come the revolution.

It took a while on the foggy, darkened streets, but I found it. A Hoover Appliance sales and repair shop of the mom and pop variety, with a half-dozen upright vacuum cleaners standing in the window behind protective metal gates.

I parked around the corner, and on my way back went out into the street a few steps and looked in at the closed and curtained window of the apartment above. A dim red light burned behind diaphanous curtains. Just to the right of the vacuum store was a five-foot-high gate that led to a narrow, thirty-foot path between the Hoover building and the apartment house next to it. At the end of the path a steep flight of stairs climbed to the front door of Miller's apartment. The structure was rickety and run down with peeling paint in large, sickly blotches.

I rang the buzzer on the outside gate and a dog next door started barking. There was no movement from the rose-lit apartment. Whoever was home wasn't in the mood to answer their door.

I lifted myself up over the gate and dropped down quietly on the other side. Except for the yapping dog everything was calm and still. The wind had died completely. The fog that had been blowing so hard in front of the Gingerbread House now hung motionless in the damp night.

I unlocked the gate I'd just jumped, leaving it slightly ajar, and proceeded directly up the flight of stairs and knocked on the door with the unabashed confidence of an encyclopedia salesman who believes in his product.

There was a stirring within. Then the first of several locks began to open.

"Who is it?" a female voice asked.

"Friend of Jeff's."

"Who?"

"Friend of Jeff's. The bartender at the Gingerbread House sent me."

Hesitation. Murmured conversation between the girl and a man. Ten seconds. Twenty. Then the last lock clicked open and the door swung inward. A girl stood there, sullenly rubbing her eyes as though roused from a deep, drug-induced sleep. She was thin, dirty, barefoot, wore a faded blue robe and had long, lank, mop-water blond hair. The hollows of her eyes were dark and defeated. She peered over my shoulder and down the stairs.

"How'd you get in, anyhow?"

"The gate was unlocked."

"Bullshit it was."

I slowly closed my eyes. "So I got tired of leaning on the buzzer."

"I could call the cops on you for that."

"Let's quit playing games. It's important that I talk to Jeff."

"What do you want him for?"

"He could be in trouble. Big trouble."

Suddenly, mechanically, she positioned her body as if to block my passage through the front door. The gesture was ridiculous. Barricading the fortress with a dress from the discount rack. Her bloodshot eyes flicked up over my right shoulder. It was a lousy stab at looking casual. The silence deepened. Time to leave.

I turned without a word and took the steps two at a time, moving as fast as I could without giving the impression of flight. No footsteps followed me down. I hurried to the gate and pulled and nothing happened. It had been closed and relatched.

I should've simply vaulted over the same way I'd vaulted in. But civilization got the best of me. I reached down and fumbled with the latch. Then the bush to my left came alive in a wild rustling of leaves and branches. I whirled, but it was too late. The weapon that swept across the foggy sky was just a darker object in a dark night, and I fell hard into the cold mud.

"What's the verdict?" Hank asked as I passed through the swinging doors of the emergency room at S.F. General.

"That promising xylophone career?"

"Yeah?"

"Finished."

Carol came up from the waiting room area and put her hand on my arm and peered with grave concern at my head. "How many stitches did they put in?" she said.

"Ten," I said. "Will you still like me when I sport a six-inch scar?"

"It's high enough on your scalp that nobody'll notice," Carol said. Then she smiled. "Anyway, I like a face with character. Look at Marlon Brando after his nose got broken."

"Thanks," I said.

The three of us walked down the long, antiseptic halls

and out into the midmorning sun, Carol reassuring me that—as much as my face needed the character—there wouldn't be a trace of a scar in a couple months. I breathed a little easier. Vanity, vanity.

Whoever had clobbered me had taken my wallet and left me there. I had come to just before dawn and somehow managed to find my van and drive to Hank and Carol's house. Carol had cleaned the wound, and together they'd driven me to the hospital. Nothing was fractured, but I'd have a hell of a headache for a few days.

Hank climbed into the van and started the engine while Carol and I got in back. "Where to?" he said.

"Let's get it over with," I sighed. "Mannion's office."

Hank whistled through his teeth. "The lieutenant's going to love this. You've scared Jeff Miller back into the woodwork for good."

"You're a great comfort, Hank. A regular Florence Nightingale."

But he was right. While Hank and Carol waited safely outside with Irma, Mannion paced the room and chewed me out and asked me who I thought I was, running around like a one-man posse. Movies and television were making his job impossible, what with every Tom, Dick, and Harry fancying themselves supersleuths. Then he ticked off on his fingers all the possible disastrous results of my foray into the Haight. Stupid. Foolish. Unbelievable.

Finally he cooled down. Went to the yellowed window and stared for a while. Quit tucking in his shirt. Okay. He understood why I might not have unwavering faith in the police, given the drivel we the public were spoon-fed every night on television. Fine. All he asked was that from now on I stayed out of it. No, he wasn't asking. He was telling.

I behaved the way he wanted me to, nodding like a contrite child and emptying my pockets of all the information I had about Ludmila, Ronald Hemming, Jeff Miller, and the earringed bartender. Mannion wrote it all down while shaking his head and then told me to go. Even Irma was mad at me.

On the drive back to the apartment Hank said, "I could have told you that you were doing the wrong thing."

"Don't start."

"I'm serious. What's the point in getting tough with a troglodyte bartender?"

"Troglodyte?"

"Cave dweller," Hank said. "From the French *trogle,* meaning hole."

"Never mind. The point is, it proved Jeff Miller had reason to be afraid of me."

"Come on, Quinn," Carol said. "If you jumped my gate in the middle of the night I'd be afraid of you, too."

"But it was a setup. An ambush. Somebody knew to relatch the gate and hide in the bushes."

"You've got conspiracy on the brain," Hank yawned. "This is how it probably went. The bartender sees you throwing around money so he calls Miller after you leave and warns him. They decide it might be economically advantageous to render you unconscious and examine your wallet. So you were rendered unconscious and your wallet is history."

"Maybe."

Back at the apartment Hank sat Carol and me down on the couch and ran a new comedy routine past us. He had a gig that night in Berkeley. He got the inspiration for it when he went to the supermarket and saw all the generic products lined up. Why not take it a step further, he said. Imagine a generic television station that had a generic newscast, with a generic anchorman. That was the name of the bit. Generic Anchorman!

Carol and I looked at each other. Neither one of us thought it was terribly funny, and when Hank finished he gave us a long, withering stare and glumly gathered up his notes. Carol tried to cheer him up, talked about the potential of the piece, but Hank wasn't having any of it. He mumbled a gloomy good-bye and tromped back down the stairs. Carol gave me a look, shrugged her shoulders, and followed.

I spent the day in the apartment, mindlessly tending to apartmentlike details. Fixed myself lunch, watched the one o'clock "Dialing for Dollars" movie on Channel 2. Then I went into the study and rearranged my books from alphabetical order to subject matter. I had to keep busy. It was the first time I'd really been alone since Sonia's death, and my mind would now and then spring from the shadows and play a malicious trick on me. Visualizing in graphic detail the crime as it must have been committed. Wondering at the extent of her putrefaction now that the lifeless hours were beginning to pile up.

Later in the afternoon I gave Erik a call. He'd heard through the grapevine about my accident and asked how I was. Then Hank called and ran his new, improved Generic Anchorman skit by me. It was better, and I told him so.

I crawled into bed early and spent a few minutes positioning my head. I was drifting into sleep when the telephone rang. It was Lt. Mannion.

"Thought you'd want to know we have Jeff Miller and his girlfriend in custody," he said.

"Hold on a second." I sat up straight in bed and turned on the lamp. "Where did you find them?"

"Hitchhiking. They were up past Ukiah, on their way to Oregon. That's what they said, but I'm guessing Canada. Turns out Miller gets arrested so much he's practically on a first-name basis with the boys at the jail. Small-time hothead. If you'd just told me about this guy from the start you'd have saved yourself a few stitches."

My alarm clock said nine-thirty, and Mannion was obviously calling from his house. Children were making a ruckus in the background, and once in a while an irritated female voice shouted for them to stop it unless they wanted to be sent to their rooms, and damn it, this time she *meant* it. The lieutenant sounded several hours into his cocktail hour.

"Did they admit hitting me?" I said.

"Two problems there. First, they both swear they had nothing to do with it. The girl says somebody came out of the bushes and nailed you and took your wallet and ran off."

"And they just left me there to bleed to death?"

"Jeff Miller doesn't lose sleep over people bleeding to death. Anyway, the second thing is that even if they did hit you—which I think they probably did—you were technically trespassing."

"Oh, come on!"

"Don't 'come on' me. You jumped their damn gate, for Christ's sake!" Mannion paused and I could hear the strong rattling of ice in a glass being drained to the last drop.

"So what are you saying?" I said.

"You can press charges if you want, but they won't stick. Simple as that. You jumped the gate and they were protecting themselves."

"But what if Miller killed Sonia? Isn't that the larger question here? Shouldn't I go ahead and press charges just to keep him under wraps until he's checked out?"

Mannion chuckled condescendingly on the other end.

"What's so funny?" I said.

"What do you think was the first thing I did when I got Miller's name? Christ, the boob tube's got you all thinking we're a bunch of morons. I hate to tell you this, but Jeff Miller didn't kill Miss Lucia."

I took a second to absorb the information. "What makes you so sure?"

"On the night Miss Lucia was murdered, Jeff Miller had been D&D and was under lock and key at the city jail. Alibis don't come much more ironclad than that."

7

I WOKE WITH A START to a room flooded with sunshine, the shards of an unremembered nightmare still jabbing at the brain. My head was throbbing, and three stories below the bedroom window cars and buses accelerated up Van Ness Avenue.

I made some coffee and took the cup in the bathroom while I changed my head bandage. I examined the damage in the mirror and decided it looked worse than it felt—swollen, waxy, purple and green. Ten little stitches meandered through the middle of it all. I thought of Brando and his broken nose. The wallpapered nymphs looked concerned, and I assured them everything was okay.

At the stroke of nine I gave Lt. Mannion a call. He was curt and irritable. No, nothing had changed on the Sonia Lucia case overnight. He emphasized the word "overnight." Jeff Miller was due to be released at any time, if he hadn't been released already.

"What about Ronald Hemming?" I said.

"He's cleared."

"What do you mean?"

"I mean Professor Hemming spent the evening of Miss Lucia's murder having dinner in Piedmont with the head of his department."

"The *whole* evening?"

"He had too much to drink and was requested by the host and hostess to spend the night, which he did."

"That was convenient."

Mannion cut me off. He had a million things to do and couldn't spend his time explaining himself to anybody who happened to dial his number. I was warned again to keep my nose out of the investigation. And no more wise-ass messages left with Irma, by the way. He hung up.

So there it was. Miller innocent, Hemming innocent, Parker back at square one with nothing to show for it but a bill from S.F. General. And Mannion was starting to make me feel like a waterboy tugging on the jerseys of the big guys who really play the game. Maybe it was time to take the lieutenant's advice. Butt out.

I wandered into the world headquarters of Amalgamated Tropical Enterprises, Inc. Feeling guilty, I gave Andrew Baxley a call. Mr. Baxley was a hundred-grand-a-year acrophobe who had to quit riding trains everywhere if he was going to get further in the company. He wasn't in the office, so I left a message and hung up gratefully.

Just before noon Hank came by, a bottle of champagne under his arm.

"I won't forget you, Quinn."

"What?"

"When you're huddled outside the studio door in the freezing slush with all the other autograph hounds, I promise I'll sign your book first. Swear to God." He put the bottle of champagne down on the table and rubbed his hands together.

"Let me guess. Your gig in Berkeley went well?"

"Killed 'em," Hank said. "Destroyed 'em. The manager should've stopped my routine to protect the audience from going into mass cardiac arrest. In fact, that's it. I'll demand a registered nurse and EKG machine from now on wherever I play."

Together we walked to the kitchen and Hank unwrapped the protective foil from around the champagne cork. "I'll never forget my humble roots. Care to join me?"

"Not in the morning, thanks."

Hank got up, walked to my wall clock, unhooked its plastic covering, and pushed the hands forward to read twelve noon. Then he rummaged through the cupboards and came back with two champagne glasses. He popped the cork and filled our glasses to the brim.

Hank didn't have that many triumphs, so I took a sip. My throat said absolutely not, and I spit the mouthful of champagne back into the glass.

Hank stared at me. "You're all class."

"I didn't know Head & Shoulders made a champagne."

"The very finest three ninety-nine can buy. Carol's got me on a tight budget. How's your head?"

"Better."

"Looks like hell."

"Thanks. Mannion called last night. They found Jeff Miller, but he didn't kill Sonia. He was in jail the night of her murder. And Hemming's cleared, too. Spent the night with friends over in Piedmont."

Hank tried the champagne, shuddered, puckered his

lips, held his glass up to the light for inspection. "On a morning like this I should be drinking Dom Perignon. Why is greatness so rarely recompensed in cold, hard cash?" He put his glass back on the table and nudged it away, as though it was a tidy mess the dog had made.

I steepled my fingers under my chin and watched a cloud skirt the top of Mount Tamalpais.

"All right," Hank said. "Let's have it."

"It's the newspaper article," I said. "Why would they talk about a serial killer for no reason?"

Hank exhaled loudly and folded his arms across his chest. "Do we have to go over this again?"

"Yes."

I ignored Hank's dirty look and reached for the phone and dialed Erik's number. Ludmila was back at work. She thanked me for coming by and we talked a minute and then she put me through.

"What's up?" Erik said.

"That article in the *Chronicle* . . . it's been bothering me."

Erik didn't answer for a while. Then he said, "Something else should be bothering you. I got a phone call from Mannion this morning."

"And?"

"He was asking questions about you."

My stomach went a little cold. "What kind of questions?"

"You told me once that you went to medical school, right?"

"Premed. But that was a long time ago, and it was only six months."

Erik cleared his throat. "Well, Mannion knows about it."

"So?"

"So Mannion is paying attention to people who might know how to wield a surgical saw. Sonia was taken apart with reasonable precision."

I held the phone in my hand, letting it all sink in. Hank stood and took the bottle of champagne into the kitchen. "Are you saying I'm a suspect?"

"I'm saying what I said. Mannion called and asked some leading questions about you."

"But . . . I was the one who called the police."

"Hate to pop your balloon," Erik said. "But police look doubly hard at discoverers of bodies. I mean, put yourself in Mannion's shoes. You were the last person to see Sonia alive. Your fingerprints, and *only* your fingerprints, are all over the room. I've seen the preliminary reports, and Sonia had been sexually assaulted. But there were no bruises or signs of a struggle, which makes an investigator tend to think that she first willingly made love to whoever killed her. You two had a past history of intimacy."

"Whoa," I said. "Suppose I'd made love to her that night, left, and then somebody else murdered her?"

"Look, Quinn. I'm just presenting Mannion's case. No matter what it says on some piece of government paper, homicide investigators think the absolute worst of everybody until given reason to think otherwise. Another thing. There was no break-in. Means she probably knew her killer. You have a key to her apartment. Want more?"

"Give it to me."

"Mannion thinks it's odd that you stayed up till two in the morning and then went boxing five hours later and hurried to be the first one to 'discover' the body."

I felt myself sink deeper into the chair. Hank strolled back out of the kitchen and looked down at me curiously.

"You still there?" Erik said.

"Still here."

"And you going off to interview Hemming and then traipsing around the Haight didn't help. Investigators are always leery of people who go high-profiling how much they're trying to track down a killer."

"Hold it, Erik. Did Mannion say all this to you?"

"No. Not all of it, anyway. But I know what's going on in his head, and I'm just laying it out on the table for you."

"What else is there?"

Erik sighed. "Am I scaring you?"

"Damn right. Now what else is there?"

"Well, . . . he did say that the stuff about the cassette sounds screwy to him. He doesn't entirely buy that you automatically click everything to zero-zero-zero and then notice it the next morning. Reeks of smoke screen."

"But I *did*! I *always* do! You know that yourself."

"Doesn't matter. You have to admit, it sounds a little odd. Always zeroing things out."

"Odd? What about Mannion? You know how many times a minute he tucks in his shirt? We all do screwy things."

There was a pause. Then Erik said, "Are you finished?"

"Yes."

He cleared his throat. "Another thing. The Tarot cards under her body . . . they brought in an expert to see if there was some kind of, you know, message to be decoded."

"And?"

"No. The expert said the cards were in the exact order they are when packaged. In other words, they were taken right out of the wrapper and put there. Planted."

I took a deep breath and looked out the window. "Sounds like he's about to arrest me," I said at last.

"For Christ's sake, Quinn, don't panic. Mannion doesn't have anything solid, and since you didn't do it, he'll never find anything solid. All I'm saying is be careful. You're definitely in his sights."

The cobwebs were clearing. I sat up on the edge of my chair and held the phone tight. "But what about the serial killer angle? The article in the *Chronicle*? Remember we were—"

"Forget it," Erik said.

"Forget what?"

"Forget what some overeager reporter wrote. There's been only one murder in the last few months that even remotely resembles what happened to Sonia."

"Which one was that?"

Pause. "Quinn . . . "

"Come on. Which was it?"

Deep sigh. "A woman was murdered a few months back. Pitchforked, decapitated, in a barn down in Woodside. But—"

"How many favors do you owe me, Erik?"

"None."

"What about the All-Star game tickets?"

Pause. "Okay, what do you want?"

"Particulars on the Woodside murder. Who I might talk to, what happened—"

"Didn't you hear what I just said about high-profiling your own investigation?"

"I'll keep it low profile, okay? I'd kind of like to have a few things to say on my behalf when Mannion comes to arrest me."

Erik exhaled loudly on the other end. "You don't breathe a goddamn word of this to Mannion. Nothing. Understood?"

"Understood."

"He'd have my little blond behind tacked up onto his office wall if he found out I was helping you. Let me look up my Woodside connection. I'll call you back."

I hung up and wandered into the kitchen. Hank was pouring the champagne down the sink.

"Eighty percent of my take for the night," he said wistfully. "You won't have clogged drains till next summer."

It was cold, and the wind was picking up. The sun began to sink into the watery horizon, and as it did the beach slowly filled with people. Couples in love, couples falling out of love. Tourists with cameras, children bending down at the edge of the shore, letting cold sand sift between their fingers. Sunsets urge contemplation. It was a safe bet I was the only person on Carmel Beach contemplating pitchforks, surgical saws, headless women.

The sun picked up speed as it hit the horizon, then was gone, and in its wake the earth hummed like a tuning fork. People stood motionless, gazing at the spot where the sun had been until at last the ubiquitous jogger, oblivious to all but his cardiovascular system, gallumphed sweatily across everyone's pensive field of vision and broke the spell.

I looked down at the scrap of paper in my hand. Kate Ulrich, friend and former roommate of the woman who'd been pitchforked and decapitated in the Woodside barn. It was all Erik was able to dig up. So I'd driven the hundred and twenty miles south to Carmel. If nothing came of this I'd leave sleuthing to the professionals. Slink back to Erik's office and kneel at the shrine of his glass-encased diplomas. Trust that Mannion would find his own murderer and get me off the hook.

I walked back from the beach and called D'Joint, the restaurant where Kate Ulrich worked, from a public phone at the end of Ocean Avenue. A woman with a phony British accent told me Ms. Ulrich wouldn't be in for another hour.

Okay. It wasn't going to be a pop-in, pop-out interview, so I tooled the van back out to Highway 1 and began to look for a reasonable hotel. Carmel was out. Too many years of living on a tight budget had spoiled certain extravagances for me. All I need for a good night's sleep is a firm bed, clean sheets, and the reasonable expectation that my car battery will still be there in the morning.

I found a Best Western on the outskirts of Del Rey Oaks and checked in. Then I sat on the bed and gave Hank a call. Carol answered, and we chatted a minute. Then she told me to hold on and Hank came on the line.

"Where the hell are you?" he asked.

"A Best Western in Del Rey Oaks. I'm going to talk to the friend of the lady who got killed at Woodside and then head on back. She works at a restaurant in Carmel. The way things have been going, she'll probably toss a drink in my face."

"Just do me a favor," Hank said. "If the bartender is wearing an earring, turn around and walk out."

I showered and shaved and slapped some cologne on my face. As I was dressing the phone rang. It was Hank again.

"You aren't depressed, are you?" he said.

"No."

"You sounded a little depressed when I talked to you."

"I'm okay."

"If you do start to feel depressed, this ought to keep things in perspective. Our solar system is only a few million years away from crossing the plane of the Milky Way galaxy."

I sat down on the bed and put on my shoes, holding the phone between my shoulder and neck. "What happens then, so I won't be taken by surprise?"

"Go ahead and joke, but it's probably what killed the dinosaurs. Our solar system hits these huge interstellar clouds of galactic gas about every thirty-five million years, and all hell breaks loose. Temperature changes, comet showers—pretty grim stuff. In a few million years we're all going to be shaken like apples off a tree."

"Gosh, I feel better already."

"Perspective, Quinn. All I'm trying to do is offer perspective."

I thanked Hank for his perspective and hung up. Put on a little more cologne. Got in the van and headed back to Carmel. The dark highway sped beneath me, and the scent of the cologne seemed like the fresh promise of a happy world. It soothed my growing unease over pitchfork deaths and Carmel chic and some of the more final, best-ignored truths of astronomy.

It took a while to find D'Joint. In the frenetic scramble to be unique, the businesses of Carmel blurred together in one hazy jumble of cookie-cutter individuality. Not so many years ago they'd come thundering across the Great Plains from New York, Paris, and London—stagecoaches crammed full of ferns and Tiffany lamps and imported paté. They came, they saw, they set up shop. And, inevitably, they ruined. In their wake lay a handful of once-lovely towns—Santa Fe, Provincetown, Key West, Aspen—now priced out of control and emptied of the very people who originally made the places what they were. Attila the Hun in designer jeans, and one by one the little towns fell before the slings and arrows of Italian labels.

At last I located D'Joint. It was right on Ocean Avenue, but set back about twenty feet from the vulgarities of the sidewalk, hidden in a grove of eucalyptus trees. I asked for Kate Ulrich at the maître d's station, and a cadaverous, elongated character straight out of El Greco requested that I wait a moment.

I strolled the waiting area. Framed photographs hung on the wall—people laughing and throwing their arms around one another, all smiles and tans and emaciated good looks. Their expressions seemed to say, "We are who we are, and all you poor suckers out there aren't." A plaque hung on the far wall proclaiming D'Joint as the honorary consulate headquarters of Tahiti, and below that was a framed copy of the London *Times* sports section from the night Muhammad Ali knocked out George Foreman. I was crouched down reading the Ali article when nyloned legs were suddenly beside me.

"Can I help you with something?"

I stood up. A woman was looking at me with folded arms and dubious eyes. She was tall, slender, with shoulder-length sandy hair. Maybe thirty-five years old.

"Kate Ulrich?"

"Yes."

"My name's Quinn Parker. I'd like to talk to you for a few minutes."

"I'm on duty," she said, pausing to look me over. There was an urban savvy in her demeanor. Chicago, New York. Definitely not Carmel. "What is it you want to talk about?"

I took a deep breath. "There's no easy way to say this. I live in San Francisco. A close friend of mine was murdered a few days ago. The way she was killed, the circumstances . . ."

Kate Ulrich began shaking her head. "If this is about

what happened to Sherri, I don't want to talk about it."

"The same person who killed Sherri might have killed my friend."

"I'm sorry." She stood looking down at her shoes, biting her lower lip. "I'm really sorry, but I can't talk about it."

"It would help me enormously."

"Look," she said. "I really have to get back to work now. Excuse me."

Kate Ulrich began to walk away and I asked her to wait a second. She stopped. I took a pen and wrote my name, address, and phone number on a paper napkin from the maître d's station. "If you change your mind, this is where I can be reached. I'm staying at the Best Western in Del Ray Oaks tonight."

I handed her the napkin and she took it the way you accept a street-corner leaflet you have no intention of reading.

"I'm sorry to be rude," she said. "And I'm sorry about your friend. I know exactly what you must be going through. But it's taken me a long time to forget about Sherri and that whole terrible business, and I don't want to go through it again. I *can't* go through it again."

"Okay," I said. "If you can't, you can't. All I ask is that you think about it."

She nodded, paused as though she were going to say something, and then briskly turned away.

I watched about ten minutes of television. Good old boys yukking it up to a banjo soundtrack while automobiles crashed into each other. I thought the canned laughers were going to split their canned guts at the gosh-durn hilarity of it all. Finally I heaved myself up out of my chair and shut the damn thing off.

I went to the bathroom, leaned on the sink, and stared at myself in the mirror. My psyche was in need of a pep talk. Locker room at halftime. Parker with his fire poker, pushing at charred logs, compounding the sorrow of other people by rekindling the embers of past tragedies.

While I stood there waiting for the reflected image to say something, the phone rang. I sighed. Hank. Some new esoteric evidence of cultural decline.

I picked up the receiver.

"I'll talk to you if you want," the female voice said. "Why don't you come by the restaurant?"

"Right now?"

"Right now."

8

WE DECIDED ON A café around the corner from D'Joint. Lots of plants, dim lights, quiet. We found a table for two at the back and settled in.

"What made you change your mind?" I asked.

Kate sighed and swept the hair out of her eyes. "It's Sunday. Business was slow and I was upset, so the manager told me to go ahead and take the night off. Thought I might as well be constructively upset and answer your questions."

"I'm sorry about barging in like that."

"It's okay. After Sherri died I did a lot of barging myself. How did you get my name?"

"Police records."

"Anybody can just call up?"

"I have a friend."

We ordered two glasses of wine from a waiter who insisted on telling us his first name and that he would be serving us. When he flitted away Kate gave me a long-suffering look and shook her head. She was an attractive woman. Healthy, full-bodied—a durable beauty rather than delicate. She had a strong jaw and dark, vibrant eyes that radiated a kind of street-smart independence. She was not the lily white, ethereal stuff of which sonnets are made. This woman would not wilt in the sun.

"What happened to your head?" she asked.

"I tried to talk to somebody else about my friend. He wasn't as cooperative as you've been."

Kate Ulrich thought about it a minute, then nodded her head. "Mind if I smoke?" she said.

"Go ahead."

She lit a cigarette and leaned back in the chair. "I'm down to about four or five a day now, usually only when I'm having a drink in the evening."

"You don't have to explain yourself."

"I can tell you're not from Carmel," she said. "Pull out a cigarette here and people look at you like you've just tunneled out of a leper colony."

"Where are you from?"

"Detroit."

I nodded diplomatically, and Kate laughed.

"What's so funny?" I said.

"Everybody reacts that way when I mention Detroit. It's like telling somebody your parents used to beat you. Avert eyes. Shift feet."

"I've never been there."

"Well, don't make a special trip, but it's not all that bad. The longer I'm in California the more of a Detroit chauvinist I turn into. At least Michigan is real. Out here I keep expecting to see Dorothy and the Tin Man skipping down Ocean Avenue. I mean, look at the ferns in this place!"

"They did overdo it a bit."

"A bit? Any moment some lost Japanese World War Two soldier's going to come stumbling out with his rusted rifle, looking for the emperor." Kate exhaled and ran the long, slender fingers of both hands through her sandy hair. "Bottom line is I'm living out here and not in Detroit, so maybe I should put a lid on it."

The waiter brought our wine, told us to "enjoy" in the cozy-up style he was so enamored of, and faded off.

"Well, then!" Kate said, smoothing the tablecloth in front of her. "What questions did you have?"

"Only three."

"Fire away."

"Did you or Sherri know anybody named Jeff Miller?"

"No."

"Professor Ronald Hemming?"

"No."

"Sonia Lucia?"

"No."

I leaned back in my chair. "That concludes my line of direct questioning."

"What about indirect?"

"The obvious. Did Sherri have contact with anyone who might have wanted to kill her? Enemies? Somebody with a grudge?"

"No. There were some curious types hanging around Sherri, but I gave all that information to the police a long time ago. I assume the peripheral oddballs were checked out and cleared."

There it was. One sip into our wine and the Great Interrogation was over. There was no good reason not to say *adios*, but we were oddly reluctant to part. Our eyes assessed each other. Two glasses of wine were never consumed more slowly.

"And what is it you do, Quinn Parker of San Francisco?"

I dug out my card and handed it to her. Kate ran her fingers over Oscar's embossed beak and down the leaning tropical palm.

"You breed parrots?" She smiled.

"How did you guess?"

"What is it really?"

"Hard to say. Outdoor psychology is closest to it."

Kate wrinkled her brow. "Come again?"

"The opposite of indoor psychology. Indoor psychology breeds indoor solutions, indoor courage. A false sense of emotional well-being that can be snapped too easily outdoors. Anthropologists will tell you that the meekest accountant sitting third desk from the right has a few brain cells kicking around from the old days, and that it would probably do everybody a lot of good to bonk a leopard over the head with a club once in a while. I guess you could say I put a club in their hands and lead them to the leopard."

Kate kept staring at me. "Really?"

"Really."

"You just find these people on the street?"

"No. I work in conjunction with a psychologist friend in San Francisco. She gives me a call when she wants to find out if her couchside solutions are going to hold up in the big nasty world."

Kate smiled, picked up her wine, kept her eyes on me as she sipped. "Just when I thought there was nothing new under the sun."

I paid the bill and as we were walking out Kate mentioned that she had some of Sherri's personal items in her apartment.

"If you want to come and have a look at them, you can."

"When?"

"Tonight, if you feel like it. I have a little wine in the refrigerator. We could . . . I don't know. Go through Sherri's things together. She kept a diary."

I stopped in my tracks. "A diary?"

"Before you get excited, the police had it a month and gave it back. It's strictly 'dear diary' stuff."

I walked Kate to her car and then followed her up Ocean Avenue in my van. A wind was picking up, the kind of wind that brings rain. For some reason I had assumed her apartment was nearby, but instead she headed out to Highway 1, turned south, then swung left a few miles later onto Carmel Valley Road. Fifteen minutes into the Valley we passed a darkened golf course, and she turned left into the parking lot of a large, futuristic apartment complex. Together we walked through a landscaped pool-Jacuzzi area till we reached her door. Kate unlocked it and told me to sit on the couch while she got out of her D'Joint clothes and dug up Sherri's things.

I plunked myself down and looked at the apartment. Solid, hard-to-damage furniture, wall-to-wall carpeting, all-electric everything, a hokey little chandelier hanging over the dining room table. On the living room wall —prominently displayed above the phony metal fireplace—was a painting of an ocean sunset with oranges and yellows vomiting all over the horizon. It was a tiny, modular living space where the Good Life had been predefined, and it was up to the tenant to accept it or move elsewhere. An overstuffed armchair was the only thing in the apartment that seemed out of place. It was old and ratty and comfortable-looking. Above and beyond it, curiously positioned in the middle of the bookshelf, was a broken wine glass.

Kate came back into the room a few minutes later

wearing faded jeans and a gauzy, cotton blouse that looked vaguely Indian. She had a couple of books and a folder in her hands.

"How do you like my apartment?" she said.

"The cold and bitter truth?"

"Nothing but."

"I'd suggest an air-sickness bag at the front door."

"Well, we agree on about everything so far." She put a finger to her chin and turned this way and that. "What's your least-favorite detail?"

"Jury's out. Probably that nine-ninety-five flaming sunset painting."

"You know what? That thing is *attached* to the wall! I'm not *allowed* to take it down!"

"Come on."

"Try it."

I got up and tried it. The painting was bolted into the wall. "You're right."

"Scary thing is, I think they're afraid people will try to steal it." Kate put the books and folder on the coffee table. "Anyway, these are Sherri's things. Can I get you that wine I promised?"

"How's your vodka and tonic supply?"

"Ample. With lime?"

"Please."

While Kate fixed my drink I picked up Sherri's diary and checked the last entry. February eighth. Then I went back and leafed through the first few pages. The writing was wooden and self-conscious—a nervous explanation to herself of why she was keeping a diary. Then it began to flow into a chit-chatty narrative about men and work and places she visited.

"Here you go," Kate said, handing me my drink.

"Thanks. What exactly was Sherri's job?"

"Like it said in the papers about fifty million times in bold, bold print. Sex therapist."

"That's a pretty general title. Can you narrow it some?"

Kate settled into the overstuffed armchair, stared into the phony metal fireplace. "Well, my own personal knee-jerk opinion was that it was kind of trendy and self-indulgent. I don't think Sherri was ever trained in a clinical sense. She took courses at Santa Cruz and Esalen, went to Gestalt workshops, knew how to rolf and grov and primal scream. Her walls weren't exactly lined with scholarly textbooks."

"She just hung up her shingle?"

"Kind of. I don't want to knock Sherri too much. I imagine she was pretty good at what she did, and she took it all very seriously. I was just a little dubious about her credentials. In Detroit I don't think she would have lasted a month." Kate paused, looked at the diary and sighed. "So speaks the cocktail waitress."

"And you shared a place in San Francisco?"

"Uh-huh. Pacific, near Fillmore. After she died I didn't feel like living in the city anymore, so I came down here. I don't know why. I just did it." Kate nodded at the diary. "Any clues springing out at you yet?"

I shook my head and put it aside. "Not yet."

"Why are you doing this, anyway? Aren't the San Francisco police working on it?"

"Not as enthusiastically as I'd like."

"That's it?"

"No." I fished the lime out of my drink. "There also seems to be a notion in the air that I might have done it, and it would be in my interest to prove that notion false."

Kate was silent for a while. "Were you ... involved with the woman who was killed?"

"Used to be."

"Well," Kate said, raising her glass of wine, "here's to those of us who've managed to stay alive."

An hour passed, and the drinks went down painlessly. At some point Kate switched to brandy and soda. She sat in the ratty, overstuffed armchair with her feet tucked up, and the rain that had been threatening since D'Joint began to beat against the windows.

"Don't tell me that chair came with the apartment," I said.

"Are you kidding? I had to sneak it in under cover of darkness. Literally! You laugh, but I'm serious. Tenants of Devonwood, you see, are not allowed to bring in their own furniture." She ran a soft hand over the threadbare upholstery as an old woman might fondly stroke the dog who keeps her company. "If the management found out I had this in here they'd probably take me down to the Jacuzzi and boil me alive." Kate got up and walked half-way to the kitchen. "I'm making popcorn. Buttered or plain?"

"Buttered."

She disappeared into the kitchen and I picked up Sherri's diary again and took a closer look at the last entry.

Feb. 8—It was a bad morning. I don't know how much longer I can keep things secret. Why did it even start? Some strange jealousy once P managed it with someone else? Who knows? Mixed-up situation. I think L is still watching me. Just a hunch. Scares me. I took C out for a ride and that made me feel better, as usual. Then a long, boring afternoon thinking about how I'm going to handle P. D came by later in the evening and we went to dinner in Palo Alto even though I wasn't really in the mood. Got into an argument. I think he knows something's up.

Kate came back into the room with a huge bowl of popcorn. I put the diary back on the table.

"Who were C, D, P and L?" I asked.

"Cinnamon and Doctor Dave. Cinnamon was Sherri's horse. Dave was a horse's ass."

"Boyfriend?"

"More or less."

"And P?"

Kate paused. There was an uncharacteristic hesitation in her face, and when she spoke it was with a kind of resigned reluctance. "Sherri was having an affair with one of her patients. She told me so one night, and I had to swear to never breathe a word of it to anybody."

"Why did she tell you?"

"Who knows? I was her friend. Her roommate. It must have been a terrible burden and she needed to get it off her chest. Sherri had a pretty good hold on what the relationship between a therapist and client should be, and she felt guilty as hell about what was happening."

I looked down at the diary. "You think the client might have been P?"

Kate nodded. "I'm sure of it."

"Did you ever see him?"

"Once. At least, I think it was him. I was at the apartment one night when Sherri thought I was gone, and she brought home this man. When Sherri saw me she hustled him right out. Two minutes, that was it. Judging by the general uncomfortableness, I assumed he was the mystery client. Sherri never mentioned the incident and I never saw the man again."

"And the police know about this?"

Kate rolled her eyes and laughed. "Do they *know* about it? Jesus, all I did for a week was look through mug books down at the police station. I must've seen two thousand photos. He wasn't there. Then I spent a day with the police artist, but I couldn't get it right."

I closed the diary, looked at the front and back covers. "Who was L? She said she was scared of him."

Kate shrugged. "No idea."

"How long after this last entry was Sherri killed?"

"The next day. Go back through and you'll see she never missed a day. Never. God, I remember once we went to L.A. together to see friends of hers and we got a little tight at the reception—it was a wedding—and when we got back to the hotel room she pulled out her diary and started writing. I mean, she could barely sit at the desk without falling over."

Kate settled into her chair, thought about what she was going to say, then said it.

"Sherri always got in too deep with men. Half her life was spent extricating herself from awkward love affairs. I always thought it was odd that she could be so detached in her profession and yet have such problems out of the office. It was tough being her friend because every time it happened, some new guy, she acted like it was the end of the world. That's why we quit rooming together. I couldn't handle it. That, plus I was tired of city living."

"How long did you share the apartment in San Francisco?"

"Almost a year."

"And her practice was there?"

"On Bush Street. She made a lot of money and it was kind of like a favor to me that we shared a place."

"What about Doctor Dave, the horse's-ass boyfriend? Sounds like she was getting ready to dump him."

"Dave didn't do it."

"What makes you so sure?"

"I dated him a couple of times myself. He actually met Sherri through me and zeroed in on her. Sherri was the kind of woman men tended to zero in on."

Kate nervously poked at the single cube of ice in her glass so that it went to the bottom and drifted slowly back to the surface, like a body that refused to be drowned. I watched it go down and up, down and up.

"Oh, Dave was all right, I suppose," she went on. "Not the man I wanted to walk hand-in-hand with through life. Or even have a third date with. But he was all right. I'm being too harsh."

I wanted to say something, but the way Kate was working her jawbone and staring down at the rug made me hold off. Then the jawbone went slack and the eyes lost their focus and whatever shred of memory that had intensified her for the instant was gone. She sighed and leaned back in the chair.

"The popcorn's starting to get dry," she said.

"I'll suffer."

"No, I hate it when it gets dry. The top layer absorbs all the butter. It'll just take me a second to melt some more."

And off into the kitchen she went. We all have our defense mechanisms, and apparently Kate's was to find immediate, headfirst refuge in the mundane. Ruminate the importance of properly buttered popcorn. I sat alone in the living room and stared at the empty armchair. She'd snuck it in under cover of darkness, risking eviction, banishment, and probable Jacuzzi execution. I felt better about the little apartment now. It was doubling as a halfway house for furniture riding the underground railroad to Oregon or Montana, where they might be free.

In a few minutes Kate came back into the living room holding a small pan of hot melted butter.

"Who knows," she said, pouring the butter into the bowl of popcorn with a slow, circular motion, "Dave might've been the most horrible pitchfork murderer in history. Impaled little boys and put them in his soup. I'm not the world's best judge of men."

"No?"

"No."

She set the pan down on the end of the coffee table, settled back into her chair. "Are you in the mood for a sad, sad story?"

"I like sad stories. Especially when it's raining."

"Then here's mine. Once upon a time in a land far, far away from here—Connecticut—this reasonably good-looking fairy princess walked down a flower-strewn aisle and pledged love to a not-so-bad-looking prince till death did them part."

"You were married?"

"Yes. But never did the course of true love run smooth, and now the princess's lawyers are fighting with the prince's lawyers and the tiara has been put in mothballs." She stopped and sipped from her brandy and soda, the lines of her mouth confused as to whether this was a ha-ha joke or a bitter memory.

I considered her confession for what I thought was an appropriate time, then held aloft my empty glass.

"I'd better fix another," I said.

I wandered into the kitchen, put together another vodka and tonic, and came back twirling the ice and looking at Kate curled up in the illegal armchair.

"Was my story that heart wrenching?" she said.

"Forgive this calloused heart for not being wrenched," I said, "but the newspapers tell me these days you flip a coin when you get married."

"Fifty percent of all married couples can't be wrong?"

I shrugged. "Depends on which fifty you're talking about."

"Well, . . . I suppose I lived for a long time thinking I was the exception to the rule. Trends happened to other people. Statistics were made up of other people. I really, truly thought that when I got married I would stay married, and that there was something wrong with people who got divorced. You know, that they had been stupid or unthinking or were just enamored with the thought of wearing a long white gown and being queen for a day. They didn't understand the *gravity* of marriage." She laughed and swept a judgmental hand at her apartment. "And now here I am. One of the crowd, reading trendy articles in trendy magazines because they apply to me."

"Welcome to the human race."

Kate paused, licked her lips. The brandy and soda was kicking in. "You know a way to tell you're in trouble?"

"I know several dozen."

Kate bent down and pulled out a magazine from below her coffee table and waved it in the air. "When articles in *Cosmopolitan* start to become relevant. *Cosmopolitan!*"

I smiled and pointed to the broken wine glass resting on the bookshelf above the armchair. "What's that?"

"Oh, that." She smiled and looked at the glass a little wistfully. "Testimony to a brief, isolated moment of lust on the part of my former husband. Seems he couldn't control himself one night at the dinner table. It was pretty nice, actually. Messy, but nice. I shouldn't make fun. The prince did have his moments." Pause. "So I kept it. Why not? Some people have stuffed fish, I've got that. Jesus, you're getting all the details tonight, aren't you?"

Yes, I was, and it was time to stop. Steer the nice

woman away from any further frank appraisals of herself. She was just a teeny bit drunk and probably talking a lot more than the sober Kate Ulrich would.

It was late. The rain was really coming down and I'd had enough vodka to make the winding, slippery, twenty-mile drive back to my hotel a little more interesting than I'd prefer. But when I stood to leave Kate looked irritated and said absolutely not. I wasn't going all the way to Del Rey Oaks at this hour. Every drunk in Monterey County would be on the road, and the Carmel Valley highway was treacherous even in the best of weather. I was sleeping on her couch, and that was that. She hauled out some sheets and blankets, waved good night, and disappeared into her bedroom.

It was a nice-enough couch. Small, but soft and cocoon-like, and I could burrow right down into the dark warmth and smell the distinctly different smell each living space has. The genius who'd devised the bolted-in painting was doubtlessly hard at work figuring out a way to neutralize scents. Blast mono-odorizer through the vents. Suck out cooking smells, nuance of perfume, the acrid pungency of love.

I pulled the end table up closer, turned on the lamp, and spent a half hour or so perusing Sherri's diary. David, the horse's ass, popped in and out with regularity. She and D going to the beach. She and D attending a concert. D surprising her with an unexpected gift. But when L or P were mentioned, the tone of the diary changed dramatically. A cautious watching of words. And throughout the entries one could not help but feel the presence of something else. Something bad. It ran through the diary and darkened her life like cloud shadows on a hill. There was a hastiness in some of the entries. The writing of someone constantly glancing back over the shoulder. But that was it. Clues, as Kate had said earlier, were not leaping from the page.

I put the diary away and turned off the light and lay there in the rainy dark. It was very still. I thought of Lt. Mannion's smiling reassurance that I was not a suspect. Smooth. I remembered what Erik had said about the fingerprints. How mine, and *only* mine, were in the bedroom the morning after the murder. The illogic of it nagged at me. No fingerprints meant the killer had wiped down the apartment after the murder. Fine. Murderers do that sort of thing. Except this killer would have worn gloves. Sonia's murder was executed with a chilling perfection and attention to detail. Whoever did it wouldn't have realized at the end of the carnage that, oops, I forgot to slip on my gloves. The only other fingerprints would have been Sonia's. She was the victim. Hers belonged there. So what was it?

And the business with the nightgown . . . puzzling. I knew Sonia. We'd practically lived together for six months. The lack of evidence of a break-in strongly suggested that she knew her murderer, had opened the door to him. Evidence of sexual assault. Okay, assume the murderer was a lover. Sonia was the kind of woman who would have greeted a lover naked, not kept him waiting in the hall at two in the morning while rummaging through a closet for a nightgown almost never worn otherwise. It didn't make sense.

I could hear Kate's body shifting in her bed, rustling the sheets and blankets. Her presence diverted me. The broken wine glass sat on the bookshelf. She'd packed it three thousand miles. A relic from the rubble of a marriage gone bad.

I tried to imagine the moment. Was it something she

had said? Or the way she looked? What was it that had caused the prince to climb over the broccoli and knock over the yams and get gravy on his gray pinstripes at the chance of ravishing her right there on grandma's tablecloth?

The rain beat harder on the windows. Adrenaline was flowing from somewhere, and I tossed and turned another hour before going to sleep.

9

"SO P MIGHT HAVE KILLED THE WOMAN," Hank said. "But there's no apparent link between the Woodside murder and Sonia's."

"That's the way it looks."

Hank nodded, pursed his lips. I couldn't share his investigatory zeal. Not this afternoon. I'd come directly to the Bus Stop from Carmel specifically to have some quiet time. Let the dust settle. Mull over love, lust, murder, and the crooked side streets of desire. I assumed Hank would be elsewhere. He wasn't.

It had been an awkward morning with Kate. What looks right by night often looks wrong by day, and the sight of rumpled bedsheets on her couch and a strange man rumbling around the kitchen fixing coffee had turned her cold and cautious and arm's length. We had a formal, studied breakfast, and afterward Kate shook my hand and smiled a nice, polite, please-kindly-exit smile. I exited.

"Okay," Hank went on, standing and beginning to pace. "A sex therapist. Means she dealt with some real screwballs, right?"

"Or people who acknowledge they have a problem and are taking steps to overcome it."

Hank gave me the look he always gives me when I'm being Reasonable and Mature About Things. "Like I said, screwballs. It's probably a good bet one of her patients killed her."

"I'm sure that possibility has occurred to the Woodside police, Hank."

Hank continued pacing. He was one of the world's great pacers, unable to keep still when dreaming up a comedy sketch or contemplating Swedish actresses or watching a sports event. I've seen him pace at restaurants and in the aisles of planes. Once at Candlestick Park an usher had to ask him to leave because he couldn't stay in his seat.

I took a sip from my drink. "Why aren't you home playing ride-the-horsey with your kids?"

"They're in school."

"Then how about ride-the-horsey with your wife? My male intuition says she could use a little attention."

Hank smiled. "You trying to get rid of me?"

"Yes."

"Fine." Hank finished his drink and climbed off the barstool. He had to get to work on a comedy skit, anyway. Somebody from Palo Alto had caught his show-stopping act in Berkeley the night before last and wanted him to perform at a new comedy showcase that had just opened near the Stanford campus.

"Another night, another five bucks," he said, pulling on his jacket.

"Think of it this way. Three or four more shows and you'll have enough to buy a decent bottle of champagne."

Hank shook his head. "I never expected sudden riches. Just sudden fame. I'm going to swing by your place and pick up some papers, then I'll be home all night."

"Why the detailed itinerary?"

"I never know when you might need a ride to the emergency room. Head's looking better, by the way."

I handed Hank my extra set of apartment keys and he left. Roger strolled over with a cold Dos Equis.

"On the house," he said.

"Thanks."

He pulled out a handful of limes and began slicing them. "Hear any more about your friend who got killed?"

"No."

I watched Roger slice the limes. He was a good bartender. Interested without being nosy. Where I drink has always depended on who's doing the serving, and when Roger moves on from the Bus Stop, so will I.

"Do bartenders still give advice to paying customers on matters of love and war?"

"No." Roger gathered up the sliced limes and dropped them in a bucket. "The union cut all that stuff out. Contract says I only have to talk sports and astrology. But in your case I'll scab. What's the problem?"

"Let's say this hypothetical guy meets this hypothetical woman and they seem to hit it off right away. She even has him over to her apartment the first night and they drink together and share a few stories and the hypothetical guy is invited to sleep on her couch."

"So far, so good. Did the hypothetical lady also sleep on the couch?"

"No. She slept in her own room and woke up the next morning cold."

"How cold?"

"Ice cubes wouldn't have thawed on her hypothetical face. The man on the couch was given a quick breakfast and whisked out the door with barely a good-bye."

Roger nodded and folded his arms across his chest. "Fire and Ice Syndrome. Well documented. Doctor Roger says drink your beer and don't worry about it. She really loves you and you'll have eight kids."

Forget it. The Bus Stop was not in the cards, so I thanked Roger for getting me current on the sociology of modern love and left the Dos Equis untasted.

Instead of going straight home I wandered along Union Street. Boutiques and singles bars, fancy cars and fancy people. Yet in a curious way it interested me more than Fisherman's Wharf or Chinatown or the cable cars clanging away. Those things were just dusted-off postcards —badly preserved relics of another age, maintained begrudgingly by merchants honing in on the tourist dollar. Union Street was the new San Francisco, like it or not.

I ducked into Springer Brothers, Union Street's version of a supermarket. If you want marinated New Zealand fish scales, you can buy them at Springer's. If you want a loaf of white bread, good luck. The stockboys look like Mercedes-Benz mechanics, and the wine department comes complete with a white-smocked specialist with a clipboard. The cashiers are gaunt and aloof and full of diminished aristocracy, standing by their cash registers, arrogant as only true greatness is arrogant.

I picked up a few things, including a bottle of nice champagne should Hank have another hit at Stanford, and headed back up Union Street toward home.

I walked past the Bus Stop and waved through the

window to Roger and made it about another ten steps when I heard him calling my name. He was out on the sidewalk, jogging up to me, still holding his white bar towel.

"Erik just called. He's been trying to track you down. Said it was important."

"Where is he?"

"At the office."

I went back into the Bus Stop with Roger and dialed Erik's number. My pulse was going. In the world of Erik J. Paige there are no urgencies except fourth-and-inches, and it was too early in the year for football.

He answered immediately. "What's up?" I said.

"They found another girl out on Clement, killed just like Sonia. Exactly."

I rose from my barstool. "Just now?"

"An hour ago. And they got the guy, Quinn! They got him!"

I sat back down. My head felt like cotton candy. "The killer?"

"Of course the killer! It was in an apartment building and a woman next door heard the commotion and called the cops. They nailed him right at the scene. Word I get is he's already confessed to Sonia's slaying and maybe another. Signed, sealed, everything."

"Who is he?"

"Don't know yet."

I stared at the beer mirror hung on the wall over the bar. So that was that . . .

"You still there?" Erik asked.

"Still here."

"I'll know more in the next few days, so stick around."

I paused a moment. "Was there a VCR in the apartment?"

"A what?"

"A VCR."

"Christ, Quinn! They caught the guy with blood up to his elbows and a goddamn saw in his hands! What do you mean?"

"But don't people sometimes imitate crimes?"

There was a pause at the other end, and when Erik spoke again his voice had changed. It was a tone I'd never heard him use with me before.

"You sound disappointed they got him, Quinn."

"Don't be ridiculous. I just want to be sure."

Silence.

"Look," I said, rubbing my eyes. "I'll be in the city for a while now. Give me a call when you find out anything else."

"Sure," Erik said flatly, the way your father used to sound when he was very disappointed in you. "Don't let Mannion know I called. He'll probably contact you tonight or tomorrow, so please try to act surprised and at least a little glad when he gives you the news, okay?"

He hung up. I must have radiated something because Roger kept his distance. He was talking to a couple of fashionably dressed women at the far end of the bar and there was some kind of joke in progress involving how many olives they could crowd onto their martini toothpicks.

I called Hank at his house and gave him the news. His reaction was one of unqualified relief. Terrible another person had to die, but at least they got the bastard and the nightmare was over. Hank said to wish him luck on his Stanford routine and hung up.

I climbed off the stool and gathered up my groceries. The cobwebs still hadn't really cleared. Roger left the two women he'd been talking to and moved close.

107

"Everything okay?" he asked.

"You know Erik." I smiled. "The Giants are thinking about moving to Denver. Big emergency."

Roger nodded. "Whatever he really said, don't let it get you down. We'll talk later, hey?"

"Okay."

Roger winked and turned his attention to the two women. As I walked past, one of them turned on her swivel stool and put her hand on my arm.

"We need a judge," she said. "Who wins, me or her?"

The woman had four olives on her toothpick. Her friend had five.

"Your friend wins," I said.

"No, but look!" she protested. "Her last olive, if you turn the toothpick upside down, it falls off. Mine stays."

She demonstrated. The olive fell off, bounced, and rolled crazily away.

"Then you both lose," I said.

Her eyes clouded a little. "What?"

"Nobody wins."

Roger came into the picture in a hurry. He laughed, said something about how everybody wins at his bar and it all depended on which version of Martini Toothpick Championship rules we were following, French or American. Ha ha ha. The woman kept her hand firmly on my arm and looked at me. It was a look she'd seen someplace and adopted. It was supposed to make me think that she found me raw and complex and this, in turn, was supposed to make her irresistible, she who found me so raw and complex.

I looked down into her half-stoned, come-hither eyes. All of her sexuality sucked up through a straw from a half-dozen books and a lifetime of lousy movies, all snug inside her, a big strawberry milkshake of memorized lust.

You poor, stupid woman, I thought. Grab a stranger by the arm and have him judge your olives. Maybe I'll smile. Maybe I'll sit next to you and be so relentlessly witty and funny and haphazardly handsome that you'll lead me home. Maybe we'll make love. Maybe I have a scalpel in my coat.

She took her hand off my arm. I had a reasonably good idea of what my eyes must have looked like. Then I turned and went out the door. As I left I could hear Roger the good-time maker telling a joke and they resumed their mirthless laughter. The women bit off the shish-kebabbed olives, one by one, and rolled them in their mouths.

Stretch out. That's it. Legs up, head back. Comfortable? Good. Now let me get out my pen and pad and I want you to tell me all about it.

I wandered up Union Street, thinking about what Erik had said. Maybe he was right. Maybe I *was* disappointed. Forget that my own ass was under Mannion's micro-scope. Maybe my "investigation" into Sonia's death had also been part diversion, as almost everything becomes a diversion once you are freed of money problems. Solvency is a double-edged sword. It catapults you out of the main-stream forever and forever and forever, and if you don't have to ride nose-to-nose in a crammed commuter bus, neither do you have the tedious but very real safety net of a life that has boundaries and soothing borders of cans and cannots. I was like a general without a war, a revo-lutionary in a world without oppression, and perhaps was prepared for the killer to run loose just a little while longer so that I might lose myself in the chase.

At the entrance to my apartment I put the groceries down, fumbled with the keys, pulled the door shut behind me with my foot. I was so distracted by the state of my miserable soul that I didn't notice anything wrong till I was halfway up the stairs.

I stood very still. It was a scuffling noise, like somebody down on all fours. One of those alarming, distinct sounds that only humans make.

I took the carpeted stairs slowly and carefully. At the landing the noise grew louder. It was coming from the study.

I edged around the bannister and crept down the hall to the living room. Unbolted the auxiliary door off the kitchen in case I needed a quick exit. Then I went into the living room again and unhooked the fireplace poker from its stand.

At the door of the study I hesitated. From the sound within I decided it was only one person. I looked at the poker clutched in my hand. It seemed a feeble weapon. The sound was now at the far wall. That meant the intruder probably had his back to me. Assuming a gun, that wouldn't leave much time.

I burst into the room and rushed the solitary figure huddled at the far wall. Kate screamed and jumped to her feet and pushed back, flat against the bookcase. We stood facing each other, frozen in ridiculous melodramatic postures—my weapon held high and menacing, her face wide open with fear.

"Dinner!" was all she could manage. "My treat!"

10

THERE ARE ADVANTAGES that come with living in the shadow of the nuclear mushroom. It must work on an unconscious level, this perpetual threat of any moment being blown back among the dinosaur bones. Schedules of events get accelerated. Like courtship, for example.

Kate lay on her stomach to my right, face turned away, shiny light-brown hair spilling onto the pillow. Her bare shoulder curved in a graceful, fleshy arc, tapering and disappearing beneath the single sheet that reached to the middle of her naked back. City sounds filtered in the bedroom window. Distant, drowsy car horns. The curtains were bright with captured sunlight.

She had come to San Francisco on a mission of apology, having decided that the unceremonious scooting-out I'd received in Carmel Valley had crossed the border of acceptable schizophrenia.

So it had been dinner at Scott's. Wine, candlelight, good talk, more than one inappropriate, gauche-as-hell belly laugh, and eventually an arm-in-arm stroll back to the apartment and the presumably innocent nightcap.

Innocent nightcap . . .

Well, Parker . . .

We had been like two starving animals tearing into a slab of raw meat, losing in the ferocity of the consumption the very pleasure of having hunger alleviated. Clutching, grappling, our respective orgasms were almost afterthoughts, abandoned in the thunderous fury like bags of popcorn in a burning movie theater.

I lay on my side and watched Kate. Her breathing seemed the rhythm of lovemaking itself, the very inhale and exhale of sensually interested life. She groaned, turned to me, opened her eyes.

"Hi," she said.

"Hi."

Kate was silent a moment, thinking. "Do you go in for postcoital banter?" she asked.

"For example?"

"Oh, you know. The woman makes slightly naughty comments on the man's abilities and the unladylike way he made her behave."

"And the man shakes his head and makes references to soreness and potential broken bones?"

"Exactly."

"No," I said. "I don't go in for that."

"Then you won't be offended if we get straight to the coffee?"

"Straight to the coffee."

I began to climb out of bed but Kate reached out to stop me.

"I didn't mean *that* straight." She held the sheet to her

breasts in a curious gesture of modesty and sat up to kiss me. It was a good kiss. "There. Now you can leave."

I got the coffee going while Kate drew a bath. I was halfway through my second cup, staring at the Golden Gate Bridge, when Kate came out. She was steamy and flushed. Her hair was damp, and she was wearing one of my robes.

"You've got some awfully intimidating women living in your bathroom," she said.

"I'll introduce you sometime."

In the distance the thousand metallic glints of cars commuting across the bridge moved as slowly as the minute hand of a clock. Lola appeared and went straight to Kate. She knelt and picked her up and the two ladies rubbed faces.

"What's her name?" Kate asked.

"Lola."

"Why Lola?"

" 'Whatever Lola Wants, Lola Gets.' " It was Sonia's line, a refrain she went through every time she fed the cat. Just saying it made my body contract a little . . . made the receding pain take a small bite once again.

Lola purred and burrowed in deeper. "Funny," Kate said. "I wouldn't have taken you for the cat type."

"Man of mystery."

Kate stroked the soft fur, then put Lola down and joined me at the dining room window.

"Your friend said that if you stare at the bridge long enough you'll swear it's sinking in the ocean. That you only get the sensation of weight by concentrating on the girders and beams."

That sounded like Hank. From the Bus Stop he had gone to the apartment and was almost out the door when Kate made her unexpected visit. He let her in, suggested that she might want to wait for me in the study and put my books back in alphabetical order, and continued on his merry way.

"Beautiful apartment," Kate said.

I nodded. "Thanks."

"I mean, really beautiful."

"Thanks."

Kate looked at me and I looked at her and we laughed at the awkwardness of it all. None of us likes to admit that we need, and to have made love so eagerly and explosively had been an admission of need in its most fundamental sense. Hard to pretend you can take it or leave it while sipping coffee in the strange robe of a strange man the morning after.

Kate looked up at the kitchen clock and wrinkled her forehead. "Is that the right time?"

"No." I'd forgotten about the clock. "Hank fiddled with it."

"Why?"

"So we could drink champagne."

Pause. "What?"

"Never mind," I said. "It's a long story."

Kate took my word for it and eventually we relocated to the living room and sat around for an hour, talking. It was not carefree and breezy. We couldn't decide whether we were strangers or lovers or both, and the Ping-Ponging began to take its toll.

After a particularly chair-squirming fifteen-second pause, Kate stood and made a move toward the bedroom.

"Better get dressed. Romance is wonderful, but the rent must be paid. My calling-in sick routine with D'Joint has about been pushed to the limit."

She dressed and I threw together something of a breakfast. I'm not a cook. Barbecuing steaks on the roof is about as far as I go, and beyond that the kitchen is little more than an awfully large room in which to store ice and a coffee machine.

After we ate I walked her to her car.

"When can I see you again?" I said.

"Whenever you want," Kate said, leaning up against the hood. "Or is that being too easy?"

"That's being too easy."

"Yeah, well . . . story of my life." She smiled up at me, shielding her eyes in the bright morning sun. We kissed.

"You know that postcoital talk neither one of us can stand?" she said.

"Yes?"

"I just want you to know that if I was the kind of woman who said those things . . . I would have said those things."

"Drive safely."

"*Ciao.*"

Chunk of door, rev of engine, one last wave of five separate fingers, and then I was standing alone on the corner of Union and Hyde watching her bright white Honda disappear down one of San Francisco's picture postcard hills.

It was not an entirely comfortable walk back to my apartment. The flavor of one-night stand was in my mouth, and I couldn't figure out why. Perhaps things happened too fast. The threat of radioactive evaporation pushed up certain timetables, but you paid for such acceleration. It's not nice to fool Mother Nature. Like freeway-reddened tomatoes, so the post-Hiroshima sexual terrain. Bright, alluring . . . and tastelessly perfect. Some things simply need to ripen on the vine.

I trudged back up the fifty-four steps and stood for a moment in the door of the bedroom. The bed was rumpled and sexy-looking. A note was on my pillow.

Started to make the bed, but decided maybe you'd prefer to leave our wrinkled sheets as they are for a while. The world's too smoothed-out as it is, don't you think?

—Kate

I sat on the bed and reread the note. Premature harvest or not, I suddenly wanted Kate Ulrich back in the unsmoothed bed very, very badly.

The phone rang. I put the note in my pocket and picked up the receiver next to the bed. It was Hank.

"A woman is rearranging books in your study," he said.

"I found out."

"Meant to tell you yesterday, but the Stanford gig was on my mind."

"How did it go?"

Hank sighed deeply and his voice lapsed into an exasperated ennui. "I was thinking . . . you know what we need?"

"What?"

"Some kind of refuge. The government should declare intelligent people an endangered species and then we'd be protected. Make it a theme park."

I stretched out on the bed. "You bombed at Stanford?"

"They do it for bald eagles. A sanctuary, that's all we—"

"Listen," I said. "I hate to cut this off, but I've got to go see Erik."

"Erik? What for?"

"Sonia."

"I thought they got the guy," Hank said.

"They got *a* guy."

Hank was silent a moment. "Kate was nice."

"I'm glad you approve."

"She understood about the Golden Gate Bridge. How it gets heavier when you stare at it."

"Good-bye, Hank."

Ludmila and Erik were together in his office when I let myself in. Erik was standing behind his chair, and Ludmila was sitting on the edge of the desk, coffee in hand. There was a kind of subdued relief in their faces and postures, and they greeted me with weak smiles, like we were all hostages who'd just been rescued, able to smile in retrospect at the perilous ordeal we'd managed to survive.

"You lawyers are workaholics," I said, pushing a magazine off the chair and settling into it. "What's the latest with this character they found?"

"We were just talking about it," Erik said, rubbing his eyes all-night-session style. "Name's Mark McCumber. Early twenties. Lives down in Fremont with his senile aunt. The Wendy Hanson killing's in the bag. She was the girl on Clement. We've got him, Quinn. I really think we've got him."

Silence. I didn't share their weary enthusiasm, and it showed. Ludmila gave me an unpleasant look and slid off the edge of the desk.

"I think I have some work to do," she said. Her body swept past and the door closed behind her. Hard. Erik stared at the closed door for several seconds, then plunked down in his swivel chair and turned his gaze on me.

"I knew I should have worn my black hat today," I said.

"She just wants it over and done with. You can't blame her."

"That's the point. I'm not blaming anybody for anything. Not yet."

We stared at each other across his big, polished desk.

"Let's have it, Quinn," Erik said at last. "Why don't you think McCumber killed Sonia?"

"I don't know who killed Sonia. Do you?"

"We have a confession."

"Big deal."

Erik held his palms out. "A confession is a confession."

"Okay, and I'm the guy that took care of Jimmy Hoffa. Now you have two confessions."

"Don't be condescending with me, Quinn. McCumber murdered Wendy Hanson. We know that." Erik held up his right hand and began counting off fingers. "Weapon, blood, fingerprints, scene of the crime, admission of guilt, everything." He'd used up all of his fingers and put the hand down.

"So what does Wendy Hanson have to do with Sonia?"

"So when Mark McCumber confesses to another identical murder we poor idiots in criminology tend to pay attention. Please tolerate our flights of fancy." Erik fumbled for a cigarette. "I'm due to see him in two hours. I'll know more then."

"How did you manage that?"

"His lawyer is a friend. Correction. I'm acquainted with his lawyer."

"What are the chances of me coming with you?"

"Zip."

"Why?"

"Right now Mark McCumber is more popular downtown than Sophia Loren. Anybody who sees him had better have a damn good reason. You don't. Anyway, what's the big problem? This sure as hell gets you off the hot seat."

"Something tells me if McCumber proves false my hot seat will get hotter."

"Maybe so," Erik said. "Maybe so."

I leaned forward, rested my elbows on Erik's desk, put chin on knuckles. I stared at the little framed photograph Erik kept propped up on his desk. It was a shot of Mr. Paige and his Irish lass, Brigid, standing before a blustery Donegal castle. Erik's long-standing bachelor status had been threatened during his leave of absence. He'd fallen madly, uncharacteristically in love with Brigid O'Malley, the mayor's daughter. But legal technicalities and residual Erik Paige cold feet had kept the relationship on trans-Atlantic hold for six months.

"Heard anything from Brigid lately?" I said.

Erik shook his head. "Not for a month. She's pissed."

"Why?"

"She wants to leave Ireland. Come to California. I suggested in my last phone call that she had it all backward. I was the one who was going to do the emigrating to Ireland. Why in God's name would anyone want to voluntarily leave Ireland? It's about the last outpost of sanity in this frigging world."

"Maybe Brigid wants an outpost of sanity where people get tan once in a while," I said. "One with bright lights and fine restaurants."

Erik smiled, shook his head again. "Nah. It's the greener grass syndrome. But I'm thinking that maybe I should change my strategy. Have her come for six months. Get a taste of it. She'd be on a plane back to Ireland in a week."

I walked to the window and looked down on Market Street. "Your windows need cleaning."

"Tell me about it. Thousand bucks a month and they never wash the windows. A thousand bucks!"

A woman was waiting for a streetcar five floors below. Pale, emaciated, stretched tense as tennis-strung cat guts. Junkie. She blinked, chewed gum, vanished into the first streetcar that pulled up without bothering to see where it was going. A million stories in the Naked City, and I wasn't in the mood for any of them. I turned back to Erik.

"What if I all of a sudden remembered seeing a guy hanging around Sonia's street the night of her death, and it might've been McCumber?"

Erik blew smoke in the air and watched with absolute and total absorption as it curled toward the ceiling. He didn't say anything till the smoke touched the ceiling and dissipated.

"How tall was this guy you might've all of a sudden remembered seeing?"

"Five ten?"

"Unh-unh. If you noticed him in all that fog and dark I'm sure he must've been more like six five. And big. Sloppy-looking."

"That's right. Now that I think about it, the guy was around six five. Big. Sloppy-looking."

"What an opportune memory you have, Quinn."

"I try."

Erik nodded to himself as he gazed at the ceiling. "Yeah, that could do it," he said. "Let me check it out. But forget today. Today's out."

"Just as well. I've got some unpleasant business to take care of this afternoon."

"What sort?"

I went to the door and leaned on the knob. "Nothing much. Just apologize to somebody for maybe ruining his personal and professional life. Catch you later."

Ludmila kept her eyes down when I came into the

reception room. I stopped, leaned both hands on her desk, and cleared my throat.

"Still friends?"

Ludmila smiled, but kept her eyes down. "Yes, Quinn. Of course."

"I only want to be sure, Ludmila. That's all."

"But I think this man did it," Ludmila said, facing me for the first time.

"Why?"

Ludmila bit her lower lip and looked off at the far wall. She was intensely concentrated, thinking about the words she was about to speak with great care.

"There was something I failed to tell you that morning you came to see me in Sausalito. I remembered it later. Something bad was happening in Sonia's life. She spoke of it, and it involved a man, but she would never say much. She wouldn't look me in the eyes, and for Sonia that was strange. Sonia would always look me directly in the eyes. I think the man was this person in jail."

"But why are you so certain the man Sonia was afraid of is McCumber?"

Ludmila shook her head and continued to stare at the patch of wall across the office. "I don't know. It is what you call intuition, I suppose. I feel it."

I waited for more, but that was it. Ludmila's intuitions were not wordy. I took my hands off the desk and left the room without speaking.

It wasn't hard to track down Professor Hemming. The card on his office door pointed the way. Medieval Literature, Room 117, Political Science Building.

The lecture hall was quiet and uncrowded, and I was

able to ease in the back door unnoticed. Hemming had his back to me, gazing up at an overhead map hanging from the wall behind the podium, talking about the migration pattern of some nomadic tribe. The girl sitting to my right scribbled furiously in her notebook. A sea of heads bent to the task.

Then Hemming turned and smiled and made what must've been an inside joke because it meant nothing to me while the whole room rumbled with laughter. The girl on my right looked down at Professor Hemming with glistening, adoring eyes, lips parted a fraction of an inch.

I thought of what Hemming had said in his office about his public-figure role. I pictured Sonia sitting in a room like this, day by day, class by class, gradually losing her footing as the strengthening waves of Ronald Hemming's humor, intelligence, and good looks washed over her.

The lecture seemed to go on forever, and that old restlessness with school in general—whether stacking blocks in kindergarten or researching a master's thesis—began to gnaw at me. Hemming went from tribal migrations to theology. What this had to do with literature I couldn't fathom, but when he said turn to page three-fifty-five, the textbook pages flipped in unison throughout the room like the beating wings of a pack of quail flushed out by hunters.

I snuck a look at the girl's book to my right. RELIGION, in bold, dark lettering, and below it a Madonna and Child in that smashed-flat Middle Ages one-dimensional style, the Christ child, omniscient, full of slumbering retribution and static, blank-faced wisdom that combined to make him look like something that had strolled off the set of "The Alfred Hitchcock Hour." The other page had a print from *The Divine Comedy*. A man standing before Dante and Virgil holding his own severed head out before him.

Nobody died normally these days. Not even in college textbooks.

The lecture stopped abruptly. I stayed in my seat while everybody filed out. Three girls lingered at the podium, mouths moving all at once while Hemming nodded and continued to write on the back of his class notes. Eventually he shooed them away and I started down the aisle. Hemming glanced up at me off-handedly and his face changed.

"Well, well," he said. "If it isn't Quinn Parker, private investigator."

"Good memory."

"Oh, I don't know." He slid the stack of papers in a brown briefcase, clicked it shut, lifted his eyes to meet mine. "My mind has this peculiar retention of people who accuse me of lurid murders."

"You go off on a tangent, Professor."

"Do I?"

"I never accused you of anything. I only came by to say I'm sorry you had to be involved at all. They've arrested someone else, someone who's confessed to Sonia's murder."

Hemming paused. It was hard to read his reaction. There was relief in his face, but also suspicion. It was not the way a totally uninvolved person would react.

"They've arrested someone?" he said.

"That's right."

"Who?"

"His name is Mark McCumber."

"Well . . . " Hemming exhaled deeply, and his face shifted back. "What a shock. And all this time I was sure I was the one who'd done it. What happened to your head?"

"I found Jeff Miller."

Hemming nodded. "Then I guess I can be expecting a visit from Jeff, too? Or was Lieutenant Mannion the last?"

"This is a murder case, Professor Hemming."

"Oh, pardon me. Sorry. Slipped my mind completely. Murder case, you say?" He pursed his lips and stared at the floor, nodding. Then his eyes snapped up. "As opposed to?"

I gestured at his satchel. "As opposed to a briefcase full of homework papers. Tenure. Final exams. Report cards with A's, B's, and C's."

Hemming's eyes narrowed. "And I guess you suppose that murder just sort of 'happens' out there for no reason at all. That it doesn't have its origins in something as tedious and 'unimportant' as A's, B's, and C's?" He hoisted his briefcase and held it before me.

"Sonia was killed," I said. "I want the person who did it locked up. She was . . . important to me."

"How noble of you."

"I have a selfish reason, too. I'm suspected of killing her myself."

Hemming looked at me sharply. For a second I had his complete attention. "Did you?"

"Did I what?"

"Did you kill her?"

"Are you trying to be funny?"

Hemming didn't answer me. His eyes were trained on me with such intensity that my mind went blank. The way X-ray machines wipe clean the image from an undeveloped photograph.

"So that's it," I went on, avoiding his eyes. "If your tenure got trampled on in the process, I'm sorry. But I did what I had to do."

Hemming broke off his stare. If he had been looking for

something in my face, he hadn't found it. Instead he let his shoulders sag and his eyes drifted off to the left, gazing at nothing in particular. When he spoke his voice was quiet and distant, as though addressing somebody else. "That's the bottom line of philosophy, Mr. Parker. We do what we have to do. That's all there is."

11

THE WAVES TO MY RIGHT sped by at seventy miles per hour. They shimmered white, breaking in small, phosphorescent curves on the dark shore of Monterey Bay. The night was warm, and I had the windows down, vaguely listening to the Giants game on the radio while the wind whistled through the van.

I sent my mind crawling back to square one for the twentieth time. A false note is a false note even if you have trouble shoring it up with a reason. I simply wasn't buying Mark McCumber. Sherri's murder, Sonia's murder . . . they were executed with a chilling, traceless perfection. McCumber? Here's a guy banging into things, disturbing the neighbors, smearing his guilt all over the apartment before trundling down the hallway into the waiting arms of the police. Unh-unh. It had the stink of an amateur sociopath trying to imitate the exploits of a professional sociopath.

It was nine o'clock when I turned down Ocean Avenue and coasted past boutique row toward D'Joint. I found a parking place around the corner and went in and sidled up to the dimly lit bar. After ordering a tequila from a beachboy bartender I dialed Erik collect.

"Did you see McCumber?"

"Sure did. Where the hell are you, since I'm paying for the call?"

"Carmel."

He paused, and in the background I could hear the television tuned in to the Giants-Pirates game.

"They only gave me ten minutes," Erik said at last.

"And?"

"And he says he killed Sonia."

"I know what he says. What do you think?"

Erik cleared his throat. "Let's just say I'm a little less convinced than I was before."

I edged forward on my barstool. "Why?"

"It's the top of the ninth, Quinn. I got an interview with McCumber for you, so you can see for yourself. How did your makeup session with Professor Hemming go?"

"Strange," I said.

"Oh?"

"He was ticked off. Mannion questioned him and now Hemming sees his tenure going belly-up."

"What's so strange about that?"

"Nothing. But when I mentioned that I was one of the suspects myself, he was all of a sudden very alert. I mean, right in my face, intense, like I was slipping a message to him. That, and his chicken shit alibi about boozing it up with his department head in Piedmont . . . I don't know . . . "

Erik was silent awhile. "Watch yourself."

"What do you mean?"

"I mean watch yourself. Like I said, I'm not quite as convinced about McCumber as I was when I woke up this morning. And you'll get your shot tomorrow. So in the meantime, watch yourself."

"What time do I see McCumber?" I said.

"Quarter after two, tomorrow afternoon. They've got him scheduled like he's the goddamn U.S. Open. But it's all hinged on the newly revealed information that you remember seeing somebody hanging around Sonia's apartment, so at least go through the motions of trying to remember."

"I'll squint and scratch my head and everything. Besides six five and sloppy, what does McCumber look like?"

"Robert Redford has nothing to worry about." Erik paused. "And Mannion's pissed. Thinks you're making up stories so you can get in and take a look at McCumber."

"Why would he think a thing like that?"

"Cops have suspicious minds. Listen, I wasn't kidding about top of the ninth. Come by the office a little before two and we'll head over together. Keep a low profile in the meantime, and don't sleep in."

"Why would I sleep in?"

"Lawyers have suspicious minds, too."

I hung up and polished off the tequila and nodded at the blank television screen overhead. "Giants game on?"

The bartender put down the pamphlet he was reading. "Lemme check."

He came over and flipped through the channels, eventually found the game, and stood next to me making an earnest effort at knowledgeable small talk. But it only illuminated the fact that he'd probably never seen a complete baseball game in his life. Eventually he came to grips with his ignorance and wandered back to the pamphlet.

With two outs in the bottom of the ninth and Pittsburgh making ominous signs of tying the score, Kate materialized by my side. In the darkened bar she took on a luminous quality, like a face rising to the surface of a nighttime lake.

"You certainly didn't waste any time," she said, smiling.

"I came to spirit thee away in my shiny white van in the night."

"Tell thy shiny white van to cool its heels for another three hours and then it can spirit me anywhere it wants."

"Three hours!"

"My shift ends at midnight."

I turned around completely on my barstool to face her. "A mere technicality, my dear."

"Some of us are poor working stiffs," Kate said, holding her smile. I wanted to reach out and link my arms around her waist, the way normal people do when they like each other, but the pamphlet-reading bartender lurked in the semidarkness like some furtive agent of the Thought Police.

"I think we're in enemy territory," I whispered.

"Definitely."

"Midnight's a long ways away. Sure you don't want me to bust you out of here?"

"This damsel in distress would be walking the unemployment lines tomorrow if you did."

I hate logical arguments. Too much money had made me expect spontaneous behavior from everybody. Damn the consequences, because for me there were no consequences.

"But three hours—"

"Now, now." Kate put two fingers to my lips. I could feel the bartender watching us. "A resourceful fellow like you shouldn't have any problem passing the time. Sit here and behave yourself and I'll see you later. I'm glad you came."

I watched the rest of the game. The Giants almost snatched defeat out of the jaws of victory, but held on to win despite a last-ditch Pittsburgh rally. Now they were almost next to last in their division. The announcer was encouraged.

I was hunkering in for a mediocre, made-for-TV movie when Kate was back at my side, holding her coat.

"Let's go," she said.

"What changed your mind?"

"Life is short, and youth is shorter."

My shiny white van had spirited us about halfway to Big Sur when I decided to tell Kate everything. The Clement Street murder, my theory about the VCR, Mark McCumber and the scheduled meeting with him tomorrow—everything. I told her about Hemming and Miller and the earringed bartender.

Kate stared straight ahead at the headlights cleaving the night. She didn't move or speak or make any facial expression. I sensed disapproval. Bad News Quinn, and her silence would remain stony until I got it through my head that she considered the issue closed. Past history. Finished. Done.

I concluded the monologue, and the dark, quiet miles slipped behind us. I looked at the odometer and guessed what the mileage reading would be before either one of us spoke again.

We sped through the town of Big Sur. Motels, gift

stores, a couple of "country" markets all clustered along the shoulder of the highway. Just us plain folk out here, ya'll, but I knew for a fact that they were mostly run by ex-realtors and commodities brokers with lots of disposable income and a passion for substance abuse.

A few miles south of town I made a sharp left onto the twisting canyon road that climbed a tortuous, engine-straining half mile to the Ventana Inn. We parked and walked through the restaurant to the outside terrace and ordered a couple of drinks. It was chilly, and the deck was all ours. Mozart-to-digest-food-by was piped through the speakers to nobody but us. Ocean fog rolled and tumbled everywhere, great ghostly waves breaking on a landless shore. It lent the night an unnatural sense of brightness and commotion.

The odometer had come and gone and Kate still hadn't said a single word. Just as I was getting ready to suggest a quick trip home, she turned to me.

"Would you have married Sonia?" she asked.

"Where did that come from?"

"If you don't want to talk about it just say so and I'll shut up."

"Married Sonia . . . " I took myself through the ceremony, slipping on the ring, greeting teary aunts in the reception line. Honeymoon, settling in, babies and white picket fences. "No, I wouldn't have married Sonia."

"What was she like?"

"Bright. Fun. Energetic. Always picking up stray people and cats and taking them in. She had about twenty gallons of the milk of human kindness to everybody else's spoonful. But she was elusive."

"Elusive?"

"Once—this was when I first got involved with her—we

were sitting around her apartment and she had one of those things. What do you call them? You look through it and see nine images of everything?"

"Kaleidoscopes?"

"Right. Kaleidoscopes. I looked at her through it. Nine Sonias, and I asked her if I could have one. I was just joking, but she answered very seriously. I don't know that I ever saw her more serious. 'You can have eight,' she said. 'You can have eight.' " I paused, took a sip of my drink. "That was Sonia."

"The cat in your apartment . . . was it hers?"

"Yes."

Kate nodded. She'd won a bet with herself. "Fog's getting cold," she said. "Let's go in."

We moved to the restaurant bar but the sudden bright light made it hard for us to look each other in the eyes. We didn't want things too defined. It was a night for blurred edges, features unfocused.

We took a room at the inn. The Ventana brochure boasted handwoven rugs from Peru and goose-down quilts from Norway. But we didn't see any of it. The lights stayed off, and the heavy wooden door closed behind us with a solid, decisive click.

The lovemaking was slow and patient. Gone was the calorie-burning fury of Union Street, and, in a sense, good riddance. Union Street had had too much gimmickry—a couple of baton twirlers showing how high they could throw the damn thing. We had indulged fully that first-time inclination to demonstrate to the new partner the tools of the trade, the sexual portfolio, how it was okay to do this and this and even this. Not to worry if 28 percent of the college-educated population don't do such and such. If you want, we can, and here's a little sample. Union Street had been a covering of the bases, a laying down of ground rules so that in the future one could relax and be assured that no red flags would go unexpectedly flying in the heat of battle.

Fine. But all that had been dispensed with. Now our lovemaking was straight and direct. It was less the breathtaking exploration of breasts and thighs and lips than it was the holding in my arms of a woman who preserved broken wine glasses and saved old armchairs and left beds unmade in the face of a world that would iron everything to a starched anonymity. A woman who turned away with tears in her eyes at the memory of a lost friend.

And when it ended we rolled apart and gazed at the lofty ceiling. No speaking, no laughing. Bit by bit, Kate's fingers grew loose in my hand, and then were limp. Her breasts rose and fell in the shadows as though drifting on a gently swelling sea.

I woke at four in the morning. Troubled sleep. I climbed out of bed, pulled on my clothes, and quietly rolled open the sliding glass door that led to the terrace. The night was cold, imprisoned in a still blanket of dense fog. Nothing else feels like four A.M. except four A.M.

I sat on the deck chair for what must have been an hour. I couldn't keep my mind on any one thing for very long. Images merged together in a bizarre collage—Sonia dressed in white, standing at the altar; McCumber sawing through arms and legs; Hank and his sinking bridge; and a transplanted brain in Moscow with wires running from it to a tape recorder. Impaled martini olives. Around and around and around they went, and I sat in the fog, imagining the cold, dark ocean less than a mile away. How deep it was. How forlorn on the bottom.

This was where the woman is supposed to wake and

notice her man is missing and come to the terrace and listen to his eloquent sorrows. But no. I sat there till the gray began to touch the edges of the ocean, then went back into the room and crawled into bed as though there was no problem. As if all was well with the world.

12

OUR FOOTSTEPS ECHOED in the hallway, just like they're supposed to. McCumber was being held in a special cell at the far end of the jail, away from the rest of the prisoners. The Princess Suite, the cop at the desk had called it.

"How long do we have?" I said.

Erik shrugged. "Till they tell us to get out. Fifteen, twenty minutes."

Except for a tour of Alcatraz years earlier, I'd never really been into the guts of a jail before, and I was struck in the mundane, predictable way of how horrible it was, how small the cells were, how dreadful the utter lack of privacy, and how I'd never breach the finely painted lines of law and order, cross my heart and hope to die.

The guard escorting us stopped at a cell that was at least three times the size of the others. He clicked professionally through his enormous ring of keys and let us in. A man stood in the cell. He wore a dark, three-piece suit, and had his hands buried in his pockets, nervously fiddling with what sounded like a half pound of change. He was alone.

"Afternoon, Erik."

"Quinn Parker, Bill Jameson. Bill Jameson, Quinn Parker."

We shook hands. McCumber's lawyer. Tall, pale, thin, all forehead and ears. Early fifties. Mostly bald. You had the feeling he'd been bald since high school. His pallor was that of damp clay, and I couldn't shake the sensation that if I squeezed his face it would mold easily into another position and stay there.

"Where's your boy?" Erik asked.

"In the potty."

Erik hooked his thumbs in his pockets. "Let it be duly noted that your client is taking a shit on our time."

"I'll see that you're given credit."

Jameson turned to me. "I understand you saw Mark in the vicinity of Ms. Lucia's apartment the night of the murder."

"I might've."

Jameson watched me with a fixed half smile, head bobbing. "According to Erik it sounds more than might've. You gave a pretty accurate description."

"The fog was thick," I said.

"May twentieth, one A.M., it was clear as a bell."

"I guess it seemed thick."

" 'Seemed thick,' " Jameson repeated. "The night was clear and you've given an accurate description of Mr. McCumber, placing him at the scene of the crime. Those are the facts."

"You seem anxious to incriminate your client," I said.

"Of course he does." Erik yawned. "No way McCumber's innocent in the Wendy Hanson case, so Bill here just wants to hook him into all the bizarre-o murders he can. Plead insanity. The more McCumber did, the crazier he looks. Right, Bill?"

"Better stick with your Market Street wetbacks." Jameson smiled. "I'm defending my client to the best of my ability."

I wandered over to McCumber's cot. It was a mess. Rumpled sheets, magazines, erratically folded newspapers, dice, and a deck of playing cards so filthy you could barely tell a spade from a heart. A foul odor hung over it all. Next to his small writing table a newspaper lay open, and an article had been circled in red. I took a look. Murder in Daly City. An old man, killed and stuffed into his own kitchen oven and put on slow broil. Identification withheld pending notification of next of kin. It was today's paper.

A key rattled the lock and McCumber came shuffling in. He made quite an impression. Stringy dark hair, terrible teeth, fingernails all but bitten off. He wore thick glasses and there were red sores around his eyes. His five-day beard grew in wispy patches, and the rear of his pants collapsed into nothing. No ass at all.

Bill Jameson said, "Mark, you remember Mr. Paige?"

McCumber nodded. It was like a father talking to his six-year-old son. "And this is Quinn Parker. He saw you near Ms. Lucia's apartment the night you say you killed her."

Our eyes met, and McCumber's thoughts could not be concealed. He looked at me as one conspiring liar to another, wondering what my scam was that I was placing him at the scene of a murder he knew he hadn't commit-

137

ted. The knowledge was passed in an instant, then Mc-Cumber shifted quickly back into his bumbling, yeah-I-did-it routine.

"I didn't see nobody," McCumber said.

"No, Mark, no," Jameson soothed. "He saw you."

McCumber blinked. Nodded. There was a kind of film on his glasses. Like they'd been smeared with week-old bacon grease.

"Where did you meet Sonia?" I said.

"Didn't. Followed her around awhile and saw that she was a sinner and I delivered her to heaven before it was too late."

Erik and I glanced at each other. Jameson wouldn't look at us. He was concentrating on his client.

"How did you know she was a sinner?" I said.

"Fornicated."

"Who did she fornicate with?"

"Everybody."

"Who specifically?"

"The devil."

"What was the name of the devil?" I said.

"Devil don't have a name. Just the devil."

"What did the devil look like?"

"Everybody."

McCumber turned and slouched into the vile cot and began rolling the three dice over and over again across the blanket.

"I think that's all for now," Jameson said.

Erik pushed himself up off the stool with a groan and signaled the guard outside. The four of us waited in the cell. Dead silence but for the muted thump of the dice rolling across the blanket. The guard unlocked the door.

I turned to McCumber and said, "Where's your tape recorder?"

He quit rolling the dice. "What?"

"You know what I mean. Or are you going to tell me you didn't tape a cassette for Sonia to take with her to heaven?"

Jameson intervened. "I *said* that's enough for now."

We left the cell and Jameson was right on our heels, striding with us down the hall.

"Okay!" he said. "Let's have it!"

Erik wrinkled his forehead, kept walking. "What are you talking about, Bill?"

"What I'm talking about, 'Bill,' is this 'tape recording to heaven' crap! What's going on?"

"You said Quinn could ask a few questions, and he did."

At the door Jameson reached out and physically stopped Erik, turning him around.

"Damn it, Paige! Don't play innocent with me! You're screwing with my client's head and I don't like it. You level with me *right* now about this tape recorder shit or you've seen the last of Mark McCumber. Or future Mark McCumbers!" A little blue vein rose on Jameson's temple.

"Bill," Erik said, pushing the door open. "It would be my infinite pleasure to have seen the last of your distinguished clientele. Go ask McCumber about the tape. Now if you'll excuse me, I have some wetbacks to attend to."

"He didn't do it, Erik."

We pulled onto Third Street and merged into the flow of traffic. Erik adjusted the rear-view mirror.

"I know," he said. "I knew before we went in."

"How?"

"The lab reports. Like I told you before, Sonia was

taken apart with reasonable precision. Wendy Hanson was a total hack job. Same guy didn't do both. Of course, that's just my opinion. Jameson'll find some way of making them look like fingerprints from the same hand. And besides that, McCumber was too predictably eccentric."

"How do you mean?"

"He had all sorts of gruesome things tacked on his bedroom wall at home. I don't know. It rings phony. Pathological killers who tack things on their walls are mostly movie creations. Makes for a nice camera sweep and fill-in soundtrack. I've strolled through the bedrooms of some of the most gruesome human beings this planet has seen and they usually look like something out of 'Leave It to Beaver.' " Erik took a deep breath and squinted into the sun. "Besides, most serial killers slip one cog at a time, clink, clink, clink, like a machine coming loose, and the general public has time to have them dealt with or put away. The true monsters generally come unraveled all at once. Boom! Speck or the guy in the tower in Texas, no way to anticipate that. I've seen the most horrendous killers coast through polygraph tests like a Girl Scout telling the different flavors of the cookies she's selling."

"So we're back where we started."

"Afraid so," Erik said. Then a smile tugged at the corners of his mouth. "I did like your bit about the tape recorder, though. Jameson's going to toss and turn a few nights on that one."

"I'd rather McCumber tossed and turned."

Erik shook his head. "McCumber's history. It's just whether he'll be in San Quentin or a mental hospital. Locked up is locked up."

"Then what's the bother?"

"Points. Law is one big Grand Prix circuit. You accumulate points all year, and at the end they tally them up and the one with the most points wins. If Jameson pulls off this insanity thing his fees'll go up three hundred percent. More. The public will scream bloody murder, of course, but that won't matter to Jameson." Erik shivered. "Incredible how long I played that game myself. Just getting near it now makes me want to go back to Ireland and wash the stink off. Hang in there, Brigid. Your man is coming back!"

"McCumber had circled another murder in the newspaper. A guy in Daly City—"

"The man in the oven."

"Right."

Erik nodded. "I heard it on the radio this morning. Jameson probably told McCumber to circle it and leave it out, real conspicuous and all, so everybody could see it and think what a nut."

"Christ, you're cynical."

"We barristers prefer 'astute and realistic.' Look, Jameson's as nice a guy as you'd want to play tennis with. But in a courtroom, watch out. We used to call him The Echo. He repeats what you say right back to you in such a way that you can't believe you ever said such a stupid thing in the first place. Amazing what a powerful tactic that is in front of a jury. 'I'm up against The Echo today,' that's what we used to say."

We parked in a public lot two blocks from Erik's office. The guy at the chain-linked entrance gave him a ticket and we walked together toward Market Street.

"What do you think the odds are that McCumber will suddenly claim to have made tape cassettes to heaven?" I asked.

Erik slowly smiled. "We'll see, won't we?" Then he looked at his parking receipt, folded it, put it in his pocket. "Pay for my own parking space. Ain't it great? Thousand bucks a month for dirty windows and no parking!"

Kate was talking to Ludmila when we got back to the office. As she'd predicted, her Big Sur walkout of the night before had gotten her fired from D'Joint. She'd taken the news as evidence of divine intervention, and had happily accompanied me up to San Francisco. She'd saved enough money to coast awhile, and it was hardly the stunning and tragic end to a potentially brilliant career.

Erik looked surprised to see her in his office. He stopped abruptly and stared.

"This is the woman you were suspicious about," I said. "Kate, meet Erik. Erik, meet Kate."

They shook hands and Erik gave me a sideways smile. "Obviously, my suspicion was justified. Hold on a second."

Erik ducked into his office and Kate came straight up to me and planted a hard, how-do-you-like-it kiss on my lips.

"What's that for?" I said.

"Serendipity," Kate said. "Unemployment euphoria. It'll wear off in a few hours."

Erik came out of his office, rubbing his hands together.

"Lieutenant Mannion called," Ludmila said. Erik put on the brakes and started to head back into his office but Ludmila stopped him. "No. For you, Quinn. He wants you to call him at his office. Immediately."

Erik hooked a thumb and pointed to the phone inside. It was the way a teacher would ominously send you to the principal's office.

I dialed and Irma put me through without a moment's hesitation. Uh-oh.

"Understand you just had a nice, long talk with Mc-Cumber," Mannion said.

"It wasn't long and it wasn't nice."

"Do you mind a hell of a lot telling me what you were doing there? Forgive me for prying, but this is a murder case and I was assigned to it."

"I wanted to have a look at him."

"How'd you get in? Paige?"

"No. I thought I remembered seeing somebody standing near Sonia's apartment the night of the murder. I guess I was mistaken."

Mannion controlled himself pretty well, considering. He started shouting, but not real loud. I held the receiver a few inches away. I didn't catch all the particulars, but the gist of Mannion's fury was that if I didn't knock it off he'd haul me in for obstruction of justice, and that went for Erik Paige, too. I hung up and went back out into the reception room.

"Well?" Erik asked.

"He was mildly distressed."

Ludmila and Kate stood around with the soberest expressions I'd seen in a while. Erik had filled them in about McCumber.

"So," Erik said into the gathering silence. "Who's up for a basketball game?"

Ludmila sighed. "Erik . . . "

"Five tickets." He reached into his coat pocket and pulled out a Ticketron envelope. "Seven o'clock tonight. San Francisco State versus San Jose State. Hank and I are going, that leaves three tickets. Perfect."

Silence.

"Whether you know it or not," Erik said, "this game is important. And then afterward maybe we can all go out and have dinner somewhere. Relax."

The prospect of dinner loosened us up, and Erik moved quickly to expand his beachhead. Top off the evening with cocktails at Julius' Castle. Watch the lights of the ships coming in.

The deliberations began. Ludmila asked how long a basketball game took. The correct answer was "not very long," and that's exactly what Erik said. Hell, it's over before you even know it. The two women looked at each other. Kate asked if there were extra innings, because once she'd gone to a baseball game in New York with her ex-husband and it went on an hour and a half longer than usual because of extra innings. Erik laughed and said there wouldn't be any extra innings. He didn't mention overtime. I let it go.

Erik was right about the importance of the game. A conference semifinal, and the San Francisco State gymnasium was filled to capacity. Our seats weren't all that great—way up in the rafters at the south end—but Erik said not to worry. We'd find something better once the game started. An old operagoer's trick. Buy cheap seats, then fill up the empty expensive ones during the first intermission. Ludmila nodded. Kate nodded. They sat with hands clasped in laps and watched the sweat-suited players warm up. Hank sat at the end wondering aloud at the possibility of a TV sitcom about a college basketball coach.

"They're missing a lot," Kate said.

"This is just practice," I said.

"You mean it hasn't even started yet?"

"In a few minutes."

"Oh."

Kate asked again about the time element. The New York baseball game was scorched into her consciousness like a traumatic childhood experience. "Extra innings" loomed as a real and present threat that any sports event had the capacity to go on and on indefinitely. I explained again about how basketball was different, and Kate nodded uneasily.

A few minutes before tip-off Hank and Ludmila headed off to restock the beer and peanuts. Kate watched them leave.

"I thought Hank was married."

"He is."

"But not to Ludmila?"

"No."

Kate arched her eyebrows. "Different strokes for different folks, I guess."

"It's not how it looks," I said.

Kate gave me a doubting glance. "Of course it isn't."

"Believe me, unlikely candidate though he may be, Hank's the original family man. Carol, his wife, is one of the world's great human beings."

"And she knows all about this?"

"I didn't send out a questionnaire, but yes. I assume so."

Kate folded her arms and looked back at the basketball court. "I guess I should admire her trust and open-mindedness, but there's no way on earth I'd let my man go on the town with a woman like Ludmila."

"You don't know Carol. Or Ludmila."

"Maybe not," Kate said. "But I know men and women and the trouble they can get into."

Our conversation was cut short by Hank and Ludmila's return. He'd said something to her while coming down the aisle and she was laughing. They were carrying two paper cups of beer each, and Ludmila was giving Hank hell for making her laugh when she was trying not to spill beer. They sat together and passed our beers down to us. I watched Hank. I watched Ludmila. Was I being naive? No, they didn't have anything going. I'd only just reacquainted the two of them a week ago. Impossible. Shame on Kate for her impure thoughts.

The game started and looked to be an immediate blowout. San Francisco took a huge lead and the rafters of the gymnasium shook with galvanized cheers. Kate was into it from the tip-off, appreciating the sport more than the score, the athletes more than the sport, gripping my arm and marveling at the speed, grace, and precision of the pituitary cases racing up and down the court.

Midway through the second quarter Erik bit his lower lip and nodded emphatically. "There! I've found our new seats."

"Where?" Kate said.

Erik pointed. "Other side, down about the tenth row. Right behind that really blond woman in the white sweater. Three empties side by side, and another two right in back. We'll get to stay pretty much together."

Kate gazed in the direction Erik was pointing. There was distraction in her eyes, then a sudden tightening of the muscles of her face. Her hand clutched my leg.

"My God! Quinn!"

"What's the matter?"

She shook her head, not quite able to speak. Her face was drained of blood. "It's him! The man in the rust-colored turtleneck. Next to the woman with the really blond hair. It's him!"

I saw the woman with the really blond hair first. She was hard not to see first. Then my eyes went left. Sitting next to her, in a rust-colored turtleneck, was Professor Ronald Hemming.

My mind was like a solid steel room into which somebody had just fired a half-dozen bullets. Shrill noises, ricochets, dangerous confusion.

"This is the man you saw with Sherri?" I said. "The man she kept secret?"

Kate was frozen in place. Then she seemed to register my question and dully nodded.

I fought through the vibration in my head. "Has he seen you?"

"What?" she said, very quietly.

"Has he seen you? Just now?"

"I don't . . . I don't know."

"Let's go. Keep your face shielded and toward me."

"Hey!" Erik said as we stood. "What's all this?"

"We have to go."

"Jesus, the game just started! Seventeen points isn't all that—"

"I'll tell you later."

Erik saw the urgency in my eyes and fell questioningly silent. Hank began to stand and I waved him back down. Then I took Kate by the hand and led her away as inconspicuously as possible, blocking her from Hemming's view with my body. At the exit door I paused. Whether he had seen us or not, I couldn't be sure, but after San Francisco had scored another basket Hemming didn't cheer. He didn't watch the action rumble down to the other end of the court. He didn't do anything. His gaze lingered on the empty net, and I was too far away to read whatever expression had settled on his face.

13

I FELT LIKE AN ASSASSIN. The cold-blooded hired killer who has his gun and his bullet and calmly waits for the prey to make its inevitable appearance.

I stood in the hallway of the English building and gazed at the pale wooden door of Room 311. Beyond it, through the tiny soundproof window, I could catch a glimpse of Professor Lawrence J. Morse conducting a graduate course in James Joyce. In two minutes the class would be over. I'd take my bluff from its wrapper, load it, line up the professor's jowly brain in the cross hairs, and pull the trigger.

Kate and I had gone over it a dozen times. Was she positive the man at the basketball game was the man who had spent two awkward minutes in her apartment months and months before? Yes, Kate said. She was positive. Positive enough to go to the police and put her finger on Hemming? Hesitation. And as the night grew late she became less sure. Maybe it wasn't. Maybe it was. The intensity of her conviction petered out and she was left a confused husk. Believing, but not believing. Sure, but not sure.

I took a deep breath, looked at my watch, then again at the pale wooden door. It was with Morse that Hemming supposedly spent the night of Sonia's murder. It was with Morse that Hemming supposedly wined and dined, and wined some more, and then wined so much that it was deemed more prudent for him to spend the night in Piedmont than attempt to weave back home across the Bay Bridge.

There was a sudden muffled commotion, and the door flew open. Students spilled out and hurried off down either end of the hallway. Professor Morse was among them; austere, silver-haired, he wore an immaculate dark suit and was about as easygoing as reinforced concrete. Enormous bags sagged under his eyes. He was very heavy, but his weight was impressive rather than grotesque; the physical manifestation of an intellectual, spiritual, and moral fact. It lent him a kind of gravity and bulk, and I didn't notice any of the students attempting to talk with him.

"Professor Morse?" I said as he brushed past. He stopped, turned, examined me unsmilingly.

"Yes?"

"My name's Quinn Parker. I'd like to talk with you for a minute."

"Unfortunately, Mr. Parker, a minute is something I don't have. My office hours are posted." He resumed his stately walk down the hall.

"It's about Ronald Hemming and Sonia Lucia."

He couldn't have stopped more abruptly if he'd walked into the back of a parked beer truck.

149

"What did you say your name was?"

"Quinn Parker."

"And what is it that you want, Quinn Parker?"

"Let's talk somewhere," I said.

Professor Morse was trying like hell to find his imposing self again. The little bravado men who turn on the chest helium were working overtime. "Anything you have to say to me can be said right here."

"In the hallway?"

"Absolutely."

I shrugged. "Okay. Why are you lying about Ronald Hemming being at your house the night Sonia was murdered?"

One and two and three and four . . .

The pouch under Morse's left eye began to twitch. A quick glance left and right. He all of a sudden didn't seem quite so anxious for this conversation to be public. "If this is a game, I'm not amused. I told the police all that was pertinent to their case. I need not say a thing to you."

"Ronald Hemming was on the corner of Twenty-third and Ortega at one-thirty in the morning on the night Sonia died. I saw him."

"Did you?"

"Yes, I did."

You don't often seen two men standing in dead silence, staring at each other, and we were beginning to draw the curious attention of passing students. Professor Morse had a change of mind about his open-hallway forum.

"Come with me," he said.

We went down the hall, up one flight of stairs, and he put his key into the office door on the right. He motioned me in first. The office was twice the size of Hemming's. No frills, no clutter. Lots of books, all clothbound. There were no posters, no "relevant" Doonesbury cartoons. This was the sanctuary of a scholar.

Professor Morse shut the blinds on his window and motioned me to the chair opposite his desk. Then he eased his own massive bulk into an oversized swivel chair.

"I can assume you were a friend of Miss Lucia's?" he said.

"That's right."

"Then first of all, allow me to express my condolences, however belated."

"Thanks. What's second of all?"

He steepled his plump fingers beneath his chin. "Second of all is this nonsense of seeing Professor Hemming on the corner of Twenty-first and whatever."

"Twenty-third and Ortega, and it isn't nonsense. I saw him as clearly as I'm seeing you now."

"Really?" Morse leaned back in his chair. "And how did this preposterously remarkable coincidence happen to come about?"

"I spent the evening with Sonia. When I left I saw Professor Hemming on the corner, near where I parked my van."

"I see." Morse was outwardly calm, slowly nodding his head as I spoke. "And why am I privy to this fascinating news? Why isn't your story being breathlessly gushed to the proper authorities?"

"I thought before I did any gushing I'd give you a chance to go back over your social calendar and realize your innocent mistake. The proper authorities take a dim view of accessory to murder."

Morse creaked forward to the edge of his seat. "I'm going to tell you something, whoever you are. Ronald

Hemming possesses one of the finest minds this university has seen in a long time. A very long time. I've taken a personal interest in him. He's a hard worker, a dedicated scholar, and is admired and respected by every single person he has come in contact with here."

"Sounds like a hell of a guy. Too bad he unwinds by slicing coeds into bite-sized chunks."

Morse flared up out of his chair. I wanted to see how far he would flare. "Professor Hemming made a mistake! That's all! Whatever his brilliance in his field, he's young and he made a mistake. A faculty member becoming involved with a student happens more often than you can possibly imagine. I won't have his reputation, his entire career, jeopardized because of this . . . this girl. I won't!" He slammed his pudgy fist onto the desk.

In the silence that followed Morse seemed to regret his outburst. I stared at the clenched fist. Then his voice became calm, memorized, methodical.

"I am going to tell you exactly what I told the police. Professor Hemming dined with me at my home in Piedmont on the night of May twentieth. He had a little too much to drink and we offered him our guest room, which he wisely accepted. Whoever you saw that night wasn't Ronald Hemming." Pause. "Good day, Mr. Parker. Get the hell out of my office and don't ever come back."

Hemming had done a good job. A cover-up worthy of Howard Hughes. Somehow he'd scrupulously avoided being photographed through three yearbooks, two alumni bulletins, and a half-dozen biannual faculty updates. I sat in the university library among the fruits of my fruitless labor. Even a college newspaper snapshot of the English Club—of which Professor Hemming was coadvisor—had left him out. Not pictured, unavailable for photograph, absent . . .

I leaned back and stretched my neck. The library was crowded. I'd gone there directly from my talk with Professor Morse to dig up a photo of Hemming. The Piedmont alibi was an out-and-out fabrication. Morse was trying to help his star protégé out of a jam. But Kate's tentative identification wasn't enough. Not with Mannion about to toss me in the clink. Armed with a photo I could try to get a positive second identification that would place Hemming firmly in Sherri's life. Get the lieutenant's attention once and for all.

In the most recent yearbook, next to the blank space where a photograph should have been, was a three-line sum-up of Professor Hemming's academic career. B.A. at the University of Colorado, M.A. at Berkeley, Ph.D. Harvard. Rhodes Scholar. Twice winner of awards from the National Endowment for the Arts. I try not to be impressed by credentials, but Hemming's accomplishments took some of the wind out of my sails.

"If only my students showed this kind of zeal."

Hemming's voice snapped me to the present. He was leaning on a file cabinet a few feet away. It was too late to cover up the yearbook. He wandered over, hands in pockets.

"Who the hell *are* you?" he asked.

Our eyes locked. Ten seconds passed, and a darkness settled over Hemming with stunning swiftness. It was as though he had jumped too fast and too deep into his hatred, and his insides had ruptured from the pressure. A case of the psychic bends. It was a depth of malevolence I had never seen on a human face before, and my attempted stance of cavalier confidence withered before it. I pushed my chair out as if to go. The movement jostled Hemming from his trance.

"Hold it!" he said.

Other students were looking up from their books. Hemming licked his lips, steadied himself, and lowered his voice. "Keep pushing, I'll push back," he said. "Don't think I won't."

I got up, a little unsteady on my feet, and walked past him, out of the library. I didn't look back, but I could feel Hemming's eyes on me every step of the way. My pace increased in spite of myself, and by the time I reached the van I was practically running.

It was almost five o'clock in Boston, but I took a chance and put the call through anyway.

I'd met Steve Patnode years ago in Guatemala. He was installing potable water systems in the highlands. Gravity-flow. Nothing fancy. No sophisticated made-in-Germany pumps that break down and then rust in the Mayan sun for lack of a trained-in-Germany engineer.

The last letter I'd gotten from him was almost a year old. Postmarked Ecuador, it was full of an exhausted, toss-in-the-towel nihilism I wasn't accustomed to. A weary, rambling thing that had the stamp of too many roughly handled dreams, too much killing witnessed, too much booze consumed solo. Development work was hopeless when the military was always closing you down. No personal life because you have to travel all the time. The hell with it. He was going back to Harvard. Some kind of job they'd offered him. Advisor. Consultant. Something. Sit in an office and watch snow fall on the unbloodied ivy.

"Quinn!" Steve's voice burst on the line. "Son of a bitch! I thought you'd dropped off the face of the earth!"

"Just sitting here watching the fog roll in."

"Save the poetry. I'm not moving out."

"How's Boston?"

"Boston's great," Steve said. "No more boiling toothbrush water. No soldiers shooting at your ass. It's good. Eight thousand channels on the cable TV."

I paused. "Listen . . . I need your help."

Steve's voice lowered a notch. "What's up?"

"What kind of access do you have to the files of former students?"

"Depends on how 'former.' "

"This guy graduated in 1978. Ph.D. in English."

"Seventy-eight's no problem. What's going on?"

"It's a little involved to go into on the phone. Maybe nothing, but I need to check it out."

Enough years of living in politically sensitive countries had given Steve a natural sense of discretion.

"What's the name?"

I gave him the information I had. "What I really want to know is his personal background. Where he was born, grew up, that sort of thing. If he has any family . . . "

I heard Steve scribbling away. "Okay. Want me to call you back when I have it, or mail it out?"

"Call me." I gave him the number and he repeated it back.

"It's nice to have a little mystery again," he said. "That's one thing you always had down south. Mystery."

"With eight thousand channels on television it's hard to have mystery."

"You got that right," Steve said. "You got that right on the nose."

14

NOTHING CLARIFIES LIKE DISTANCE, and that was precisely what I was putting between us and Professor Hemming. I had the window seat, and while Kate read the novel she'd bought at the airport I gazed down at the United States slipping by.

Steve had called back two hours later with the information. Ronald J. Hemming had been born in Luray, Virginia, in 1949, graduating from Luray High School in 1967. That was it. The family part of it was a complete blank, but Steve had a friend of a friend in New York who could look into it more if I wanted.

I hadn't wanted. At least not right away. Instead I'd made reservations for Washington, D.C., the nearest airport to Luray, Virginia. Before going, I asked Carol if she'd be willing to get her telephoto camera out of mothballs and get a few good shots of the unphotographable

Professor Hemming. Carol had done free-lance photo-journalism once upon a time in the years before family-hood, and she jumped at my request.

After a routine landing at National Airport, Kate and I rented a car and headed south out of Washington, D.C., for the resort town of Front Royal. The lodge we'd booked reservations into was built on a scale to comfortably accommodate medium-sized dinosaurs. Enormous rooms. Enormous windows. Fireplaces you could drive a Jeep through. We hadn't needed the formality of reservations. It was midweek of the off-season and we had the run of the place.

We unpacked and showered and then went down into the cavernous dining area to warm ourselves with steaks and red wine. The room seated six hundred, and after we got our table that left room for five hundred ninety-eight. Three waiters got the fireplace going. They tossed hand-fuls of logs in, all at once, the way you throw meat to voracious zoo animals.

"You haven't said fifty words since we left Washington," Kate said, staring at me from across the table. "What's on your mind?"

"I'm trying to be a good patriotic American and presume innocence, but it's coming hard."

"Why?"

I ran my fingertips along the length of the heavy wooden table. "The only way to presume innocence in this case is to write it all off to wild coincidence. Hemming just happened to go blundering into scenes of murder and mayhem by accident. But let's go ahead and be dirty rotten pinko communists for a second and presume guilt. Then the pieces start to fall together."

"Explain."

"Okay. Let's assume a few things. First assumption is that Hemming is the murderer, and that he murdered both Sonia and Sherri."

Kate nodded. "I'm with you so far."

"Let's also assume that the professor has not been on a rampage his entire life. That the homicidal behavior is a recent development."

"Why assume that?"

"Because I don't think anybody could be so competent as to kill lots and lots of people in such a high-profile way over many years and not have at least somebody sniffing at his trail."

"Okay," Kate said. "So it just started. Next question is: why did it just start?"

"Exactly. Let's assume, because of the bizarre nature of the killings, that the reasons are primarily psychological. In other words, it doesn't really have anything to do with money or greed or the normal reasons people get murdered. There is a demon inside of the professor. A real demon. And when this demon gets released, Hemming starts his murderous ways. We've seen the work of this demon. Believe me, it showed its horrible face for a second at the library. But what releases it? What sets it off?"

Kate leaned forward and nursed her wine with both hands. "How is this trip to Luray going to tell you that?"

"You're getting ahead of me. We still have more assuming to do. Hemming was a patient of Sherri's. That meant he had sexual dysfunction of some sort. What sort?"

Kate shrugged. "From what Sherri said there were mainly two sorts. It's not working right, or it's not working at all."

I shrugged. "Okay. Let's say in Hemming's case it's not working at all. Let's say it's *never* worked."

"You mean he was a virgin?"

"Maybe."

"If he was a virgin, how did he manage such a passionate love affair with Sonia?"

I leaned forward on my elbows. "Remember the night I asked you about the initials in Sherri's diary? The first night at your apartment in Carmel?"

"Yes?"

"You were positive that P was the client Sherri was having an affair with. Suppose P was Hemming. P for Professor. Sherri said in the diary that she swore she wouldn't let it happen, but it was happening, and maybe it was because she was jealous that he was finally managing it with someone else. 'Finally managing it.' Those were her words."

Kate looked at a spot on my chin. "What are you saying?"

"Hemming needed sexual therapy of some sort. And if he *was* a virgin, then it's not entirely ludicrous to think that Sherri and Sonia were the only two women he'd slept with."

Kate looked at me, dubious. "What are you getting at?"

I leaned forward in my chair. "Why can't *that* be the thing that releases the demon? The orgasmic state! The guy was a frustrated virgin all his life, finally manages it with Sonia, and boom."

I was suddenly conscious of the waiter standing by our table, waiting to set down the steaks. How long he'd been listening in was anybody's guess, but he gave me a long, long stare, dropped off the food, and disappeared.

"So when he goes into this orgasmic state," Kate said, "does that mean he's unaware of what he's doing?"

"Exactly. Something gets triggered in him."

Kate shook her head. "Not logical. Professor Hemming

doesn't drive around with a trunkload of saws and video equipment just in case his demon gets triggered. That's pretty off the wall, even for a communist."

I leaned back in my chair and pouted for a second. "So my orgasmic theory has some holes in it. Why don't you come up with something?"

Kate smiled. "I still don't see how coming to Luray is going to tell us a thing about Ronald Hemming, least of all his sexual preferences."

"It probably won't. But I want to know more about the guy. He covered his tracks well in San Francisco. . . . There must be a reason. He's very careful about his past."

"And if you discover something peculiar, then what?"

"Depends. If Carol manages to get a good photograph, we can see about getting a second identification. And I was thinking on the flight out if there was any way I could get my hands on Sherri's files. The files she kept on her clients."

"I might be able to help you there," Kate said. "Sherri worked closely with another female therapist in the same building, and they had some crossover with their patients. If one went on a vacation, the other'd take over. That sort of thing. I imagine the other therapist has duplicates of Sherri's files."

I nodded, sipped my wine. "Worth a try."

"And after that, then what?"

"Then I just go to Lieutenant Mannion and take my chances. He's the professional, and I think I can give him enough circumstantial evidence to get the heat off my butt."

"What about me?" Kate asked. "Do you think I'm in danger?"

"I don't like the track record of women who've been around the professor."

Kate turned away from her food and looked into the fire. "Is there a phobia dealing with fear of pitchforks?"

"Not funny, Kate."

"Wasn't supposed to be. I'm getting it."

We ate, and after we ate I held Kate's hand and we took a walk. The night was bright with stars, and very cold.

"It feels good to be here," Kate said, taking a deep breath of the pine-scented air. "You're not going to go out tomorrow and play superhero, are you?"

"Quinn Parker? Someday I'll take this shirt off and show you my yellow streak."

Kate smiled. "All I'm saying is don't go breaking your leg or be in traction or anything."

"I'll do my best."

"It'd put a crimp in our love life if you're all wrapped up in gauze."

"I don't know. Depends on what you're into." We stopped, I squared her shoulders, and we kissed in the crisp cold starlight. When I pulled back, her eyes had a glazed, unfocused look.

"Maybe we should cover ourselves tonight," I said. "Just in case I break something tomorrow."

"Boy, I've heard some lines in my time . . . "

Kate linked her arms around my neck, drew me very, very close, and we kissed again. Her lips felt unnaturally warm in the chill night. I thought of the human engine beneath the skin, keeping the temperature steady, all systems going. Frail and self-contained and utterly separate from the rest of the world. "Want to know one of my deep, dark secrets?" she murmured.

"Immediately."

"Well, . . . I have this thing about making love outdoors."

"Yes?"

"Yes." She gazed dreamily into my eyes. "The thing is, it has to be at least seventy-two degrees Fahrenheit, twenty-one Celsius. Let's go back to the room. I want to see that yellow streak you were talking about."

We went to the room and made love ferociously and quickly, then fell apart. It had all the tenderness and fragile nuance of two cars broadsiding each other in the middle of an intersection at sixty miles per hour.

"Did you get the license of that truck?" Kate said.

"Careful. You're getting close to postcoital dialogue."

"Coital? Is that what we did?"

I laughed and rolled over and pulled her atop me, thigh to thigh, face to face. Her breasts were warm and heavy on my chest. Soft, moist, webbed with delicate blue veins. My hands slid down her back and rested on the pliable rise of rump.

"I wish I could tell you I loved you," Kate said. "But it sticks in my throat."

"Why's that?"

"I've said it one too many times before, I guess. I made a vow last time that in the future I'd keep it generic."

"Generic?"

"Like this." Kate rolled off me, onto her back, took a deep breath, and looked at the ceiling. "I enjoy you. I like my body on your body. I think your voice is sexy, and I usually laugh at your jokes. I admire how you took in Lola. There. Isn't that better than 'I love you'?"

"It's longer."

Kate bounced over onto her side and looked at me with a big smile. Sandra Dee at a slumber party. "How many women have told you they loved you?"

"You want a number?"

"Yes."

"I avoid that kind of arithmetic."

"Come on. Fess up."

I looked over at her. "You know, sometimes the Detroit in you just comes crashing out."

"Thanks. How many?"

"A couple."

"Liar, liar, pants on fire . . . "

"Fifty."

"Who were they?"

"Nobody you know."

"What were their names?"

"Come on, Kate."

"Who were they?" She smiled and rolled over onto her stomach, propped up on two eager elbows.

"Sandy and Connie. Theresa and Gail. Uh, Tina and Carmen. Take your pick."

"Why won't you be serious?"

"Are you always this curious about the men you bed?"

" 'The men I bed'? Don't be so free with the plural. And no, I'm usually not this curious. Take advantage of it." She rested her chin on her hands, thinking something over. "Really only a couple?"

"As far as I remember, Your Honor."

"Funny. I would've thought a lot more."

"I guess I'm the type that inspires women not to make declarations of love."

"Hmmm." Kate stared at me, long and hard. Her eyes scanned my face, forehead to jaw, several times.

"It's getting cold down here at the end of your microscope," I said.

"Maybe it's because women respect you."

"That's it. I resign from this conversation." I turned away, feigning deep and immediate sleep.

Kate rose to her knees, pulling blanket and sheet up over her shoulders so that as I looked up she resembled nothing so much as a naked witch with a flowing, billowy cape. She planted a knee on either side of my waist and looked down at me.

"You can run," she whispered. "But you can't hide. Joe Louis said that. Native of Detroit, Michigan."

On one's deathbed certain images will come back. A kind of review of your life, how it was lived, the people and things that urged it toward one permanent road rather than another. This was one of those images. File it under Youth. File it under that stupid, oh-so-Western belief that youth is better than age, that what is new is better than what is old.

Kate's skin was smooth and brown. The breasts taut, full, and firm. The long legs, dancer's legs, parted so shamelessly innocent. There was no wavering in the face. It was confident of the body's wants, and the body's ability to fulfill those wants. She was years away from the wrinkles, the sagging, the nip-and-tuck to cling to what was always taken for granted. Yes, we age. And yes, we should age gracefully and enjoy sex and white-water rafting and contemporary music well into our seventies. Ann Landers is full of crusty octogenarians writing about how they're carrying on in bed, and over breakfast tables throughout the country is a collective "Good for you!" Feisty. Scrappy. And we cling to their dubious experiences the way you desperately want to believe the stories of those who died on the operating table and then came back to life to talk about warmth and light on the other side.

"Where did you go?" Kate asked. Her voice was low, as though speaking in church.

"Somewhere I shouldn't have."

"Want to come back?"

"Yes."

Kate lowered herself onto me, pulling the blanket overhead till it covered us like a tent. A circus tent. Her lips went to my chest and I eased her down fully. All is possible under the Big Top. Any kid can tell you that. Fantastic stunts. Feats of balance and derring-do.

Acts dizzying and death defying.

15

L URAY, VIRGINIA, is one of those nondescript towns you pass on the freeway when you're on your way to someplace else. Most of us have only a passing, freakish acquaintance with them. The kid has to use the bathroom. The car breaks down. In the normal course of things a place like Luray goes by the window at about seventy miles per hour.

The Blue Ridge Mountains to the left were gray and ashen, with patches of snow and cold overcast covering the peaks. The easy, drawling radio announcer out of Front Royal didn't mince his words. Rain was not called fog in this part of the country. It was just plain, flat-out cold.

I turned off State Highway 211 and drove past a mobile home park named for what the countryside used to look like before they bulldozed it down to make room for the mobile home park. A huge, ugly factory to the left belched toxic smoke into the raw, pale sky. To the right were sagging signs. VISIT WORLD-FAMOUS LURAY CAVERNS! The women came in two sizes; fat and skeletal. The men worshipped the gods of Ford and Chevy, hanging around their pickups, hands red and busted up and knuckly.

"Da da da, dum dum." Kate hummed softly the "Dueling Banjos" theme from *Deliverance*.

"You're not helping things," I said.

"Where have you taken me?"

"To a place where you don't have to ask permission to smoke."

I had to stop for directions twice, but at last located the high school. It was a surprisingly nice, two-story structure way up the slowly ascending hill, as far away from the highway as you could get and still be in town. Beyond the school, the hill slanted steeply and disappeared in a thick tree cover. We parked and got out. You had a full view of the factory, the town, the ribbon of highway a few miles distant. On the factory grounds I could make out a real, honest-to-goodness mansion. The forty-room kind. It was surrounded by a half-dozen large circular pools of eerily colored liquid. Reinforced barbed wire all the way around.

"That smokestack almost looks alive, doesn't it?" Kate said, standing close, leaning into me. Her face was red with cold, her breath vaporized.

I nodded. The smokestack did look alive. Some towering, spewing thing rising far, far above anything else in the town. Somewhere in the past a battle had been fought, and Luray lost. The little wooden houses huddled in the gray. Terms of defeat required that the homes spit out their inhabitants five days a week to work in the shadow of the smokestack. The high school behind me was the only structure that didn't seem defeated. Guerrilla warfare from the outback. Educate the young and send them far, far away from Luray. I suspected that when push eventually came to shove, the smokestack would march up the hill and crush the school into another liquid vat of chemical color.

We drew a blank at the school. Luray seemed to me to be the kind of town where people tended to stay in whatever jobs they landed at an early age. Minnie, the waitress. Gus, the mailman. Joe, the history teacher. But nobody at the school had been there when Ronald Hemming had graduated in 1967. That was that.

We drove back into town and found a place to eat. It was an old-fashioned diner. Jukebox selectors attached to every table. My beer came with one of those bar napkins that have cartoons of big-busted women in compromising positions uttering double entendres that might've been dreamed up by a seventh grader.

I judge the quality of a diner by the number of adjectives they feel compelled to surround the food with, and this one didn't bode well. Everything on the menu was sizzled or smothered or crisp or golden. All the sauces, without exception, were zesty. A suspicious waitress took our order and disappeared.

"Will you get mad at me if I ask a simple question?" Kate said.

"Of course not."

"How in the world are you going to find out anything about Ronald Hemming? My God, Quinn. This is ancient history. He hasn't been here for twenty years."

I chewed on my lower lip and flipped through the jukebox selector. "Just start asking. People like to talk."

"People can only talk about what they know."

"I think in Luray they know a lot. A few hours here

and I'd be able to tell you the color of Hemming's under-wear."

Kate informed me that she didn't care about Hemming's underwear, and that I was welcome to snoop around all I wanted. She was going to wander and absorb Luray's special charms, and then we'd meet back at the freeway hotel we'd decided on earlier.

We ate the golden, crisp, zesty food and then kissed good-bye in front of the car. Kate gave me a strangely earnest pinch on the arm and a warning to be careful. I told her that I would, and she drove off.

Molly's "Just One" was the only bar in town I could find. A small, ramshackle place near the entrance to the tannery. Neon martini glass with a neon olive and the broken remnants of what used to be neon bubbles. A ratty yard in back with a busted-up tricycle, and enough screwy trinkets on the shelf in the second-floor window to give the bar away as doubling as somebody's apartment.

I pushed open the door and was hit with that distinctly sickening smell of an unventilated bar at midmorning. Cigarette smoke, spilled whisky marinating between the floorboards, the vague stench of urine from toilets left drunkenly unflushed. It was dark, and a static-filled television bolted to the wall droned into the shadows. Bar to the left with ten or so stools, to the right a pool table and a couple of little tables. Two men in the far corner were examining pool cues from a wall rack.

I took a stool and waited for somebody to show up. A minute passed with nothing happening, then one of the men walked past me, leaned into a half-opened door at the end of the bar, and yelled, "Darlene!"

"What?" A voice from upstairs.

"Customer!"

"Shit."

He walked past me back toward the pool table without so much as a glance.

"Thanks," I said. He didn't say anything. Cozy little place.

I shifted my butt on the barstool and sighed. Drink a beer and leave, Parker. From the outside, Molly's "Just One" looked like the kind of place where some gnarled old coot would be tending bar and could tell me all about Hemming. Heavy footsteps clunked down unseen stairs and the door opened and in came Darlene.

She was a chunky blond about my age with a sloppy, plaid shirt hanging untucked over soiled jeans; a pug nose; and a puffy face the pallor of raw oysters. She moved with a slow, raunchy sexuality . . . like a big, dirty, sleepy cat who lives in the street and takes it when it's given out.

"What'll it be?" she said.

"A beer."

"What kind?"

"What kind do you have?"

"What d'you want?"

I took a breath. "Dos Equis?"

"Get serious."

"Michelob?"

She nodded and dug below for a bottle. Pendulous breasts shifted freely beneath the plaid shirt.

"Ninety-five cents," she said.

"Cheap."

"We're in business to do business."

Behind me the two men began to play pool. From the window-rattling break I assumed they were pretty good.

Darlene watched them over my left shoulder. I turned halfway on the stool to watch myself.

"What you doin' in Luray?" Darlene said. "Tannery stuff?"

"No. Just passing through and thought I'd try to look up an old friend."

"Which old friend?"

"Ronald Hemming."

She shook her head. "Never heard of him."

I shrugged like it was no big deal. "Knew it was a long shot, but what the hell. Give it a try, right?"

I watched the game. The men called each other Jesse and Carl. Carl was the older and better player. A lived-in face, ravaged by sun, booze, and acne. Like he'd stuck it in a microwave for thirty seconds. He chewed on a cigarette and didn't say much, squinting through the smoke and drilling the ball with machinelike regularity into whatever pocket he wanted.

"Where you headed?" Darlene said.

"Florida."

"Florida . . . ," she repeated. "Never been there. I probably must live the most boring life anybody ever thought of."

"Oh, I don't know, Darlene. Some people wouldn't think it was so bad. Mountains, fresh air, no rush hours. Luray Caverns."

"Luray Caverns!" she mocked. "Them caverns is just a big, long fancy hole in the ground, you ask me."

Carl won the game, and he gruffly told Jesse to set 'em up. A five-dollar bill changed hands.

"Don't know why Jesse keeps playing against Carl," Darlene said darkly. Something told me she owned a piece of the lost five bucks.

"Carl's good."

"Go and try and tell Jesse that."

"No thanks. I get the feeling Jesse doesn't take constructive criticism too well."

"Boy, you got that right."

Just then Jesse missed a shot and cracked the cue down on the table. "Darlene! Shit! How about a little goddamn light in here!"

"Open the goddamn window yourself!" she yelled back.

Jesse turned, his words came out slow and serious. "Get some fucking light on this table. Now!"

Good old Jesse. Genus: wrong side of the tracks. Habitat: backroads of America. Diet: chili dogs and beer. Characterized by foul language, greasy hair, Lucky Strikes rolled up in the sleeves of white T-shirts. Known to attack man if provoked. Darlene flicked some switches behind the bar and lights came on overhead. Jesse sarcastically thanked her. Anger brought some color to her face, and her eyes shone with a pure, unfettered hatred. Time to leave. I drank the rest of my beer quickly and waved her off when she started to grab another.

"On the house," she said under her breath.

"Better not. Say, who do you think might know about my old friend in town? This goes back a lot of years."

"Easy. Walt over at the barber shop. He knows everything about everything."

"Where is it?"

"Out the door and two blocks left and that's it. But wait. How much longer you gonna be in town?"

"Another day or two."

"Look. You . . . you can't find your old friend, you interested in maybe, you know, making a new one?"

I paused. Behind me Jesse swore and smacked down his pool cue.

"I'm with someone, Darlene. Bad timing."

Darlene looked down at the bar top. "Still could have a little fun. Take a drive. Nobody needs to know nothin'."

Jesse was all of a sudden right next to me, leaning his elbows on the bar. He had tight, angry muscles under translucent, tattooed skin. I moved a little to the right. He was staring at Darlene. It was a pretty ugly profile.

"What's doin' at the bar?" he said. "Little early to be hustlin' up action, ain't it?"

"Why don't you just shut up, Jesse Hatcher!" she flared. "Go on and lose some more of my money!"

Jesse just stood leaning, nodding his head up and down with gradually accumulating fury. "Peddlin' your goddamn ass . . . eleven in the goddamn morning . . ."

"Take it easy," I said.

He whirled on me. "Lookit. You don't want another asshole tore for you, just shut up!"

I sighed and looked over at Darlene. "Thanks for the beer." I rose from the stool but Jesse put one hand on my shoulder and shoved me back down.

"Not so fast, pal," he said.

"C'mon, Jess," Carl said sleepily from the pool table. "Let's git playin'."

Jesse just stood there and glared at me. "Peddlin' her goddamn ass . . ."

"Jesse," I said, "she didn't peddle anything but twelve ounces of beer, which is what usually gets peddled in a bar."

He made a motion to grab at my shirt and I clipped his hand off with one short chop, brushing by him and heading for the door, not looking back.

I heard it. The fraction of silence, then the whistle of sliced air. You don't turn around when you hear that sound. You get left or right.

I chose right, and almost made it. The pool cue shattered across my left shoulder, broke in half, and I fell against the bar. Pain tore up the side of my left arm, but that's not what I was worried about. I was worried about the jagged half of the pool stick that Jesse, looming over me, still held in his hands.

Darlene screamed, and then there was an ugly, dead clonking sound and a pool ball dropped at my feet. Jesse's eyes emptied, he weaved like a drunk, then hit the floor so hard he bounced.

Carl ambled over from the pool table. "Git the police," he said. Darlene shakily obeyed. I got up and brushed off my pants. A line of fire burned the length of my shoulder.

"You okay?" Carl asked.

"I think so. Thanks."

"Sure thing."

Darlene hung up, peered down over the bar to where Jesse lay, out cold. "You better not've kilt him, Carl Petrie!"

"I didn't kill nobody, Darlene. Just git me a beer."

"That pool ball's like a goddamn rock. I seen a tee-vee program says you can get a brain clot real easy like that. The blood gets all pressured up."

Carl took a long drag from his cigarette, adjusted his haunches on the stool. "You rather instead Jesse here runs this feller through like a stuck pig and gits sent to jail for twenty years?"

Darlene stood there, not knowing what to say. "You coulda missed him, throwing a pool ball like that."

"So?"

"So you coulda busted my mirror!"

Carl looked pained. "Just shut your damn trap, Darlene, and git me a beer."

Darlene came out from behind the bar and dragged Jesse to a corner and propped him up. She'd forgotten all about how she and I were going to get to be friends and take a drive together. Just as well. Nothing could rend that love asunder.

16

W ALT'S BARBER SHOP was exactly where Darlene said it was. When I opened the door a little bell jangled, and a lanky old codger who'd been sitting in the only barber's chair snapped to. He was about six six and bowed like an old clothes hanger. An undernourished, swayed-in-the-middle look that reminded me of Don Quixote's horse. He scooted the magazines off the chair. They were all pretty smutty. When I didn't pick one up he quickly apologized for them, saying that his clientele were factory workers, and they liked to look at the pictures. I speculated that there might be worse things on this troubled planet than women taking their clothes off for a camera. He relaxed at that. Nodded his head like there sure as hell were.

After it was confirmed that he was, indeed, Walt, I settled into his chair and we threw the bull back and forth for a while. It wasn't often, he said, that somebody like me came in for a haircut. I asked him who I was "like."

"Oh, you know. City type. And not Charlottesville. When you first come in I thought you was one of them New York people down t' inspect the tannery."

"New York?"

"Group owns this and a couple other tanneries somewheres. Ever so often a couple bigwigs come down, walk around awhile, fly back home. Big owner is Mr. Benson. He don't show his face around here no more, though."

"Why not?"

"Month or so ago he come down and got himself in a big stink with Wilbur. Wilbur's the loading foreman down t' the tracks. Got a little spur line here. Zigs quarter mile up t' the factory, then back out." He illustrated with his finger how it zigged, then zagged. I watched him demonstrate in the mirror. "Anyhow, Wilbur and Mr. Benson got into it, jawbone to jawbone. Wilbur's got a temper on him. I seen him punch out a car window before. Anyhow, Wilbur tells Mr. Benson he don't care how much money he's got. Wilbur says you say one more thing at me and I'll knock you coldern a nun's ass. So next day comes along, here's Mr. Benson walking around with Wilbur, inspecting or whatever, and he sees all these pipes layin' around—windowsills, tables, stairs—everywhere. He says, 'What the hell's all this, Wilbur?' And Wilbur, he says, 'Just to have something handy, sir, case you mouth off t' me again.'"

Walt put down his razor and laughed at the memory. "That's the last we seen of Mr. Benson in Luray, I'll tell you!"

"You know," I said, laughing along, "I just put something together. The caverns, the factory. An old school buddy of mine came from here. Sure. Luray, Virginia."

"What's the name?"

"Ron Hemming."

Walt turned off his electric razor. Walked around to face me head on. Mouth so wide you could've pushed a golf ball through it without touching skin. "Ain't polite to pull an old man's leg."

"We went to college together. It *was* Luray, wasn't it?"

"Well, I'll be a son of a bitch if this world don't get littler every day! Ron Hemming got his first haircut in this self-same damn chair you're sitting in!"

Walt paused to let the immensity of the fact sink in. I shook my head. "Amazing."

"Have to tell the wife about this," Walt said. He put down his razor and went over to the cash register and wrote in a pad. "Don't write a thing down now, I forget."

He finished, recapped the pen, resumed cutting my hair. "Ron Hemming . . . ," he mused. "If that don't take everything!"

"Don't suppose Ron's around now?"

"Hell, no. When he left, he left."

"What about family? His mother and father?"

Walt stopped snipping, backed up a couple of steps and gave me a closer look. There was caution in his voice that hadn't been there before. "You two was friends?"

"Well, we were friends, yes, but he never spoke about his family. Never. I always thought it was a little strange."

Walt pursed his lips. "Strange ain't the word for it. I guess it's natural enough you wouldn't know. Suppose it's not the thing you talk about . . . "

"Was there a problem?" I said.

"Well, . . . normally I wouldn't be saying nothin', but it's such common knowledge around here I don't see how it especially matters. What happened was, Elliot—Ron's daddy—went screwy and killed Ron's mama and then himself. Happened right down the street here on Arrowhead Lane."

"My God . . . " I blinked at my reflection in the mirror. "Ron never said a word about it."

"Hell, I guess not," Walt said. "Would you?"

"How long ago did this happen?"

"Shoot, got to be thirty year. Ron was just a kid. Lucky he wasn't in the house or it would've been three dead, not just two. This was just after the war. Korea. Fifty-six or fifty-seven."

"Jesus . . . Why do you think his father did it?"

"Loony as a coot, that's all. Always was. When he was young, he's always getting into it—bustin' windows, drunk, fights, you name it. Worsen Wilbur ever was, and Wilbur's bad, believe me. Vi didn't calm Elliot down a bit. Least not at first. Ever day the police was up t' the house, dousing water on some family to-do. Elliot worked over t' the tannery, bend-stacker, and all the time he was comin' in with a black eye or gashed-up forehead, so everybody figgered little Vi could dish it out pretty good herself."

"What happened the day he flipped? Was he drunk?"

"Who knows? The Hemmings pretty much kept to themselves. Got stranger and stranger. Elliot quit his job at the tannery because the other bend-stackers wouldn't take down the pictures of nekkid women they got in there tacked on the walls. I don't know. Queer bird."

"What happened to Ron after the tragedy?" I said.

"The what?"

"After Elliot killed himself and Mrs. Hemming."

"Ron went to live with Vi's folks."

I sat there in the chair trying to absorb the information. Walt continued to snip at my hair, but I could sense distraction in his movements. Finally he stopped altogether, came around to the front of the chair, and sat on the ledge of the shelf in front of the mirror, facing me.

"How good a friend of Ron's are you?" Walt asked.

"Well, . . . not *that* good. You know, we went to school and knocked around a little bit. . . . "

"Because, I'll tell you. Something happened here that was real, real bad. Rumor at first, but then it got so everybody knew it, and the authorities confirmed it. Thing is, I don't want to go saying something that'll get back to Ronald and him thinking that I'm sitting around the old barber's chair blabbing about his life. Because I'm not. I don't."

Walt looked at me very closely. He wasn't a lovable old codger anymore. His eyes were frank and serious.

"I'll never say a word," I said.

"Telling you this so maybe you understand if Ron's kinda funny about talkin' about his past. What happened was, after the shooting, the police found a graveyard out in the back. That, and a little coffin about the perfect size for a five-year-old boy. What Vi and Elliot did was bury the boy now and then. Put him in the casket and stuck him in the ground for punishment."

I felt the saliva gathering in my throat and not going down. "Jesus . . ."

Walt took a deep breath and then came around to continue the haircut. " 'Bout all this town could talk about for a while. Amazing thing was how goddamn normal Ron grew up to be, like nothing ever happened. Hell of a football player. All-state basketball. Good-looker. Had the girls just plain eatin' out of his hand. Always readin' books about this thick." Walt held his thumb and index finger three inches apart. "I saw Ron and I says to myself, I says, 'Walt, there's one young feller ain't gonna be stacking no bends in Luray, Virginia.' "

We lapsed into silence again. Walt showed utterly no curiosity about where Hemming was now. His interest in the world seemed to extend about five miles from the patch of floor where his solitary barber's chair was nailed. Within that radius his knowledge was complete and compulsive, but beyond it the globe became a strange and unknowable place inhabited by out-of-towners and out-of-staters.

While Walt finished up my haircut he told me of the drought they'd had in Luray fifteen years ago. A lurid tale about a reservoir outside town that over the decades had claimed a number of lives in boating and swimming accidents. They'd flooded a wooded meadow when they'd made the reservoir, so when a body sank it generally got tangled in old tree limbs and never came back up. During the drought the reservoir started evaporating, dropping six inches a day, and pretty soon the tops of the submerged trees started showing. The health department had to send boats out to pluck the waxy, soapy corpses from the limbs. Walt loved the story. He told it with great care and precision.

"Are Ron's grandparents still living?" I asked at last.

"God, no. Died years ago."

"Anybody in town who'd know how to contact Ron?"

"Only Mary Douglas." Walt said it flatly, matter-of-fact, as if it was assumed I knew who Mary Douglas was.

"Girlfriend?"

This got a laugh from Walt. "Not hardly. Mary was a spinster lady. Lost her fiancé in World War Two and never bothered much with men after that. It was Mary who got on the state people and had Ron took away from Elliot and Vi. Well, tried to. She loved that boy."

My haircut was finished. I stood up and got out my wallet. "How much do I owe you?"

"Three dollars."

I paid him. "Any chance of me talking to her?"

"To who?"

"Mary Douglas."

Walt shook his head. "That'd be a little tough. She got herself buried a few months back."

He didn't elaborate. I put my wallet back in my pocket and slowly walked to the door. I figured if Mary's getting buried was strange enough, he'd get around to it. If it wasn't, he wouldn't.

" 'Fraid I've given you an earful this afternoon," he said. "But shoot—this town's had its share, and that's a fact. Suppose every town's had its share, probably. But listen. You see Ron, you say hi from Walt. He'll remember. Tell him he gets a free haircut next time he comes through Luray. You tell him that."

My resistance caved in before Walt's.

"Tell me," I said, "how did Mary Douglas die?"

"Mary Douglas?" The question caught Walt off-guard, as if he had to think again who she was. "Oh. It was cancer. Three-pack-a-day smoker all her life. Caught up with her."

I waited at the door, nodding stupidly. I couldn't quite grasp the concept of a normal death. Then I thanked Walt again for the haircut and left.

Kate wasn't in the hotel. A note on the bed said that she couldn't resist and was on her way to see World-Famous Luray Caverns. Rumor of a decent Chinese restaurant down the highway a few miles, and did I want a date for the night.

I took a deep breath and sat on the edge of the bed. Thought of little Ron Hemming. A five-year-old like any five-year-old, growing up in this oppressive yet oddly beautiful country. Under a normal roof a kid who'd go fishing, who'd watch Dad drink beer and Mother get fat in front of a black-and-white screen. He'd collect frogs and root for the Yankees and now and then sit in the immensity of Walt's barber shop, silent in the presence of thick, big-shouldered men who roared over strange magazines. A kid who'd probably learned well to fear the World Out There, and considered himself lucky to spend the rest of his years stacking bends in the shadow of Mr. Benson's smokestack.

I got up, stretched, and walked to the window. At the Nomad Inn you had your choice of a freeway view, factory view, or no view. I'd opted for no view, and now stood with hands in pockets gazing down at the ice machine. A fat woman stood before it, slamming the side. Right, left, right. Combinations. Really hard. The way you'd finish off a prizefighter if you got him in trouble on the ropes. But the ice machine stubbornly held on and the woman swore and waddled off, muttering.

I put in a collect call to Hank in San Francisco.

"About time," he said. "Where are you?"

"Sitting here at the Nomad Inn, Luray, Virginia. Panoramic view of an ice machine that doesn't work."

"Luray . . . famous caverns, right?"

I was thrown for a second. "How did you know that?"

"Contrary to widespread belief, I haven't lived my life in a damn incubator."

"How are things going back there?" I said.

"As per usual. What about you?"

"Professor Hemming had quite a boyhood. His dad flipped out and killed his mom and then himself. Turned out his folks used to bury him in the backyard for mis-behaving. His own little coffin and everything."

"Good God . . . "

"But the strange thing is he came back to Luray and seemed to have a pretty normal life afterward. High school football star, good grades, very popular. Lots of girlfriends."

Hank exhaled loudly. "What else?"

"Not much. I've been hit over the back with a pool cue, Darlene wants my body, the foreman at the factory here leaves metal pipes around so he can brain people he's unhappy with. Oh, yeah. I've got a drought story to tell sometime."

"We'll go through those one by one later," Hank said. "How'd you find out about Hemming getting buried?"

"Hedda Hopper is alive and well and posing as a Luray barber."

"When are you coming back?"

"Tomorrow."

"We Union Street Irregulars are all waiting on pins and needles." Hank yawned. "In the meantime, enjoy the rest of your visit. Hemming's been behaving himself here. Carol got some great black-and-whites of him, and he never had a clue. She's so pumped up she's about to abandon motherhood and get back into the photography. What else? Oh, yeah. All of a sudden nobody thinks Mark McCumber killed Sonia. Mannion was on the horn to Erik again, and you seem to have retaken center stage."

I stretched out on the bed and closed my eyes. "Great. Tell Mannion I'll be back soon and he can go ahead and arrest me if he wants."

"Three square meals a day."

I hung up and passed an excruciatingly dull afternoon in the hotel room, waiting for Kate. Finally, a little before six, a key rattled in the door and she walked in. I was up on the bed, watching television. She tossed something at me and it hit me in the stomach. A REMEMBER LURAY CAVERNS back scratcher.

"Just what I wanted," I said.

Kate smiled and pulled off her coat. Her face was red from the cold. "The caverns are great," she said. Then paused before leaning down to kiss me. "What are you watching?"

"Game show. They spin this giant wheel and if it's a dragon they lose all their money."

"I'm taking a shower."

She did, and I got up and fiddled with the TV, trying to find something else. This was not Steve's Boston of eight thousand channels. In Luray it was this one or that one, and neither came in very well. I resigned myself to the game show and went back to the bed.

Kate came out about fifteen minutes later, all steamy and washed and fresh-smelling. She tossed the towel back in the bathroom and stood there nude, hands on hips.

"Never thought I'd find myself in a hotel in Luray, Virginia, watching my man gape at a game show on television."

"It suits you."

"Ha ha. How did your afternoon go?"

I told her. And as I told her a change came over her. The playfulness left her face. No more casual, saucy nakedness. She began to dress with a disturbing efficiency, as though each garment crawled into was one more shield against the nightmare she found herself in. When I got to the part about Hemming getting buried, Kate left the room altogether and closed the bathroom door behind her. A minute later it opened.

"Was it something I said?" I asked.

"It's something everybody's been saying." She lay down on the other bed.

"You asked and I answered, that's all."

"I'm not blaming you," she said. Her eyes were fixed on the ceiling. "I just want to live a normal life again."

"We both do."

She acted as if she hadn't heard me. She was off somewhere. Traveling back. When she spoke again her throat was tight with emotion. "I must be working something off," she said.

"What do you mean?"

"I must've done something really horrible in another lifetime and this is the one where I pay it all back."

"Methinks the lady is too hard on herself."

"Are you kidding? This is the original derailed life. Look where I am. Sitting in the Nomad Inn with a back scratcher listening to how a little boy got buried in the backyard all the time! Jesus!"

The sound was all the way down on the television. A fat woman with ill-fitting hosiery was getting ready to spin the wheel. The camera panned the audience. They were all going nuts, jumping out of their seats.

"You know what?" Kate went on. "You want to hear something really priceless?"

"What?"

"When I got divorced, even my parents sided with Phil."

"Phil being the name of your ex-husband?"

"That's right. Him up there on the cross with his arms out and me standing at the bottom with a hammer and a half-dozen nails in my mouth." Kate shook her head and kept staring at the ceiling. "He had everybody snowed. A real charmer. But everybody else didn't live with him. I saw a side of him nobody else ever saw. As far as everyone else was concerned, he was just wonderful Phil, the life of the party."

"*Candil de la calle*," I said.

"What's that?"

"Streetlamp. In Mexico they use it to describe someone who shines for everyone except those in his own house."

"*Candil de la calle*," Kate repeated, nodding. Her eyes were a little wet. Knock aside a few emotional boulders and you never know what waters might start to flow. The talk about little Ronald Hemming victimized by his crazed parents had somehow summoned Kate's ex-husband into the room.

"You're being too harsh on yourself," I said.

"Never mind," Kate said.

Not many "never minds" are in earnest, but this one was. So I left it alone. She turned away from me on the other bed, facing the far wall. In a matter of minutes her side rose and fell in the steady rhythm of sleep. I softly called her name. No answer. I got up, covered her as best I could, and eased back down in my own bed.

On the silent television screen the old woman had apparently averted the dragon and the whole place was going berserk. Flashing lights and dollar signs and the host beaming like a hand-painted tie, hugging the lady as she shook her head, disbelieving.

I turned the television off. The screen zipped to a single small dot, then disappeared completely. I left the old woman where she was, lost in the gray circuitry of the machine, jumping up and down in the dragon-free neon.

Free, free, free at last.

17

I T WAS A CLEAR AFTERNOON, and the pilot gave us a long, slow, comfortably banked turn directly over the city. The vacationers crowded the little windows, oohed and ahhed and pointed out landmarks to one another.

It had been a quiet, sober flight. Kate distant and preoccupied, me reading the inflight magazine with much more attention than it merited.

More than ever it looked like Hemming was our man. But my hastily assembled theory of a kind of orgasm-induced altered state wasn't holding together. Kate was right. Hemming probably didn't tool around town with a saw and camera on hand in case he should get laid by accident. No. There was something definitely premeditated about Sonia's murder. The lack of fingerprints, the meticulous attention to detail that the viewing of a cassette would imply .... It was not the work of an out-of-control berserko.

I drifted in and out of sleep, opening my eyes now and then to the silent, inflight movie. The issue of the finger-prints continued to nag at me like a dull toothache. It bothered me that Hemming had been so popular in school. Girlfriends. A charmer in class. His personality profile was resisting the brooding, moody, dysfunctional cubbyhole I was trying to build for him. I preferred to remember him as he had been that afternoon in the library. The black malignancy of his totally unrestrained hatred. But no. Even that, in retrospect, was wrong. Too much. An overreaction. He had looked at me as though I had killed Sherri and Sonia myself.

We took a taxi into the city, climbed the fifty-four steps, and collapsed on the living room couch. Kate decided to take a long, hot bath and I walked to the Olympic Market on Polk and bought the two biggest porterhouse steaks they had, two bottles of good red wine, and a quart of their Greek-style salad nonpareil in the deli section.

It was dusk and getting chilly. Though I couldn't see it, I knew the fog was rolling in. The foghorns way off in the bay punctuated the noise of Polk Street. They bellowed low and deep, like primeval creatures calling to each other. When the world ends, when bridges rust and fall into the sea and the last human skeleton dries to powder and blows away, there will still be foghorns.

Kate was comfortable in a thick, flannel nightgown she'd picked up in Washington. Wool socks. Hair pinned up and dewy wet from the bath. She'd built a fire and was poking around at the phony log.

I started broiling the steaks, uncorked both bottles of wine, poured out a couple of glasses. Kate was crouched before the fire, sitting on her heels, hands on knees. Firelight danced on her face. I felt good. Glad to be home. Glad to be fifty-four steps up in the sky. Kate took the glass of wine I handed her.

"Fog's coming in," she said.

"Hank's son Matty calls it 'gloomy.' 'Wow, look at all that gloomy,' he says."

Kate smiled.

"Happy to be back?" I said.

"Happy to be out of Luray."

I stretched out on the rug in front of the fireplace. Fiddled with the drink in my hand. "You're a million miles away, Kate Ulrich."

"Not that far. Only two thousand or so."

"Hawaii?"

"Detroit."

"Ocean fog, good wine . . . tell me you'd rather be in Detroit on a night like this."

"I'd rather be in Detroit on a night like this."

"You're serious, aren't you?"

"Guess I'm like Hank's son. Wow, look at all the gloomy."

"Okay," I said. "I'm a reasonable man. Tell me about Detroit."

"Detroit . . . " Kate paused. "Big. Ugly. A lake. Domed stadium. Real people. Canada right there. Change of seasons."

"Change of seasons doesn't work with me," I said. "One winter in New York cured me of that. What else?"

"Car races in the streets. Lee Iacocca. Motown music that'll still knock you sideways." Pause. "Me, maybe."

Kate wouldn't face me. Kept her eyes on the fire.

"Really?"

"Really."

190

"Since when have you been thinking this way?"

"A while. Before I met you. California is like . . . I don't know. Having an affair. All jolt and no substance. And now after all this with Sherri and Hemming . . . It's making me a little bit crazy." Kate shook her head, held the glass of red wine up, and watched the fire through it. "I've got this fantasy."

"Tell me."

"What happens is I go down to the Greyhound station here in San Francisco and buy a ticket for Detroit, but I have to wait awhile for the bus and while I'm waiting all these creeps and horrible people come slinking around. Just when it feels like I'm about to get pulled under, this gleaming bus comes up and I get in and the door closes behind me, the whoosh of air brakes, and we drive away."

"They don't have Greyhound creeps in Detroit?"

"I said this was a fantasy."

"Wouldn't a nonstop out of S.F. International be easier?"

"No. See, this way I get to watch every last mile that goes by between here and Detroit, and when I get home I think of all that barren, empty desert between me and California, and I'm safe somehow."

"Sounds like you've made up your mind."

"Not exactly. I mean, I did. I had. But then I met you." She turned and looked at me. "If I'm way out in left field just tell me, okay? I'm one of the world's great copers, but I need to know what I'm coping with." In the pause her eyes darted ever-so-slightly toward the kitchen. "Steaks are burning."

So they were. I jumped up and rescued them before the damage was substantial. I put them on plates, dished out a hefty portion of Greek salad, and futzed around the kitchen, buying time. For too long I'd been wandering the psychotic world of Ronald Hemming, and Kate's sudden refocusing on something real and human had caught me off guard. I went back out to the living room and handed Kate her plate.

"That was the Detroit in me," she said.

"What was?"

" 'The steaks are burning.' You could be in the middle of proposing marriage and I'd tell you the steaks were burning. Relentless practicality. A Californian'd let them burn and get on with the lovemaking. I'm not like that. I'll never be like that." She looked into the fire. "You know what my job was in Michigan?"

"Tell me."

"Research analyst."

"What research did you analyze?"

"Actually, I did market studies more than anything else. Like . . . okay, there were these two hair salon places, chains, each with maybe ten or fifteen stores in the Detroit area. Both gave quality haircuts at low prices, both had good locations. You look at them on paper and they're exactly the same. Except one chain is going gangbusters and the other's losing money. The chain losing money hired me to figure out what was going wrong. Took me half a day to put my finger on it. You know what it was?"

"Not in a hundred guesses."

"The color of the cloth they put on the customer when they cut. The thing they clip behind your neck." Kate laughed, remembering it. "One used a white cloth, the other dark blue. It was obvious. The dark blue cloth made people uptight because it showed any dandruff or dry scalp while they were getting their hair cut. The white cloth hid people's imperfections. So the chain switched to white cloth and it's thriving. I got paid a lot of money for figuring that out."

"So why did you end this promising career?"

"My husband got transferred to the New York office." Kate shrugged. "I followed. Ulrich women follow their men, foolish ladies. Then when things fell apart, I couldn't face returning to Detroit. I wanted something really different, something that would shake up my life. I had this image of myself on the California coast, with fog and hawks and fascinating people." Kate paused and turned to look at me. "I don't have a lot of time, Quinn. That's why I need to know how you really feel. A wonderful, breezy, six-month affair is a luxury I can't afford at this stage of my life. Does all this sound cold and methodical?"

"No."

"So your answer's still sealed with Price Waterhouse?"

"Kate, . . . I couldn't trust my answers about anything these days. Until this business with Sonia is wrapped up . . . "

Kate put two fingers to my lips and nodded. "I understand. No more talk."

We pushed the plates and the wine aside and made love slowly and silently before the fireplace, just the way it's supposed to happen in romance novels. But no cries or gasps or breathless urgings. Silent. As though afraid of waking a sleeping, unseen party who shared the room with us.

We finished with Kate atop me, her hair in my face, the sharp wet pain of her lips and teeth on my shoulder, her body kicking into me almost angrily, the way you slam your fist on a table to make a point. Then she stopped with one taut, muscle-stretched understanding of something, and fell away. The air seemed to hum, and a quiet minute passed.

"Jesus," Kate said at last. "It seems we make love an awful lot."

"Are you concerned?"

"No." She lay on her back, trailing a fingernail along the area between her breasts. "But too much of anything makes me suspicious. It's a flaw in my character."

"What would you rather be doing?"

"I don't know. Think about someone you never make love to. Like Hank."

"Do I have to?"

"What's the glue that holds you two together?"

"Hank's inability to pay his bills."

"I'm serious."

"So am I."

Kate gave a huge sigh and rose to a sitting position. Her hair was wild and every which way. "Lucky you," she said.

"Why's that?"

"Kate Ulrich, world-famous postcoital bore, has just asked her absolutely last annoying question of the night. What's for dessert?"

Hank made his appearance early the next morning and Kate kindly begged off. She'd had enough of Ronald Hemming. She was going to swing by Sherri's old office on Bush Street and see about the possible duplicate set of patients' records, then that was it. For the first time in too long she was going to be a normal person and go meet a friend for lunch downtown and browse a few stores and maybe duck into a museum. She'd be back before dark. I asked her to check in once in a while anyway and she said she would.

Hank spent a few minutes in Oscar's room, feeding him the script of the failed "Generic Anchorman!" A scarlet macaw can live up to sixty years, and that's too long a time to sit on a perch in a cage without playthings. They need toys or they'll go nuts. Pace, pluck their feathers . . . in general behave just like humans who don't put toys in *their* cages. Oscar showed a preference for crumpled paper. He tore at it, tried to eat it, kicked it around, and generally had a grand old Mardi Gras time. It had become Hank's custom to sacrifice all failed comedy bits to Oscar's eager talons.

After the ritual Hank came out of the room shaking his head. "Either that was a particularly bad skit, or Oscar's got rabies."

"There's been tension in the household," I said. "Lola's wondering what scarlet macaw meat tastes like. Oscar's got some aggression to work off."

Hank smiled. "Lola'd better watch it. Oscar's liable to come down off his perch and drop-kick that cat down to Van Ness."

Oscar's exuberant paper-shredding of "Generic Anchorman!" was more than Hank could bear. So he turned his back on the doomed masterpiece and protested that he needed some sun on his too-white body.

We grabbed a couple of lawn chairs and went up the back stairs leading to the roof.

"What's Hemming been up to?" I asked.

Hank cleared his throat and started spreading tanning oil on his arms. "Well, I've pretty much concluded that your theory about the videotape is ninety percent accurate."

"What brought about this revelation?"

"Hemming got very nervous when I started to put a cassette in his machine. That's not to say I had *the* cassette in my hands, but his reaction was—"

"Wait a minute." I sat up straight in my chair. "Hemming's machine?"

"That's right."

"Where was his machine?"

"In his living room."

"You were in his living room?"

Hank nodded, lathered up his shoulders. "Repairing a broken cable line."

I put down my coffee. "Back up and start from the beginning."

"Like this," Hank said. "Since you've been so dead set on the video angle, I went ahead and assumed you're right. I also figured that if he did tape it, it must still be somewhere around his house, where he can watch it. He might have a suspicion that you're on to him, but the incriminating tape would still be there. Nixon taught us that much in Watergate. So I cut the cable to his house yesterday and waited till he got home and called and said I was the repairman and our computer showed a breakdown in service to his area, and would he mind turning on his television and checking. He did and I invited myself over to have a look. Fiddled with the set, pushed a few buttons and shook my head and said it looked like term box vandalism, damn punks. Like the bit about term box?"

"What's a term box?"

"Nothing. Just made it up to sound official." Hank smiled, pleased with the detail. "Anyway, he had three unmarked cassettes sitting on top of the television, next to the VCR. Right in the middle of all my blue-collar jabbering I picked one up real quick and shoved it in the machine and Professor Hemming went about six inches off the floor. That's why I said ninety percent on the probability of Sonia's death being on tape."

For a moment I simply stared at Hank, too stunned to say a word. "Anything else?"

Hank shook his head. "No. Except Hemming's got a gym in a back room and the weights on the bench press were set at two hundred ninety pounds. Means he's a very, very strong guy."

"Strong enough to push a pitchfork all the way through a girl and into a wall."

"Exactly."

"They should pickle your brain and preserve it forever," I said.

"Yes, they really should. Do me a favor and tell Carol that."

"You two having problems?"

"Not really," Hank said. "But the money's running low and I'm getting the feeling . . . I don't know. That I should put the comedy on hold awhile and go out and find a normal job."

"That's not what Carol wants."

"I know. But at five bucks per triumph the kids are going to have a tough time going to college."

"If it's a matter of a loan to get you through . . . "

Hank shook his head. "Thanks, but I don't have many spasms of responsibility. Let me enjoy it for a while."

For a few minutes we sat in silence on the roof. The sunlight was bright and cool. No clouds, no fog. I was wondering what to do next. My first impulse was to go back out to San Francisco State and confront Professor Hemming. Dish up Luray, Virginia, and put it right out on the table. Something about Walt and the free haircut.

Touch the electrode and watch Hemming react. But I resisted. It would be a cruel thing to do, and there was always that chance—no matter how remote—that Hemming was innocent. A tenure-happy teacher who unfortunately got mixed up with a girl who was destined to be murdered.

Yeah, right.

And maybe if one only reread *Romeo and Juliet* enough times Juliet would wake up five minutes earlier and stop Romeo from killing himself and they could make a down payment on a palace in the suburbs.

"Vapor Trail's out again," Hank said.

I shielded my eyes and looked east, to the top of the salmon-colored building on Hyde Street. So he was. Vapor Trail was an old man who lived in the penthouse of the tallest apartment building in the area, and he had a telescope mounted on his patio that looked powerful enough to count the craters on Jupiter. There wasn't a rooftop in the area that was safe from Vapor Trail's scrutiny, and on a day like today they would be littered with women in various states of undress. We called him Vapor Trail because he seemed to appear and disappear as mysteriously as the fog. I waved in the direction of the telescope and Vapor Trail waved back.

As Hank was getting ready to apply his second layer of tanning oil, the cordless phone rang. It was Kate. We had a ten-second conversation, then I stood and put my shirt on and stretched the kinks out of my back.

"Going somewhere?" Hank said.

"Downtown. Kate found a copy of Sherri Kaline's client records."

Lola's head suddenly poked up from the back steps that led to the roof. She came cautiously up to us, checking out the view from this angle and that. Below we could hear

Oscar screeching with delight. Hank looked down in the direction of the bedroom.

"Oscar's pushing it."

"What's the problem? You've finally found an appreciative audience." I smiled and Hank didn't smile back. "Put your afternoon to good use."

"I will," Hank said, and he gave Lola a blast of Beethoven's Fifth. Lola wandered over. Hank dug into his pockets and pulled out a ring full of keys and put his face close to Lola's. "This, my lovely cat, is a key. I'm going to teach you how to use it. No scarlet macaw in the world will be safe once you master this."

Lola looked up at Hank with moist eyes. For a second I thought they had actually communicated, but then I realized what a foolish notion this was. As I left Hank was down on all fours, taking a key off the ring. Lola pawed at it, eager to learn.

18

I HOPPED A TAXI into town and rode the elevator up
to the third floor of Sherri Kaline's old office on
Bush Street. The reception area was set up like a futuristic airline terminal—sleek and elegant and blindingly
white. The waiting room was in the shape of an octagon,
with eight doors leading off into eight offices. A single
receptionist occupied a circular desk in the middle of the
octagon. Rows of chairs formed inverted triangles leading to each of the eight doors.

I stood for a moment to quell the vertigo of such architecture gone amok, and the receptionist smiled out at me
from the depths of the Pythagorean nightmare.

"Can I help you?"

"I'm supposed to meet Kate Ulrich . . . "

"Oh, yes!" She buzzed something on a hidden control
panel. "Office five. Go right in."

I maneuvered through the trapezoids and parallelograms and went into the office. Kate was sitting there, alone, in a smaller waiting room. She had a manila folder in her lap. When I came in she stood to kiss me.

"You made it," she said.

"Barely."

"Here." She handed me the folder. "Exact duplicates of Sherri's client records. Lonnie didn't want them to leave the office, otherwise I would've brought them to you."

I sat down next to Kate and opened the folder. About forty pages, onionskin paper, with single-space typing.

"Have you looked it over?" I said.

Kate nodded. "Some. Lonnie brought me up-to-date. Naturally, the Woodside police suspected one of her clients. She had twenty-five at the time of her death. I didn't realize how well she was doing. Pretax income last year of nearly eighty thousand dollars. Sixteen of Sherri's clients were women. Lonnie said all were checked out, though because of the brutality of the murder they weren't really looking for a woman."

"Women aren't brutal?"

Kate smiled. "Women aren't strong. Not *that* strong, anyway. The pitchfork went all the way through and took out a half-inch of wood from the wall behind."

"What else?" I said.

"Of the nine left, five checked out immediately. The other four were under assumed names. Lonnie says it happens all the time, especially with sex or mental-illness things, so nothing terribly suspicious there. Two of the pseudonyms were located and cleared. That leaves two clients, both male, who were never found." Kate leaned forward and leafed through the papers in the file. "This one . . . and this one."

"Did Lonnie ever see these two clients?"

Kate shook her head. "No. Never."

"Are the police still looking for them?"

"I guess so," Kate said. "The case isn't closed. But Lonnie said the police told her that with false identities you generally either get them quickly or you never get them."

I spent a few minutes looking through the two files. They called themselves Harv Danson and Jeff Moss.

"Tell you what," Kate said. "I'm going to wander out and enjoy the city, then head back to Carmel. I've got some loose ends to tie up. Take your time. Lonnie said to just leave the files with the receptionist when you're through."

Kate stood, leaned down to give me a kiss, and left. I separated the two files from the rest of the pile and began to read.

I turned first to the patient who called himself Harv Danson. Not a whole lot to it. Your basic overburdened professional trying to function healthily in the pressure-cooker environment of modern business. I scanned the file. No sexual monsters lurking in deep, dark closets. Instead, a portrait emerged of a quiet, mild-mannered fellow who lost himself in a rich fantasy life—castles and cliffs and yearned-for loves on exotic shores. Sherri didn't quite know what to do with him. The visits grew less and less frequent, had less and less to do with sexual dysfunction, and finally Sherri concluded that Harv Danson was coming to therapy once a week for no other reason than to share a room with Sherri Kaline. Infatuation. Puppy love. The file ended with a whimper, not a bang, and the man who called himself Harv Danson receded back into the fanciful woodwork from which he came. Not terribly satisfying. I put aside Harv Danson and moved on to Jeff Moss.

He was thirty-five years old. If Hemming had been

seventeen when he graduated from Luray High School he would have been thirty-seven. Close enough. Patient was handsome, relaxed, confident. Check, check, check. His problem was a chronic inability to have sex. A virgin, consequently, and anxious for it to be otherwise. A hypothesis on page three that something had happened to Jeff Moss as a young boy and he'd been traumatized on the issue of sex ever since. Possible sexual abuse, since the patient had trouble recollecting events before the age of seven. Sherri couldn't decide if it was amnesia or simply a pathological unwillingness on the part of Jeff Moss to confront certain aspects of his past. Sherri'd made numerous attempts to break through, but it was just a long, silent fall into darkness.

Then, on page four, a change. Jeff Moss announced that he was having an affair. Sherri's notes were doubtful. Delusion fantasy. But the tone of her entries subtly changed. If I hadn't been looking for it, I probably wouldn't have seen it. Her analyses became less clinical. More personal. A touch of jealousy—even resentment—that perhaps Jeff Moss really *was* discovering the world of sex via another woman. The last office session was dated five days before Sherri was murdered, and there was nothing special about it. No dark, shadowy harbingers of doom.

But it was Hemming. There wasn't a doubt in my mind. And I was willing to bet my last dime that the other woman in Jeff Moss's life was Sonia Lucia. I put the file back together, gave it to the smiling receptionist, and began walking south in the direction of Market Street.

"Doughnut?" Erik pushed the brown paper bag toward me.

"Thanks."

He yawned, stretched, leaned back in his chair. "What brings Quinn Parker to this seedy end of town on a glorious day like today?"

I reached into the bag, poked around till I found something with cinnamon on it, then brought Erik current regarding the Luray revelations and the two missing John Does from Sherri's client list. Erik listened without expression, and when I finished he cleared his throat, linked his hands behind his head, and stared at the ceiling. "So what do you think?" he said.

"Hemming certainly fit the second profile. The age, the problem, the disturbed childhood. . . . Who knows? What I'm thinking is, maybe it's time to take a chance and go to Lieutenant Mannion with this information. He has better tools at his disposal than I do. He'd be able to follow it up. Put the necessary manpower on it."

"Quinn . . . " Erik slowly shook his head. "Do you know what a guy like Mannion makes?"

"No."

"Sixty grand a year."

"So?"

"You know how much of that is overtime?"

"How much?"

"Twenty. When there's a budget crunch—as there happens to be in a major way this year—the first thing that gets axed is overtime. Statistics show that a crime not solved within the first forty-eight to seventy-two hours is a crime not likely to be solved at all. In this city, San Francisco, forty percent of *all* homicides remain unsolved. Given those numbers, Mannion's not going to go tromping around all hours of the night ignoring wife, children, sleep, and mortgage payments looking for a killer who may or may not exist. I don't care how dedicated the guy is."

I finished the doughnut and slapped the crumbs from my hands. "Carol got some good photos of Hemming."

Erik looked at me. "She what?"

"While I was out in Virginia. Carol went to the campus and took a couple of good shots. She used to be a photojournalist, you know."

"Have you seen them?"

"No. I'm going over there now. Then I'll try to find sombody who can give a second identification, linking Hemming to the Sherri Kaline murder. Budget crunch or not, Mannion would *have* to pay attention to that."

Erik stood and wandered to the window, keeping his back to me.

I scanned the desk for his photo of Brigid. It was gone. "Hey, what happened to your Irish flame?"

"My what?"

"Brigid."

Erik turned, registered what I was saying, and managed a reluctant smile. "Out of sight, out of mind."

He wandered over to his desk and began opening drawers. The third one he tried he found the framed photo in among loose coins, rubber bands, and paper clips. He made a big procedure of how he was dusting it off, then he placed it with exaggerated finesse at its usual spot on the desk. "There."

"She do something to make you mad?"

Erik shook his head. "I got a postcard from her this weekend."

"She still want to come out to San Francisco?"

Erik shook his head. "No. She's fed up with us being this far apart."

"Can't blame her." I said. "A little tough on the hormones to keep a candle burning for someone ten thousand miles away."

"True," Erik said. He was off somewhere, way, way back in time and space. "In fact, there was a not-too-subtle implication that perhaps we should call it off unless one of us makes a move."

"So?"

Erik smiled. He was talking more to himself than to me. "Actually, I was thinking about Ireland this morning—about this old woman who came around my village every Friday, like clockwork, to collect bottles. She used them to fill with honey. Hard drinkers, the Irish. By the time she finished with my street she'd have a wheelbarrow full. Used to buy my honey down at the market and it'd come in a Dewar's bottle. Today's Friday. I bet she's doing that right now." He paused, turned to face me. "So I'm thinking about making the move. Longer this time. Maybe for good."

"You're not serious."

"Yes, Quinn. I am. And it's not just Brigid. It's probably something I'd do anyway. The old sickness is coming back again. All this business with Sonia . . . "

"No Forty-Niners games in Ireland," I said.

Erik's smile grew softer and softer. It looked like it might evaporate and take Erik with it. "I'll buy a satellite dish."

"You can't run away from the problems of the world, Erik."

He turned, leaned against the windowsill, and looked at me. "Did I ever tell you my movie-in-the-jungle story?"

"No."

"This was back years ago. Before I ever came to California. Happened down the coast of Mexico, oddly enough. Your stomping grounds. I rented a hut in a fishing village called Aticama, a little south of San Blas."

"I know it."

"Great place, right? Seafood, no electricity, wild, open beach, jungle everywhere. The perfect spot to run and hide. Except the second week I was there the traveling projectionist came to town."

"Projectionist?"

"Yeah. Since there isn't any electricity, what the villagers do is all get out and whitewash the side of a building and wait once a month for the projectionist. He comes around in a beat-up jalopy with films and a generator and you sit under the stars and watch the movie. I really got into it. Rolled up my sleeves and whitewashed the building with the local kids, all of it. That night the movies started. First was a black-and-white religious film, made in Mexico. Morality tale about how the good honest priest comes to town and converts the local heathen bad guy into a good Christian. When that was over they showed an American western. Your standard shoot-'em-up. But it was the thing they showed last . . . it was kind of a documentary. News footage of what the World War Two soldiers found when they stumbled onto the concentration camps. There I was, under the jungly night, in the middle of paradise, watching images of skeletal corpses piled fifteen feet high."

"They showed this with the kids there?"

"They showed it to everybody! And it didn't stop, Quinn. I mean . . . the goddamn thing just didn't stop. It went on and on and on, atrocity after atrocity, and the little children just sat on their benches and watched." Erik shook his head, deep into the memory.

"I remember craning around, trying to see the projectionist. He was in a little booth by himself. But all I could see was his elbow coming out the tiny window. That, and the ray of light and the curl of his cigarette smoke drifting upward in the night. I never got a look at his face, but it was like Evil itself had come into town . . . the traveling projectionist . . . that's when I knew there was no running away."

I sat silently and watched Erik. I'd never heard him speak like that before. Finally he seemed to rouse himself and he looked at me with clear eyes.

"Never knew the old lawyer could be so poetic, did you?"

"No," I said. "I didn't."

"Well, . . . enough of that."

Erik walked away from the window and began rubbing his neck. "You and Kate, you're pretty close?"

"As close as you can get in a week."

Erik nodded. "Looked that way."

"Do I detect disapproval?"

"Why should I disapprove?"

"I don't know. Something about funeral-baked meats."

"Speak English."

"Thought you might be holding out a candle for Sonia," I said. "She was your friend, too."

"Sonia?" Erik looked puzzled. "Sonia's dead."

For a moment we were silent. So she was. Then Erik walked toward the door and I took the hint.

"Sorry about going on like that about the traveling projectionist," he smiled.

"Don't be. It was a good story."

"No." Erik shook his head. "It was more than that. It was the most goddamn vivid moment of my life. That elbow, the cigarette smoke, the stars above and the withered bodies flickering in the light." Pause. "I know this sounds crazy, but I've got this fear that I'm going to see that elbow again one of these days. Sitting in a restaurant, at a ball game, somewhere. Just the elbow. I'll recognize it."

19

Hank and his family live in a modest, two-bedroom house on Woodland Avenue, about a drive and a three-iron from the U.C. Medical Center. The neighborhood is an oasis of normalcy in a city that prides itself on abnormality. Children roller-skate on sidewalks. Mothers take their babies in strollers down to the local market. On weekends the men wash cars and mow lawns and get together for barbecues. You know the paperboy. It could almost be mistaken for a middle-class suburb of Indianapolis exept for the ocean fog and the token neighborhood transvestite bar.

Carol greeted me at the door with a big hug and kiss. Matty and Cort, the two boys, appeared instantly at her side to see what was going on with mommy. She told the boys to run upstairs and play and they said they didn't want to. They wanted Uncle Quinn to pull his thumb off again. It was a trick I'd shown a few times, an optical illusion that makes my thumb appear to leave my hand and float in midair. Matty was five and Cort was three. I said that I'd do it if they went upstairs to play afterward, and they eagerly nodded their heads. It was a deal. I floated my thumb in front of them. Matty watched very carefully, Cort clapped his hands, and then they ran off together into the kitchen. Carol fluttered her eyes like it was all too much.

"Kids are growing up."

"Not fast enough for me," she said, combing fingers through her hair. "I don't really think that. But I have my days."

"Matty already suspects my floating thumb trick. I could see some doubt in his eye this time."

"Like father, like son." Carol said. Then Matty and Cort were thundering back into the living room from the kitchen. "Hold on a second. Let me get these two salted away and then I'll show you what I've got."

Carol got up and led the boys out of the room, hands cupped lovingly around their heads, talking to them softly about making deals and sticking to them.

The one that got away. Not Sonia, though at times I indulged myself by thinking so. Sonia was a pipe dream. An archetypal heartache, existing only to be yearned after and having nothing to do with the real world. But Carol was the genuine article, and she could've wallpapered her home with the chest hair of countless male trophies. Not because of her extravagant beauty, because it wasn't. Not because of her voluptuous figure, because it wasn't. She simply had the ring of authenticity. A woman whose hands you'd love to have cupping the heads of your children. How else do you define it?

She got away, perhaps, but that's not to say that long ago we hadn't circled each other. Watched our share of movies together. Logged time gazing into each other's eyes in Italian restaurants. But it was destined not to be. The minute she'd laid eyes on Hank Wilkie, Quinn Parker slipped out of the picture. She talked about Hank's "essence."

One afternoon last year I'd liberated her by hauling along a trusted babysitter and taking her to lunch. It was all on the up-and-up—even cleared it beforehand with Hank—but one drink became two, and two became three, and it could've gone anywhere. I drove Carol home, and at the door she kissed me. It wasn't passion, but it wasn't the way you'd kiss your brother, either.

"No more lunches," she'd said, withdrawing her lips. "Okay?"

"No more lunches."

And that had been it. Three drinks do not an essence disintegrate, and Hank would always be the man for her.

I sat there, lost in the land of what-might-have-been, when Carol came back into the room, rolling her eyes and slapping her hands. Cartoon theme music wafted down the stairs.

" 'Dumbo's Circus,' " she said. "That should hold them for a half hour. Sure you don't want anything?"

"Positive."

She sat in the chair across from me and glanced up at the ceiling. "Swore I'd never use that damn television as a babysitter, but Jesus . . . sometimes you don't know what else to do."

"How about Sodium Pentothal?"

"Don't think it hasn't crossed my mind," Carol said. We laughed, and as the laughter tapered off we looked at each other.

"The kids are wonderful. You don't know how good it

feels to stretch my legs around something wholesome for a change."

"I was thinking about Sonia today," Carol said. "I used to be jealous of her. Isn't that ridiculous?"

"You being jealous of any woman is very ridiculous."

"No, but I mean . . . she was so gorgeous and sexy. I don't know. Every time she walked into a room things got tense. The men would all perk up and the women would go rigid. I felt for Sonia. She seemed like a sweet girl. Beauty like hers can be a curse."

"I suppose you're right."

Carol skirted the floor with her gaze, as though unsure what to say next. "Hank said the man who confessed isn't the one who killed Sonia."

"I'm afraid not."

"You don't want to talk about it, right?"

"I'm enjoying talking to you," I said.

Carol nodded, leaned back in her chair, took a deep breath. In the silence we could hear the strains of "Dumbo's Circus." "So!" she said at last, waving her hand at the living room. "I'll let you enjoy all this wholesomeness while I get the pictures."

She got up and disappeared down the hallway and came back in a moment with a manila envelope. "I think you'll like these," she said, undoing the clasp. "I got about a half-dozen when he was outside, talking to a student, then another ten or so at this picnic bench. I think the picnic shots are clearer."

I leafed through the eight-by-ten black-and-white photos. They were excellent. If you couldn't identify Hemming from one of those, you couldn't identify him.

"Haven't lost your touch," I said.

"Thanks. You don't know how good it felt to get back into the darkroom again."

"You should do some more free-lancing."

Carol nodded. "I'm going to. Next year Cort is in pre-school and I'll have the time."

I put the photos back in the envelope and leaned back in the chair. "So how are things around the old homestead?" I said.

Carol's face darkened. "Hank's threatening to go straight on us and get a regular job."

"It's not all that strange," I said. "Most of the world's population have regular jobs."

"I didn't want to get married to the rest of the world's population." Carol bit her lower lip. "It'd kill him, you know. Putting aside the comedy."

"Can't he do both?"

Carol shook her head. "No way. He tried that once before. If he was just dabbling, or less talented. . . . You know where he is right now?"

I shook my head.

"At a job interview. For a kennel company!"

"Doing what?"

Carol shrugged and looked exasperated. "Watching the dogs, I guess. Who knows?"

Hank's car suddenly sounded in the driveway. Carol shot a nervous glance at the front door, then at me. "Don't bring this job business up," she said. "I don't want to get into it with him right now."

"Won't say a word."

Hank came through the door and dropped a well-thumbed newspaper onto the coffee table. He waved at me and gave Carol one of those perfunctory, exhausted-businessman kisses on the forehead, then went into the kitchen. We could hear the electrical hum of the refrigerator, then Hank walked back into the room with a can of beer.

"How did it go?" Carol asked. Her voice was thin and controlled, and I suddenly felt like an intruder.

"It went fine," Hank said, easing into a chair and taking a swig of beer. "I start in"—he looked at his watch—"ninety-five minutes."

Carol's eyes went wide. "Ninety-five minutes?"

"That's right."

"Tonight?"

"Tonight."

More silence filled the room.

"What about your routine tonight at Zzzanadoo?" Carol said.

Hank put his beer down. "My routine at Zzzanadoo would probably net me about seven dollars. Pozzi's Pet Resort pays nine bucks an hour, every hour, whether you're watching the dogs or just sitting around the office. *That's* what happened to my routine tonight at Zzzanadoo."

The silence got thicker. I began reading book titles from the nearby shelf.

Carol cleared her throat. "But I thought you'd been trying to get your foot in the door at Zzzanadoo for a year. Didn't you say it was a jumping-off point to—"

"We need the money!" Hank said. "Simple as that. We need the money. I've had my foot in every door in the city except this one. Enough is enough."

"That might be the first true thing you've said in a month," Carol said, lips trembling. "Enough is enough."

And with that she turned on her heels and stormed out of the room. Hank watched her go out, mouth open, shaking his head. Then he turned to me.

"Do you believe that!" he said.

"I'll stay out of this one."

"I mean . . . Jesus! She wants me to push my career and

not push it at the same time! Get this. Last night I come home after two solid hours of bullshit with the people who run Zzzanadoo. They want my act, they don't want my act. They'll pay top dollar. No, wait. They'll pay me top dollar week after next. On and on and on. Hard-assed sons of bitches. So last night I come home just to have thirty minutes to myself. Thirty minutes of people not shouting in my face. A little ESPN, catch up on the sports, have a drink. No. Carol hits the roof. Says I'm more interested in quarterbacks than my own kids. Says the insecurity of my profession is driving her crazy. She says dinner's in the refrigerator and if I want to eat I can damn well go out there myself and heat it up, she doesn't serve three shifts nightly. A half hour! That's all I wanted!"

I nodded understandingly, but kept my mouth shut. Taking sides in domestic wars might not be the stupidest thing you can do, but it's right up there. They eventually make up, but always retain the memory of how you helped kick when one was down.

"Ah, never mind," Hank said, waving disgustedly at the door through which Carol had exited. "This kennel job will take care of some short-term bills. I can always do Zzzanadoo next week. Do well there it could mean big things down the line. Things for the whole family, not just me."

"Congratulations."

"Thanks. Nice to know somebody around here appreciates me." He looked at his watch. "Shit. I gotta go."

I walked with him to the door and stood there while he pulled on his coat. "Take it easy, Hank. We've all been under a lot of strain. Erik's even thinking about going back to Ireland."

Hank stood at the door and looked out with confused eyes. "Yeah, well. I might end up going with him." He paused, turned back as if debating whether or not to seek Carol out, then thought better of it and went out the door.

As soon as the car pulled out of the driveway Carol came back into the living room.

"Sorry," she said, sitting quietly in the chair.

"What for?"

"It's so attractive when couples bicker in front of guests."

"You look on me as a guest?"

Tears were in her eyes. "I don't know, Quinn. It's changing. Hank's gotten so moody. Jesus, sometimes I just say a word to him and he jumps all over me."

I was silent for a while. "This thing with Sonia has gotten us all a little edgy."

She shook her head and dabbed at her tears. "No. He's been this way for months now, way before Sonia. He's putting too much pressure on himself."

"Hank?"

"That's just it. He never shows it. He just breezes through life with his quips and . . . " She coughed, cleared her throat. "You know how much he sees his sons?"

"No."

"Take a guess."

"Carol . . . "

"Ten minutes in the morning and ten minutes at night, that's how much! The comedy takes up all his good time. Writing it, rehearsing it, lining up acts. And then he suddenly dumps it for some stupid nine-buck-an-hour job. Does that sound normal to you?"

"I'm no authority on normal, Carol." I thought for a moment of the basketball game, Hank off buying beer with Ludmila, their laughing faces as they returned. Kate watching the whole thing with an eyebrow arched. I didn't want to be thinking what I was thinking.

"Hank's a good man," I said.

"I know he's a good man," Carol said. A single tear streaked her right cheek, and she quickly brushed it away. "I married him, didn't I? But I just can't . . . I don't think any of us can take this much longer. I believe in his talent, I really do, and I want him to do it. It's a dream we've shared together, but it's such a struggle. All that boring stuff about security that we all used to laugh at . . . suddenly it's running our lives."

Carol kept her knuckles to her mouth, clenched her eyes shut, shook her head. I went over and put my hand on the back of her neck. She leaned into me and gave a ragged sigh.

"Poor Quinn," she said. "Drop by for a little talk and you're suddenly in the middle of a lousy soap opera."

"I remember you helping me out of my own soap opera once," I said. "Name was Kim. Six feet tall, eyes of blue, and a husband she'd conveniently forgotten to mention."

Carol nodded, sniffling. "Hold on a second."

She left and came back a minute later. "Okay," she half laughed. "I'm not scheduled to cry again till six o'clock." Carol's eyes went to the ceiling, and she shook her head. "Do you have any idea what it's like to have a five- and three-year-old running around the house all day?"

"Tell me."

"Who has the most peanuts. Who'll get the blue dish. Which one gets to sit under the faucet while they're taking their baths. Always hauling food out of the refrigerator. Sometimes I stretch out in bed at night and lie there in the dark. Just lie there, wondering if I can take any more, thinking about how it was five years ago and that my life is kind of over in a way. Does that sound crazy?"

"It doesn't sound crazy at all."

"Susan, the woman who took my job, came by yesterday," Carol said. Before she'd gotten pregnant with Matty, Carol had been the publicity person for a major West Coast publishing house. A lot of travel and expense-account lunches with authors making the California talk-show circuit. "She was off to have dinner with Jimmy Breslin. Where am I? Digging through the chewable vitamins because it'll be World War Three if one urchin gets orange flavored and the other doesn't."

I started to laugh, picturing it.

"Don't laugh," Carol said, laughing herself. "This is tragic stuff. This is my life going down the drain."

"Mommy?"

The two kids stood tentatively in the doorway, watching Mommy and Uncle Quinn acting weird.

"What, Matty?" Carol said.

" 'Dumbo's Circus' is over," Matty said.

"Yeah," Cort echoed. "Over."

Matty came up to his mother and leaned on her lap. "Can we have the cake now? You promised."

Carol closed her eyes, took a steadying breath. Then she looked at her watch. "Yes. Bring it in here with two plates and a knife, but not the sharp one."

The two boys turned and thundered into the kitchen.

"Think of it this way," I said. "In twenty years they'll be big, strapping fellows who'll bear-hug you off your feet. Beat up people who say bad things about you. Take you for dinner and wine and dancing."

"Only if the doctors let me out for the night."

Matty and Cort came back into the room with the cake,

two plates, and a well-worn knife. Immediately a squabble broke out as to who would get to cut the cake and who'd get the biggest piece. Carol put her fingers to her lips and whistled. The din quieted.

"We'll do it this way. Matty, you get to cut the pieces."

Matty turned and jeered triumphantly at Cort.

"And Cort, you get to choose first."

Matty's elation faded. He suddenly knew what was required of him. No knife, dull or sharp, ever parceled out two more precisely equal pieces of cake.

"Well done," I said. "The wisdom of Solomon."

"The wisdom of Grandma Patrese of Milano. She who had eight kids of her own. I don't know, Quinn. I guess people used to be made of tougher stuff."

"Something tells me Grandma Patrese did her share of staring at the ceiling at night."

Carol rested the full weight of her head on the back of the couch and watched the kids plow through the cake. "Maybe so," she said. "Maybe so."

It was getting late and I walked to the door. Carol followed.

"Why do I feel like I'm abandoning you?" I said.

"Because you are, schmuck." Carol smiled. "Put it out of your mind. I'll be fine."

"Let's go on a trip soon. Mexico. You, Hank, the kids. Eat shrimp-meat tacos and watch the waves roll in and practice our Spanish."

"God . . ." Carol leaned against the door. "I'm there already."

"Just stay afloat in the meantime."

"Like this?" Carol gestured as one treading water.

"You got it."

"Come see me again soon?"

"Whether you want it or not. And thanks for the photos. This might just do it."

I got in the van, waved good-bye to Carol, and pulled away from the house in the oasis of normalcy in the city that prides itself on abnormality.

20

I CALLED KATE IN CARMEL as soon as I got back to the apartment. I told her about the leading but inconclusive medical records, Carol's photos, and asked if she knew of anybody who could give a second identification of Hemming.

"I've already thought about that," Kate said. "There's only one that I know of. Jimmy Hennessy, the caretaker of Innisfree."

"Innisfree?"

"The ranch in Woodside where Sherri was killed. Her parents' place. She didn't take patients there, but if Hemming was a romantic interest, they might have spent some time there together. And Jimmy, he doesn't miss a thing. He was the one who discovered the body."

Kate said she'd give a call to tell him I was coming. I got the exact address, gave Kate a long-distance kiss, and returned the receiver to its cradle. While I sat there mulling over nothing in particular, the phone rang. It was Lt. Mannion.

"Guess I didn't make myself clear the other day about obstructing justice."

"What are you talking about?"

"Professor Morse came to visit me over the weekend."

"Who?"

"Don't give me this 'who' bullshit. Hemming's alibi. The big, fat guy. Looks like Orson Welles."

"Oh, him." I rubbed my face. I needed a shave. "Did he admit he lied?"

"He said you came to the office and threatened him."

"I asked him about Hemming. That's all."

"Professor Morse said you told him you saw Hemming on Twenty-third and Ortega the night of Miss Lucia's murder."

"Maybe I did."

Mannion took a deep breath. "This is the same corner you saw McCumber?"

"Yes."

"Pretty crowded street corner for one in the morning. They all having a damn weenie roast out there or what?"

I sighed. "Look, Lieutenant. You know as well as I do that Hemming didn't spend that night of all nights in Piedmont. Morse is protecting him. He practically admitted it to me in his office."

Mannion's voice grew stern. I could almost see him shift his ass forward on the chair. I'd had my final warning. Next time I was going to jail. Period. He had the form to type out my arrest warrant, and Irma's fingertips were itching with anticipation. There was a coolness in his voice that said he meant it this time. You only rant and rave when you have conflict. Mannion had no more conflict concerning me.

• • •

Woodside is where a certain class of San Francisco's gentry keep their country homes. It's a small, meandering, well-heeled town thirty miles south of the city, dotted with ranches and mansions, peopled with equestrians and dog breeders. The cars are British, the restaurants French, and the predominant feeling drifting in the balmy air is a relaxed, serene, pipe-smoking sense of having made it with one's tweeds unruffled. Someone had once called it a hotbed of social rest.

I pulled my van up to the gate at Innisfree Ranch and cut the engine. Dust from the dirt road settled in the late-morning sunshine. A plaque hung on the gate. Carved in redwood, the letters in white relief:

I WILL ARISE AND GO NOW, AND GO TO INNISFREE,
AND A SMALL CABIN BUILD THERE, OF CLAY AND WATTLES MADE:
NINE BEAN-ROWS WILL I HAVE THERE, A HIVE FOR THE HONEYBEE,
AND LIVE ALONE IN THE BEE-LOUD GLADE.

The gate was locked, so I left the van and crawled through an opening in the wooden slats. Off to the right was the main house. About eight hundred thousand dollars' worth of clay and wattles. On the left was another structure which I took to be the stables. It was very, very still.

I walked down the road, calling out once in a while, and about twenty feet from the main house a figure appeared around the corner of the stables. He was a tall, thin, weather-beaten man of fifty-five or sixty, wearing overalls and mud-caked boots and a low-slung wide-brimmed hat. He walked with a limp and had the narrowest head I've ever seen on a human neck. A long, sharp nose dominated the face. The type who'd run tax revenuers off his land and roll his own cigarettes.

"Mr. Hennessy?" I said.

"That's right."

"I believe Kate Ulrich called earlier this morning and said I'd be coming."

"That's right." He jerked his head toward the stables. "Come on."

The stables were dark and drafty. There were stalls for ten horses—five on each side—but the place was empty of any living thing and gave the impression of having been empty for quite some time. Only a few bales of stale hay and the faint aroma of decades of manure gave any hint that animals had once been housed there.

"No more horses?" I said.

"No more nothin'. For sale, all of it. After what happened, Mr. and Mrs. Kaline upped and left. It's only me out here now. Me and the wife. What's your question?"

"Sherri had a new boyfriend just before she died, didn't she?"

Jimmy didn't answer right away. He walked slowly to a saddle, took out a pocketknife, and began smoothing out a ragged leather strap with tremendous concentration. "Miss Kaline had lots of men callers."

"But she had a new one at the end?"

Jimmy ran a pair of nicotine-stained fingers down the leather strap. "Yep. And I don't know who he was or where the hell he skedaddled to. Police asked me that a long time ago and I about wore my eyes out looking at all their photo books. So if that's your question, we're wasting each other's time."

I took the eight-by-ten of Hemming out of the manila envelope. "Was this the guy?"

Jimmy Hennessy straightened up, held the photo at arm's length, and his eyes slowly widened. "Where the hell'd you get this?"

"Is it him?"

"Sure is." Jimmy handed the photo back. His cold blue eyes rested on me. "You ain't the police?"

"No."

He just kept looking at me. My body was humming, and it was all I could do to keep a calm and controlled manner. Yes, I thought. We got the bastard! We got him!

"Would you be willing to come to San Francisco and make an identification?" I said.

Jimmy looked down at the ground. "Was up to me, I'd come right now, this minute. But I got to ask the wife. She's dead set against any more of this."

"Where did the murder happen?"

Jimmy pointed with the pocketknife at the last stall on the left. "In there."

I walked over to the chest-high door and peered in. It was your basic horse stall. The dirt floor was covered with a thick carpet of mud-smeared hay, and the wooden wall to my right was stained that rusty, faded color of long-dried blood. At the top of the stain you could see the three evenly spaced holes in the wood where the pitchfork had been imbedded.

"Cops, you couldn't believe it," Jimmy said. "Crawling all over each other in there like a friggin' Chinese gangbang."

He grunted and lifted the saddle he'd been working on and set it atop a wooden post. "Don't know why I bothered with that," he said. "Nobody's going to be riding around here for a while. Habit's a strange thing."

"You found her in here, then?"

"Nope. She was sitting over toward the door."

I looked at Jimmy. "Sitting?"

"You didn't know that?"

I shook my head.

"Hell! That was what spooked me worst of all. I come in here and there's Miss Kaline, sitting in a chair, propped up, sorta. Like this." Jimmy sat on the edge of the post and turned toward me. "Just like this."

He held out his right arm, rigid, fist clenched.

"What's that?" I said.

"Head got chopped off. Then somebody'd gone and tied the hair around her fingers and looped a rope around her arm, proppin' it up. She's sittin' like that, holdin' her own head out there like it's watching television."

Jimmy's pose took my memory and drove it in first gear into something rock hard and immovable. Consciousness jarred at impact. What? Something I'd seen before. It rang a bell. A strange and distant bell . . .

Then Jimmy was up off the edge of the post, walking me out of the stables. He seemed to regret his impromptu demonstration, clearing his throat and mumbling about having to get back to work. I thanked Jimmy for his help and said I'd be in touch about making the trip to San Francisco.

"Tell you what," he said. "You set it up, I'll identify him. Sherri was a fine girl. Nothin' please me more than putting the guy that done it behind bars. The wife don't like it, she can just sit on it. A man's got to do his duty."

I thanked him again and he nodded curtly and turned away. The last I saw of Jimmy Hennessy he was limping back toward the stables, back to the saddle that had neither horse nor rider.

It was a quiet ride back to San Francisco. The pavement hissed beneath the tires, and I fell into the trance of the road. Lulled by the smooth lefts and rights, the passing and being passed, the signs ticking past with metronomic regularity. And as I drifted deeper into the hypnotic calm of the highway, something crept up on me. Something I'd seen. Something glimpsed over the shoulder of a young girl.

I sat up straight, tackled the image as it tried to skirt away and held it firmly down on the floor of my consciousness. The giggling coed, misty eyes and lips parted, textbook open . . . Madonna and Child and a print of a man wandering in a desolate landscape, his head held before him like a lantern.

I pulled the van over to the shoulder and sat for a moment in the electric silence. The strange bell had rung.

I went into the San Francisco State bookstore via the back way. There was one textbook for English 411. A big, fifty-dollar coffee-table book, the kind students might hang on to for a decade or so after graduation, displaying it prominently in the future living room as proof of past intellectual pretense. I bought it, along with a paperback translation of *The Inferno,* and took my goods across campus to the Stonestown Shopping Mall.

I sat down in one of those Carnival of Eating places, with the cuisine of a dozen countries represented, all lined up in a row. Mexico, tacos. Italy, pizza. Like that. I settled on Germany, sausage. Got a stein of cold beer and found a table way off in the corner and spread the books out before me.

I began leafing through the textbook, starting at page one hundred, till I found it. The man holding his own severed head out before him. The image was so much Jimmy in Woodside that it startled me for a moment. It was the exact pose.

I went to the back of the book where the translator

explained in layman's terms what was happening. The man with the severed head was Bertrand de Born. In the Middle Ages he was famous for having incited John to rebel against his father, Henry II of England. And, as always in Dante, the punishment fit the crime. He who would have divided people in life is consequently condemned to an eternity of being divided himself.

I shut the book and closed my eyes and leaned back in the cheap plastic chair. What about Sonia? Using the Tarot cards as a base, I reopened the book and went straight to the section where Dante dealt with the diviners and fortune-tellers. While I read I tried to keep my objectivity: cold, scientific, step by step. But it was hard.

> And as I inclined my head and looked down from their
>   faces,
> I saw that each of them was gruesomely disfigured
> between the lines of the jawbone and where the chest
>   begins;
> for the face was twisted on the neck,
> and they came on backwards
> because they could not see ahead,
> for to look before them was forbidden.

What was it that Erik had been so adamant about? That serial killers wrote their signature on every crime they committed, and that a trained eye could see it?

Signatures come in many forms, and I'd found mine. But it didn't agree with beer and sausage. I reached deep into my pocket for a quarter so I could call Erik. It was time for some legal counsel.

21

HANK WAS ALREADY at my apartment when I returned. He was sitting at the dining room table leafing through a book.

"What's that?" I said.

He tipped the volume up so I could read it. *A Glossary of Legal Terms.* "My new passion."

"I must be hallucinating."

"No hallucination. My career at Pozzi's Pet Resort is over. Short, sweet, poignant. So meet Hank Wilkie, proofreader for a major downtown law firm."

"What happened? Nine dollars an hour, lots of goof-off time to write comedy . . . "

Hank exhaled and shook his head. "You know what they do to the dogs? They pipe Muzak into their kennels. Their *carpeted* kennels. I couldn't handle it so I shut the music off. Mrs. Pozzi turned rabid on me. Threw a fit.

Foamed at the mouth. So I've decided to turn white collar."

"What do you know about proofreading?" I said.

"Nothing. I'm cramming. I go back for my second interview tomorrow. Mrs. Anderson." Hank winced. "You know what she asked me at my first interview?"

"No."

"You're not going to believe this."

"Just tell me."

"She asked which aspect of proofreading was my favorite. My *favorite*! This with a straight face. I mean a dead, straight face." Hank shifted into his eager, by-gosh cub reporter voice. "Well, gee, Mrs. Anderson. Catching an error in diction is awfully fun, but I guess for sheer unbridled mirth nothing really touches the occasional split infinitive." He shook his head, let his voice slide back to normal. "There should be a national Bore-Off. A Bore Bowl. Get all the great bores of the world and assemble them in the Superdome and they just start talking to one another till only one is left standing."

I eased into the chair. Lola came out from down the hall and leapt nimbly into my lap. "I've got a second ID of Hemming from the Woodside murder."

Hank snapped alert. "Really?"

"Really."

"Jesus . . . then it *was* him."

"Remember what I told you Erik said in his office the day after Sonia was killed? About how serial killers always wrote their signature on every crime they committed?"

"Vaguely."

"How's this for a signature?"

I ran it past him. Dante, *The Inferno,* Sherri and Sonia

and their luckless counterparts. Hank listened without expression, gazing out beyond me at a patch of blank wall next to the television.

"So what do you think?" I said at the end of it. "Am I crazy, or what?"

"I don't think anything's crazy anymore," Hank murmured. "What scares me is that you may have hit the nail right on the head. This would also explain the video business. What makes hell such a terrible place is that it never ends. How do you make something endless in the twentieth century?"

"Plug in the video and hit the play button," I said. "Exactly."

I stroked Lola's fur and looked out at the green water of the bay while she softly purred. "What do you remember about *The Divine Comedy*?"

Hank sighed. "High school was a long, long time ago."

"You must remember something."

"Dante and Virgil take a stroll through hell. A lot of slime and ooze and people screaming. Kind of like Florida real estate. God was not one of those happy-go-lucky sorts, though as Gods go, I always liked the Middle Ages one. If you're going to have one, it might as well be big. Wrathful, fierce, take no shit. I only remember *The Inerno*, not *Purgatory* or *Paradise*." Hank paused. Halfway smiled. "Funny how virtue has a way of milking personality. Oh, yeah. Dante trained his cat to hold a candle upright on his desk so that he could write into the night."

"I just got off the phone to Erik."

"And?"

"And he says I should take everything I've got to Lieutenant Mannion right now."

Hank shrugged. "Sounds reasonable."

I put Lola down and got up and walked over to the dining room window. I pushed my hands as far down into my pants pockets as they would go and just stood there, chewing my lip. "I'm having trouble with being reasonable," I said.

"Why?"

"I guess it would strike me as more reasonable if I thought Mannion would do something about it."

"Why wouldn't he?"

I turned to face Hank. "Erik told me something else. He said that even with all this, Mannion probably couldn't arrest Hemming. That it's all circumstantial. Mannion needs something tangible. A shirt fiber, strand of hair, fingerprint. Something. Exhibit A, Erik kept calling it. You have to have Exhibit A. And medieval numerology is not exhibit anything."

"Mannion's a professional," Hank said. "Quit worrying. Besides, now you're off the hook. What's the problem?"

"The problem is I'm afraid another woman will have her head rearranged because everybody's sitting around twiddling their thumbs waiting for Professor Hemming to leave a fingerprint." I turned from the window and began to pace. "Suppose he really does see himself as some sort of angel of God. Hell's a crowded place. There's no end to the sinners who need to be dealt with."

"What's the alternative?" Hank said.

I was quiet for a moment. "I asked Erik a straight-out legal question, minus any buddy-buddy counseling. I asked him what would happen if someone were to break into Hemming's house and find a videocassette and take it and plop it on Mannion's desk. I asked him if that would qualify as Exhibit A."

Hank looked at me. There was disapproval in the look. "You can't use evidence that has been obtained illegally."

"That's just it," I said. "You can. As long as law enforcement officials had nothing to do with the break-in, it doesn't matter. In law they call it 'fruit from the poisoned tree.' If Lieutenant Mannion broke into the house, that's something else. The courts would toss it in the garbage. But if a private citizen comes into his office and plunks evidence on his desk, that's fine. In fact, Erik said it's the *obligation* of a citizen to turn over evidence of criminal activity, no matter how it was obtained. A videocassette, weapon, kilo of heroin. Doesn't matter."

"And that's it?" Hank said. "Simple as that?"

"Not entirely. The only hitch is that whoever broke in would be liable for criminal prosecution as well. Felony burglary."

Hank stood and went into the kitchen and came back with a cold beer. "I don't like it," he said.

"Why not?"

Hank drank from the beer. "And suppose you find the tape and it's inconclusive. And suppose his department head, Professor What's-His-Name, doesn't back down on the alibi. Then what?"

"I'll claim to have definitely seen Hemming on the night of the murder in the vicinity of Sonia's apartment."

Hank looked at me. "Lie, in other words?"

"Oh, come on, Hank! Don't suddenly go virtuous on me. This guy took Sonia apart! And Sherri! And maybe others that we don't even know about. So yes, I would lie. Happy?"

"No," Hank said, his voice rising. "I'm not happy. Because you know what I see?"

"What?"

"I see a guy who's losing perspective. I see a guy who's got such tunnel vision he's ready to do anything to nail his prey. Anything!"

We glared at each other, and an electrified silence filled the apartment.

"Why are you being this way?" I said.

"Did you ever stop to consider once that maybe this two-fanged monster, Ronald Hemming, is innocent? This headless stuff at Woodside. Maybe it doesn't fit as cleanly as you think. Bertrand whoever-he-was, he had his head cut off because he broke relationships apart in life. Sounds to me like Sherri and Hemming were hot and heavy. Where's the big message? Maybe Hemming hasn't done a damn thing wrong in his wrong life except diddle a coed or two!"

"You really believe that?"

"It's not important what I 'believe'!" Hank shouted. "The only important thing is what happened! The only important thing is the truth, and you don't give a damn about the truth anymore. You'll make up stories, perjure yourself, break into a house. . . . There's no justice anymore. Forget such annoying concepts as guilty or innocent. That doesn't matter anymore. The only thing that matters is who's the best liar."

"All I want to do is stop the killing," I said quietly.

"We all do!" Hank shouted. "For Christ's sake, we all do! You know what you've turned into?"

"What?"

"A vigilante, only without the gun. A paper-pushing Charles Bronson. That's all. No difference. And somewhere in your obsession you've completely lost track of the most basic notions of what is fair." Hank put the can of beer down on the table, hard, and moved toward the door. "I lost my thirst."

"Wait a minute," I said.

Hank halted, kept his back to me. "What?"

"Sit down." Pause. "Please."

"What for?"

"Because I asked you to."

Hank hesitated, put hands on hips, stared straight up at the ceiling. Then he pulled off his jacket and plunked down on the couch. "What?"

I took a deep breath and leaned forward on the chair. "The only 'truth' that matters to me now is that nobody else die like Sonia and Sherri. And I've had it up to here with legal niceties about shirt fibers and procedure and fingerprints that don't exist."

We were silent a moment. Hank looked up from his lap and focused on me for the first time in a while. "Did you tell Erik what you were thinking of? The break-in?"

"Yes."

"What did he say?"

"He told me emphatically not to do it. But he was more concerned with my criminal liability than any moral questions of right or wrong."

Hank closed his eyes. "What a nightmare this whole thing has been."

"I'm trying to end it, that's all," I said. "I'm only trying to end it."

Hank got up and went to the fireplace and looked at the photos hung on the wall. He wasn't convinced. "Did Erik buy the medieval business?" he said.

"More or less. He acknowledged the connection. That's about as much as you'll ever get out of a lawyer. He said he kind of understood why Hemming might have fastened onto that era in particular, if my theory is right."

"Why's that?"

"Erik understands how people might think the Dark

Ages weren't all that dark. No push-button wars. Society wasn't so overregulated. Right was right and wrong was wrong. Erik said that's why he likes Ireland so much. Two hours out of Dublin and you're back in another century."

Hank softly laughed and came back to the couch. "I love these people who want to live in the olden days. Take away Erik's stereo and he'd be climbing the walls."

"Maybe."

"No 'maybe' about it. Filth and disease and ignorance. Get serious, Quinn. One impacted molar and you might as well forget it. All those earnest characters down at the Renaissance Faire with their gowns and harps . . . tell them their average life span ends in four years and see how thrilled they are with the thirteenth century."

I leaned against the windowsill. "Erik would say you'd live your life accordingly. You'd live with more intensity."

"No you wouldn't. You'd die twenty years earlier, that's all."

Hank sighed and pushed himself to his feet. "I'd love to stick around and debate this point, but the brawling, two-fisted world of occasional bad grammar awaits." He stopped, smiled. "You know, there might be a skit here about the Bore Bowl. How would it be refereed? The judges would all go comatose from boredom themselves. Yeah. We could maybe hook them up with portable intravenous units. Mainline essence of caffeine. Rotate them every ten minutes or so. Put them on a straight amphetamine diet."

"When we have a firm date nailed down at the Superdome we can worry about it."

I walked Hank to the top of the stairs and leaned over the bannister as he made his way down. At the first landing he looked back up. "You're going to try to get it, aren't you?"

I nodded. "Yes."

"How do you propose to pull it off?"

"Go in Hemming's house and take it."

Hank stared at me. "Go in the house?"

"That's right," I said. "You did it yourself."

"Hemming didn't know me. He knows you. He doesn't just know you. He's probably got every line on your damn face memorized."

"So I break in when he isn't around."

Hank shook his head. "Ever heard of alarm systems? Dead bolts? Killer dogs? People are scared shitless these days. It takes a pro to break into a house that doesn't want to be broken into."

"So I'll find a pro."

"How does that work?" Hank smiled, continuing slowly down the rest of the stairs. "The classified section of the *Chronicle?*"

"No. The far end of the ring."

22

ROSCOE LAUGHINGHOUSE was there when I arrived, working the heavy bag. It was his own personal bag, which he kept stored in an oversized locker in the corner of the gym. I'd used it once and it was not unlike hitting a one-hundred-pound sack of semisolidified concrete. When Roscoe really got into it, he could bend the sack in half with either hand, and somebody had to lean against the bag to keep it from flying around.

Today Roscoe wasn't into it. Taking it easy. Popping the bag with solid, fluid jabs. Left . . . left . . . left-left, and then over the top with a strong right, rattling the metal chain that hooked it to the ceiling. Now and then he leaned in with a ducked left shoulder and pushed the bag off and let it slam back into him—a hundred bone-jarring pounds of concrete, swinging back like a wrecking ball. To "get the feel of rough stuff" in the ring, he'd once told me.

I wandered to the apron of the ring and watched him for a moment. Then he saw me, smiled, fired off a couple of lightning-quick combinations, just to show off.

"Look at this place, man," he said, strolling over. "Dead. These other guys, I don't know what they be thinking. Girlfriend bitch about take me to the movies, take me to the dance. How come you never go buy me nothin'. Next thing, poor sucker working the car wash, talkin' about what coulda been."

"Where'll you be?"

"Me? Knockin' guys out on the tee-vee for million dollar a shot." He threw a hook, looked down at the floor, shook his head sadly. "Good-bye, Mr. Mike Tyson."

Roscoe had that inexplicable quality we call "presence." Commanding presence. He was black, but his facial features were Grecian. Noble. Othello with boxing gloves. Two thousand years ago he might've been a king somewhere, in robes and jewels, a charismatic leader of thousands. But fate had popped him out of a poor woman's womb in the heart of a twentieth-century ghetto, and this boxing routine—tough, grueling, painful—was his own kind of redemption. Setting things right. Realigning a mistake on destiny's part.

"What's the weight?" I said.

Roscoe slapped his hard, corded belly. "Two-oh-two. We're talkin' Ferrari, man. We're talkin' Jaguar."

"Mr. Mike Tyson is talking two-twenty-five."

"Yeah, I know. But I be bulking up here soon. Ritchie say he want me comin' in two-fourteen, but I ain't too sure. Slow me down, man. Gotta stay lean and mean, slip inside them big fat heavies, whack 'em, slip back out. They be standin' there with a busted nose thinkin' where'd that nigger come from. Two-fourteen, man, I be waddlin' around like a fuckin' dinosaur, just like them. Lose my advantage. My edge. Ritchie say, sure, two-fourteen 'cause he don't have to climb in no ring. He just sit there on his little bucket and hair all combed, stinkin' that cheap-shit Woolworth cologne he slap on his face. Two-fourteen my ass. Ain't his fuckin' neck gonna be ripped out by the roots. Two-oh-two just fine. Two-oh-nine max."

"I need to talk to you about something."

"Sure thing." Roscoe looked down at his belly. "I mean, shit. Joe Louis only what? One-ninety? One-ninety five? Joe Louis!"

"Roscoe . . . "

"I heard you. You need to talk. What about?"

"Not sure where to start. I need a favor."

"Yeah? Me, too. Start with stickin' on the gloves and then we talk. Otherwise I don't spar today."

I started to protest, but then thought, what the hell. Since Sonia's death I'd done practically nothing in the way of exercise, and the muscles were wanting to run unleashed.

I took fifteen minutes to change, tape my hands, do some warming up. It felt good to be back in the gym, smelling the rancid smell of it, getting the body loose. Roscoe was waiting for me in the ring, shadowboxing. Tight, controlled, intense, the way good fighters do, almost like a trance.

"Okay," he said. "Ding."

For a while he stalked me, letting me get the feel of the ring, crouched low and staring at my neck in that menacing, distracting way he had. We each threw a couple dozen powder-puff jabs and he said "ding" and we stopped for a while. I was breathing heavily.

"Was that three minutes?" I said.

"Two. Don't want to tire out the white boy too soon. Respect old age."

"Thanks."

"So what you be needin' to be talkin' about, Cupie?"

"Like I said, I need a favor."

"What kind?"

"There's this guy I think murdered a girlfriend of mine."

Roscoe abruptly stopped his shadowboxing. "What?"

"Sonia Lucia. You never met her. She was killed about two weeks ago and I think I know who did it, but I don't have any proof."

"Damn." Roscoe looked off at the wall behind me and whistled low and soft. "You and this lady close?"

"Used to be. Might have been again. But that's not the point. This guy covered himself well. But I think he videotaped it, and I think the tape's in his house."

"Ding," Roscoe said. "Keep talking."

We circled each other in the ring. "I need somebody to break into his house and get the cassette. Not you. But maybe somebody you know. Somebody who wants to make some extra money."

Roscoe didn't say anything. He bobbed, slouched, gloves moving in tight, nervous circles, staring at my neck.

"I'll pay whatever's the going rate," I said. "All I want's the cassette. I'd do it myself but I don't know the ropes. I'm afraid I'd screw it up."

Roscoe fired a left jab at my stomach and I felt it. I backed up and he stayed right with me and snapped my head back with another lightning jab and I went into the ropes, sliding away to the right where Roscoe advanced on me.

"Jesus," I said. "Take it easy."

He came straight at me and fired a hard left hook to the body that I blocked and followed it with a fierce right that I managed to catch on the shoulder. It was like being clubbed with a baseball bat.

"Roscoe! Shit!"

His eyes stayed on my throat.

Instinct took over. Survival. I set myself, waited for Roscoe to begin his next assault, feigned a cowering cover-up, and then let loose with the hardest left-right combination of my life. Both shots caught Roscoe flush on the jaw and he dropped to one knee. Blinked. More stunned than hurt. Then he got up and moved toward me and I danced away, sticking long left jabs in his face. We were fighting for keeps.

Fright can do strange things. It can induce immediate catatonia, or it can turn you into the hundred-pound mother who lifts a station wagon off her trapped baby. Purely biological, the social chemists will tell you. Fight or flight syndrome. The ropes fenced me in, so there wasn't going to be any flight for this boy. I decided I'd better fight. I became the hundred-pound mother.

I kept moving clockwise, backpedaling, stinging Roscoe with a steady left jab. I had at least a six-inch reach advantage and he was having trouble getting under it. Then he cut off the ring and let go his right and I saw it coming but couldn't react and it rocked me square on the cheekbone. My legs held me up. Roscoe had dropped his hands, expecting me to crumple to the canvas. He was wide open. I nailed him with a left hook. Again his eyes went wide with disbelief. I threw a desperate right that he ducked under and then it was like a big, black fifty-pound bird flew straight in my face and I was on my ass, holding on to the lower rope while the ring whirled around me.

"The *fuck* you doing?"

Somebody was climbing into the ring. I sat there. Face warm. Everything kind of dreamy and nice. Somebody was shouting. I got halfway up and then fell down again. Fine. I'd just sit awhile.

Rough, calloused hands hauled me up. Ritchie Dalgiacomo was peering up into my eyes.

"You okay? Hey?" He slapped my cheek. "Hey! Hey!"

"Quit slapping me, Ritchie."

He backed off, bit his pudgy lower lip, and looked at both of us. "Can't believe it! Go out and buy a fucking newspaper and come back and you two dildos're killing each other! No headgear. Nothing!" He whirled on Roscoe, who was leaning on the ropes in the far corner, staring off toward the locker room.

"Where's the hell's your headgear?"

Roscoe shrugged. Ritchie imitated the shrug. "In case you forgot, asshole, you got a thousand-buck fight in less than two weeks!"

"Don't call me an asshole," Roscoe said quietly.

"I call *anybody* an asshole who pisses away a grand on a stupid, pickup gym fight!"

Ritchie Dalgiacomo was Roscoe's trainer, manager, patron saint, and so on. Considered himself a class act, but was Vegas all the way. Wide lapels, lots of gold chains, hair styled to a frizzy, billowy ridiculousness. He called women "broads" and slapped important people on the back and laughed at their bad jokes. A decent-enough guy when he wasn't trying to impress people, but almost all his life was spent trying to impress people.

"Lay off, Ritchie," Roscoe said. "We was just horsin' around."

"Horse around!" Ritchie laughed a short, hysterical laugh. "I love it! Horse around! Get a cut eye and that thousand's in the toilet! Hear me? The toilet! And not only that, but down the line promoters're putting together a card and they say no, forget Laughinghouse, guy's a fuck-up. Calls in three days before with a cut eye."

Ritchie was working himself into a genuine sweat. In a way, I couldn't blame him. For years he had hung around the Bay Area gyms, looking for fighters to represent. Now and then somebody came along, somebody good enough to get a couple of paying fights in Oakland before being salvoed back into obscurity. A lousy business, but there was always the chance that a young, raw, unformed Rocky Marciano might come shuffling through the door. Roscoe Laughinghouse was Ritchie's Marciano, and our informal gym fight was, in his eyes, nothing less than playing touch football with a vase from the Ming Dynasty.

Ritchie yelled for another minute or so, then climbed out of the ring on some predictable exit line. Roscoe still wouldn't look at me.

"Is it just my imagination," I said, "or are you a little upset with me?"

"Upset!" Roscoe whirled on me, eyes wide and disappointed. He looked like he was about to start bawling. "Jesus Christ, Cupie—listen to yourself. Got a favor, Roscoe. Round up a coupla niggers, do this dirty job for me. Pay the going rate. Going rate! Shit, man! What you think, we got a bulletin board down there in the ghetto?" He shifted into his Stepin Fetchit voice. "Say, Leroy, what a burglary go fo' now? Well, depend we talkin' house or 'partment."

"Sorry for the way I presented it."

" . . . going rate," he mumbled. "Man, if you don't take all."

"You know how this guy murdered my girlfriend?"

"Save it."

"I'm not going to save it. He cut her head off and stuck it back on all wrong. Whether or not she was alive when this started—"

"Okay, okay," Roscoe said. "I get the picture."

"Can you help me?"

A long silence filled the empty gym.

"Ah, Cupie, . . . " Roscoe said at last. "Know how long a time it took puttin' space between me and all that shit?" His head was hung low, looking at the resin-covered ring floor.

"Okay," I said. "Don't sweat it. I'll find another way. I shouldn't have put you on the spot like that."

Roscoe looked away, was silent awhile. Then he said, "Don't think I ever been hit so hard that combination you hit me with. First time I ever been off my feet, me with five pro fights."

"Survival."

"No, I mean it, man. You coulda been a fighter, you started younger. Fast, good moves, hit hard, take a pretty good shot. Ritchie have a triple hemorrhoid, he find a white boy could do all that."

"What's this thousand-dollar fight?"

"Circle Star in San Jose, the sixteenth. Got me up against this big giant. Freak. Six eight, two-sixty, like that."

"What's his record?"

"Seven-oh. Seven knockouts. That's only because everybody else shit their pants when they see him. Freeze up. Get hit once and can't fall down fast enough."

I took a quick shower and changed into my street clothes. I was starting to feel the right hand that had floored me. Roscoe was back hammering away at his concrete bag when I came out, not taking it very easy this time. His T-shirt was dark with sweat. He saw me and stopped and leaned against the bag, breathing heavily.

"Hey, good luck, man," he said. "Sorry I flipped out like that. It's just, you know ... "

"I had it coming. Good luck to you, too."

"What for?"

"The giant at Circle Star."

Roscoe smiled, put his arm around the heavy bag like it was his brand-new fiancée he was real proud of. "Aww, man, . . . piece of cake. David and Goliath, just like it say in the Bible."

"How about a prediction?"

"Don't got a prediction, except I'm gonna win."

"Look, you want the million-dollar paydays you better make predictions. Newspapers love that stuff."

"Yeah, you probably right." He whacked the bag a few times and bounced on the balls of his feet. All two hundred and two pounds went up and down in one solid mass. Not an ounce of fat. Then a smile creased his face. "Got my prediction already. Don't need more than one word. I be famous for one-word predictions."

"What's the word?"

Roscoe stood back from the bag, cupped both gloves around his mouth, tilted his head back, and yelled high into the rafters, "Timberrrrrrrrrr!"

23

THE HOT PINK THEATER on Kearny Street was so down at the heels it didn't even have a barker out front. Just a young, washed-out woman selling tickets from behind a bulletproof, grope-proof windowed area. I asked if Michelle was working, and the girl nodded without looking up.

After Roscoe, this was about as far as my tenuous footholds in the netherworld went. I'd known Michelle from my three-piece-suit days before the the power drill accident. She had worked in the accounting department, and we'd often have lunch together, brown-bagging it, and she'd tell me about how she wanted to go back to school and get her master's in architecture. Our lunches generally concluded with me urging her to go ahead and do it and Michelle protesting that there was no way she could afford it. After I left the firm we'd pretty much lost track of each other, and it was through a mutual friend that I knew she was dancing at the Hot Pink.

This afternoon the place was completely empty. I stood at the front to let my eyes adjust to the dark. A movie was running, and a hundred vacant seats flickered in the pornographic light. I found a chair on the aisle, five or six rows up from the front, and waited.

The movie went on and on. There was a general sense of energy and secretion, but the close-ups were so close it was impossible to determine who was doing what to whom. The screen was full of disembodied flesh, throbbing in a wet, rhythmic manner, and it had about as much erotic impact as a hospital film of triple-bypass surgery. Suddenly the camera pulled back to reveal two exhausted, naked people smoking cigarettes, and that was the end of the movie. Their human faces seemed like a surprise cameo appearance in a film that had nothing to do with people. A single harsh light beamed onto the stage and a Jimi Hendrix tape began to play.

I hadn't seen Michelle in months, and her sudden appearance on stage caught me off-guard. She was not a particularly beautiful woman. Not in the sense that, say, Ludmila was beautiful. Her head was too round and too small for her body, and her features seemed to crowd toward the center of her face. She wore her strawberry-blond hair in a ponytail, which gave an uneasy aura of innocence to the seedy surroundings. Heels, very tight jeans, and a loose, Day-Glo green blouse rounded out the costume. Michelle walked to the center of the stage, registered that someone was sitting in the audience, and began.

The dancing was distant and uninspired. The blouse came off to reveal a Frederick's of Hollywood push-up bra, and then she came down off the stage and gyrated up to me in a fashion that was supposed to be provocative. A ten-inch red string was connected to the zipper of her jeans, and it was my duty to pull it down. She still hadn't recognized me.

I unzipped her jeans and said, "Did Frank Lloyd Wright start this way?"

She stopped. "What?"

"Hello, Michelle."

She shielded her eyes from the spotlight. "Who's that? Quinn?"

"None other."

"Son of a bitch!" A smile spread across her face, and for a moment she made a move as if to cover her breasts. "What in the hell are you doing here?"

"Hey, Michelle!" A male voice shouted from a door behind the stage. "Hey!"

"Hold on," she said, gyrating anew at the Hendrix tape. "Let me just finish this."

She finished. It was far more graphic than I would have cared for, and there were excruciatingly embarrassing moments in the silences between Hendrix songs when she would be caught in midthrust with only the sound of the rewinding projector.

When it was over she gathered up her clothes and signaled me to follow. Together we went through the dark backstage doorway where the voice had earlier yelled.

A twenty-foot corridor led to an exit door. There was a tiny room to the left and a tiny room to the right. Two men were sitting at a table in the room on the left, playing cards. Michelle, still stark naked, ducked into the door on the right.

"I'll wait," I said.

"What for? No modesty at the Hot Pink."

That's what she said, but I noticed she pulled on her clothes as fast as she could once we were in. It was a barren, depressing room. Two chairs, a warped card table, a smudged mirror hanging on the wall.

"What's stranger?"—she smiled, more relaxed now that she was dressed—"me working in a place like this or you forking out five bucks to watch?"

"My strangeness barometer's been thrown out of whack the last couple of weeks. How are you, Michelle?"

"What can I say? Making a living."

I sat and Michelle went over to a small sink that jutted from the wall and splashed water on her face. Then she undid the ponytail and shook her hair free.

"What's with the new hairdo?" I said.

"It's the June special. Makes our distinguished clientele think a little girl is stripping for them. Pretty sick, huh?"

"Pretty sick."

"So!" Michelle plunked down in the chair opposite me, folded her arms across her Day-Glo blouse. "How're you doing with your millions? Paris, London, and all that?"

"None of that. And just for the record, my millions come to less than a million."

She fidgeted around, twirled little circles with her fingernail on the table. "When did you find out about my new career?"

"Gary told me a few months ago. Saw him at the company softball game."

"They still invite you?"

"Nobody else can block the plate."

"Gary . . . " Michelle said aimlessly. "And when he told you, you couldn't believe it, right?"

"I was surprised."

"Well, don't be. The numbers line up like this. I want to go back to school. I work here twenty minutes at a time, six times a day, and I take home seven hundred a week. That's net. Not gross. Net. It's dead out there now, but come around after five o'clock. If I wanted to get extracurricular about the whole thing I'd knock down twice as much. So before you start lecturing, go find me a job in an accounting department with those numbers and I'll gladly crawl back into my clothes."

I waited for a moment. "Is that all?"

"That's all."

"You don't have to talk like a gun moll to me, Michelle. We used to slurp yogurt together, remember?"

Michelle smiled. "Yogurt . . . yeah, I remember. Sorry for the assault. Guess I felt I needed to defend myself."

"You don't."

"It's because I'm not even here, really," she said. "You saw how I looked you straight in the face and didn't recognize you. Old Jimi starts and I tune out and when I pick up my paycheck every Friday it's like, what are you giving me all this money for?" She paused. "So tell me. How did you like my performance?"

"Kept my eyes shut the whole time."

"I bet. You didn't find it degrading and debasing and all that stuff?"

"Some."

"You know, for the first time in six months I was inhibited, knowing you were out there watching."

"I'll take that as a compliment. But what happened to feathers? I thought strippers were supposed to have bubbles and feathers and balloons and fans?"

"Unh-unh. Fantasy's out. Today's customer wants street clothes. I guess so he can think that this is something that could really happen."

"Delightful."

"Like I said . . . " Michelle dropped a hand in front of her face like a curtain falling.

We small-talked awhile. Gossip about characters we'd both known at Jendresen & Rossner. What it was like going back to school after a five-year hiatus. Then we fell silent and Michelle gave me a look.

"So what brings you down to the Hot Pink Theater at one in the afternoon? And don't tell me the cinematic brilliance."

I took a deep breath and gave Michelle the short version of all that had happened in the past weeks. It was a story I was getting good at. Like Walt back in Luray with his tale of the drought. Michelle listened with a pained expression.

"You think the murder's on a cassette?" she said.

"I'm sure of it."

"And the cassette's in the professor's house?"

"Maybe."

She thought for a moment. "So who am I in all this?"

"I need somebody to break into the house and steal the cassette. Somebody who's a pro, who can get past alarm systems. Somebody who'll keep his mouth shut."

Michelle stared at me with her little round eyes. "All I do around here is take my clothes off."

"I'm not talking about you, for Christ's sake. But there must be somebody here . . . "

"What, because I work in a strip joint I take coffee breaks with gangsters?"

"What about those two across the hall?"

Michelle scrunched up her forehead. "Rico? He's the owner. And Jack's just here to take care of trouble. I don't know about Jack, but Rico's a straight arrow. Little house in Millbrae, wife and kids, Loyal Order of Moose, the works. I doubt he walks around broadcasting he's the owner of the Hot Pink, but—"

"And Jack?"

"Like I said, he's the bouncer. Nice-enough guy. Never says five words all week."

"And at no time through these pristine halls passes someone who looks a little suspect?"

"This isn't Nob Hill, Quinn. Come on."

"Can I talk to them a second?"

"Jack and Rico?"

"I'm willing to pay. A lot. Sometimes that can un-straighten an arrow."

"Rico doesn't need it. He cleans up on this place. You're liable to have your ass thrown out of here if you go marching into his office talking about busting into houses."

"As the authorized spokesman for my ass, we'll take the chance."

Michelle exhaled loudly, gave me a long, lingering look to see if I'd withdraw my request. When I didn't, she said, "Come on."

I followed as Michelle leaned into the office across the hall. The guy closest to us looked around.

"What's up, honey?"

"Friend of mine here wants to talk to you about something, Rico."

"Sure thing." Rico had his back to the door and he wrenched around to scrutinize me. He was short, pudgy, dark-skinned. Pockmarked cheeks clustered up close to a bulbous, drinker's nose. He wore tinted glasses, but what I could see of his eyes reminded me of Hemingway's line about the eyes of an unsuccessful rapist. Straight arrow.

"What can I do ya?"

"I need a favor," I said. "It's not quite legal, but I'll pay well."

"Lotsa things ain't quite legal. How 'ain't quite' we talkin'?"

"Break into a house and have a look around. Don't take anything but a videocassette, and maybe not even that."

"Break into a house!" Rico turned to Jack sitting across the table and laughed and turned back to me. There was no transition period between Rico laughing and Rico not laughing. "I don't know what planet you come from, buddy, but here on earth that's *real* illegal."

Jack, the bouncer, sat there, stonefaced.

"I don't know, Rico. You look like somebody who appreciates the gray areas of life."

"That so?" Rico gave me a close look. "What happened? Some guy porking your wife and put it on film?"

That seemed a harmless direction to go in, so I went with it. "Maybe."

Rico turned around in his chair and reshuffled the cards. "New game," he said to Jack. "Lost my concentration."

Silence for ten seconds. Rico looked over his shoulder and acted surprised to see I was still there. He said, "Answer's no, buddy. Now why don't you just drift outta here?"

My inclination was to put his tinted glasses on a little tighter than they were, nice and snug, but this was Michelle's boss, and Michelle needed the seven hundred a week. I turned and left.

Back in the dressing room Michelle shrugged her shoulders. "Told you."

"Win some, lose some."

In the silence the moans from the picture next door

grew louder. Michelle sighed. "If I remember my orgasms correctly, it's about time for me to do my thing."

We walked out into the still-empty theater.

"Man, it's usually not *this* dead," she said, putting her hair back up into a ponytail.

"Well, I think I'm going to go have a beer at Vesuvio's and think about what comes next. Thanks for trying."

The Jimi Hendrix tape started up. Over Michelle's shoulder I could see Rico craning his pudgy head to see what we were doing.

Michelle cleared her throat and looked at me sideways. "Listen, . . . Would you mind sitting through my routine first? It's humiliating to strip for a bunch of stupid empty chairs."

"Only if you get rid of that ponytail."

She smiled sheepishly, looked back to see if Rico was watching, and undid the ponytail. Then the smile dissolved. "I hate this place, you know. I really hate this place."

I discreetly took a seat toward the back so things would be a little less gynecological. I thought Michelle might spice it up and make it funny or improvise in some small way to signal that she was on top of it all, but she didn't. The performance was a faded carbon copy of the one that went before, and when she finished she'd forgotten completely about me. No wink, no wave, no playful wag of bare tush. She walked around the stage in utter silence, gathering up the discarded clothes as a maid would pick up somebody else's dirty laundry.

24

MIDWAY THROUGH MY SECOND BEER at Vesuvio's I was conscious of a man standing by my table. It was Jack, the bouncer. I was expecting him. His expressionless interest in my proposal had been unmistakeable, and I had been careful to let Michelle know where I'd be drinking my beer.

"Michelle said you were here," he said.

"Sit down."

He sat. Rubbed the stubble of his chin with the knuckles of his left hand, back and forth, back and forth, quickly, like a woman briskly filing her fingernails. He was a man of indeterminate ethnic origin. Black, American Indian, maybe some Asian. Depended on how the light hit him and what expression he wore. He had on jeans and a rugby shirt. Not a big man—five eight or nine—but solid as granite. Dense, like six ounces of his body would weigh twice as much as six ounces of mine.

His features were hard and small and his curly black hair was cut very short.

"Forgot your name," I said.

"Jack Gilliam."

"Beer?"

"No. Rico smell it on me, I'm out the door. This is my break, only Rico don't know I come to see you."

"You liked my proposal more than he did?"

"Depends on the money."

"A thousand dollars."

Jack Gilliam absorbed the figure. "Thousand five."

"What?"

"Thousand five. I got a record. I get caught I rot awhile at Soledad."

"Okay," I said. "Thousand five."

"When?"

"I won't know till the same day. Can you take a look at the house this afternoon?"

He nodded. "Tonight. After my shift."

"Here's the address." I wrote it out for him on a napkin. "Be sure you check it out tonight, because we might be moving on this as soon as tomorrow."

Jack Gilliam studied the address with the exaggerated concentration of an illiterate pretending otherwise. "Something goes wrong," he said, "you never heard of me, right?"

"Nobody will ever know. I give you my word."

Gilliam continued nodding. "Five hundred now," he said.

"I don't walk around with five hundred in my wallet. Here." I emptied my pockets. "Take two and I'll give you five fifty tomorrow. You'll get the other five fifty after the job."

Jack Gilliam nodded through the mathematics. "*Seven*

fifty after the job. Two, five fifty, and five fifty's only a thousand three. You said thousand five."

"Right. I meant seven fifty after the job."

It was an honest mistake, but he'd nailed it like a harpooned bunny rabbit. He wasn't as dumb as he looked.

I told Gilliam to keep coming to Vesuvio's at two, same table, and the day I met him there would be the day we'd move. Gilliam took the two hundred and headed out the door and I wondered whether I'd ever see his face again. Tomorrow I could go to the Hot Pink and he'd say, "What two hundred? Get out of here before I bash your face." It was possible.

Possible? Try probable, Parker. And while you're trying things, go ahead and consider that it might be better all around if you wrote off the two hundred to foolish indiscretion. Jack Gilliam and his ilk don't have a whole lot of taxable income changing hands. They hurt each other and go to jail and their idea of earning an honest dollar is to crack skulls at strip joints.

Introspection makes cowards of us all. So I finished off my beer and walked out into the cool, breezy sunlight. And quit introspecting.

Next day Jack Gilliam was waiting for me at the same table, same time, same seat. He was even wearing the same rugby shirt. For some peculiar reason it propped up my waning confidence in him.

"Tonight's the night," I said.

"You got the five fifty?"

I gave him the envelope. He opened it, looked inside, tucked it away.

"Did you check out the house?"

"Told you I would, didn't I?"

"And?"

"Simple."

"No alarm system?"

Jack Gilliam nodded. "An easy one."

"What about neighbors?"

"I told you it was simple." Gilliam brought the envelope out again and peered in.

"The ink's not going to run," I said. "We do it at nine o'clock. There's a liquor store on the corner of Pierce and Haight. I'll meet you there at eight-thirty."

"Okay."

And that was it. He left his coffee untasted and walked out the door.

It was a street corner like a lot of street corners now in San Francisco. A grim counterpoint to the upbeat soda pop commercials that show blacks and whites and Asians and Arabs and Jews all hugging one another and wandering through improbable meadows, beaming with joy that all peoples on this planet really did know how to live together.

The corner of Pierce and Haight didn't jibe with the carbonated soft drink view of the world. On the corner of Pierce and Haight you could feel the fear, distrust, and intolerance of modern urban America. Ten minutes of waiting for Jack Gilliam had given me time to absorb the special tension of the area. Nobody smiled. Nobody greeted anybody else. A restlessness bred of not having much disposable income in a country that had the largest slice of pie of all. So blame must be attached. Damn Arabs. Damn blacks. Damn whitey. Damn everybody else but me.

It was a cold night. Clear, not much wind. Gilliam was

late, and after his punctuality at Vesuvio's I began to wonder. Then a green Ford Galaxy eased around the corner and parked at the curb directly in front of me. Gilliam got out, nodded in my direction, locked up the car, and joined me on the sidewalk.

"We move in about fifteen minutes," I said.

"Fine."

Jack Gilliam leaned against the parked green Ford and lit a cigarette, shielding the match in the soft breeze. I was struck again by the density of his body. You couldn't imagine him being a cuddly little baby. He was more like something conceived and born and reared in a marble quarry.

While we waited four guys came out of the Arab liquor store. Three were teenagers, the other maybe twenty-five. The older one had a paper bag with a bottle inside it and he took a swig. "Yaaahooo!" he yelled. The other three laughed. Big shots.

Gilliam had his eyes on the street corner. Then he looked at his watch, then the street corner again.

"What you got to do in there can't take more than a half hour," Gilliam said.

"It shouldn't."

"It can't. Half hour is it. After that we beat it."

"Okay."

"I mean it."

"I said okay."

Behind us the punks were kicking a newspaper box, trying to rattle loose the change. It smashed around till they finally knocked it flat on its side. The older guy stood over it and put his boot right through the plastic door. Reached unsteadily down, pulled out a newspaper from the ruined box.

"Anybody want to read Ann Landers?" he said. The

three teenagers laughed. Gilliam turned his gaze back to the street corner.

"Just what we need," he muttered. "A bunch of ass-holes."

"Hey, fella!"

It was the guy with the bottle. I turned around, but it was Gilliam he was talking to. Ugly character. Narrow head, snag-toothed, lank dirty hair down to his shoulders. Big man to the local kids, buying them booze and talking about all the broads he's screwed and tough guys he's kicked the shit out of.

"Time you got, fella?"

Gilliam ignored him.

"Man don't hear so good," the snag-toothed guy said to his friends. "I said, what's the time?"

"Nine," Gilliam said.

"Can't hear you."

"Nine."

He made a face and looked at his buddies. "Nine," he repeated, imitating Gilliam's clenched, clipped style. "Fuckin' Clint Eastwood in the neighborhood." The three teenagers laughed as if it were the funniest thing they'd ever heard. The big shot took another swig from the bottle.

"Friend got a problem?" he said to me.

I didn't answer.

"Hey, you! Friend got a fucking problem or what?"

He walked up to me, reeking of alcohol and marijuana.

"Why don't you and your friends take a stroll?" I said.

"A 'stroll'?"

The way he said "stroll" it had three syllables. That got them all laughing again.

"What's the problem?" the guy said. "You and Clint wanna be alone or something?"

262

"That's right."

"They wanna be alone, Brent," one of the teenagers said. Brent stood looking at me, swaying slightly.

"Don't get so many queers up here," he said. "Kick their homo asses back down the hill's what we do. But good."

The queer angle filled them with a kind of mob courage. A banner they could crawl behind. The teenagers moved closer. Okay. Time for a different approach. Be a nice guy. Reason with them. Let them feel they really told me off. Another feather in Brent's cap.

"Look," I said. "We're not queer and we don't want any trouble. Why don't you go off someplace and enjoy yourselves?"

"Maybe we don't want to."

"Let's go," Gilliam said. He put out his cigarette and started to move but Brent stepped forward. He and Gilliam bumped chests.

"Wait a minute, fella," Brent said. "Maybe I didn't make it clear. See, . . . we're a little short of cash."

Gilliam's eyes turned black. "Beat it."

"Come on, Clint. Big movie star like you." Giggling behind me. "Let's take a look."

Brent switched the bottle to his left hand and reached around for Gilliam's wallet with his right. Gilliam waited till Brent was stretched out, a little off balance, then grabbed him by the hair, yanked him squealing to his tiptoes, and slammed him face-first into the passenger window of the green Ford. A sickening crunch, and the glass webbed into a thousand veined cracks. Brent made a sound like he'd just unexpectedly pricked himself with a pin, and slumped into the gutter.

For a moment there was stunned silence. I looked from the bleeding face to the crushed window. The bottle had shattered on the sidewalk, and the stink of cheap apricot brandy flooded the night.

Then I was conscious of movement behind me. I turned and the danger of the knife registered before the brain could even identify it as a knife. It burst across the circuitry as something generic and lethal. Killing Thing.

I waited till I was certain the kid had committed himself, then lunged to the right. He had to correct by sweeping the blade across the length of his body, and he wasn't fast enough. I rolled and kicked at his ankles and he went down in a jangled heap.

When I scrambled up he still had the knife in his hand. Eyes wild with fright and blood lust. He came at me again but this time simply took a long, roundhouse, slashing swing that I easily moved under. I pivoted and launched a right hand that caught him flush in the stomach. I was accustomed to bouncing my punches off Roscoe's solid, fiberglass belly. But this kid hadn't done a sit-up in his life. My fist sank deep into his beer-softened gut and kept going through the toneless, mildewed stomach till I thought it might come shredding out his back.

The knife hit the cement and his eyes bugged and he fell with the rigid silence of a mannequin tumbling from a shop window. That was when I saw the other knife, poised, ready to fall. Another generic message crackled through the brain. It calculated point of knife, position of self, and evaluated the probable result. Forget it, the message said. You're dead.

But the knife didn't fall. From where I crouched, waiting to die, it stayed suspended in the night. Then the hand that held it slowly lowered. The fingers went loose and the knife hit the sidewalk. The kid backed away, color gone from his face. I followed the plane of his eyes to Jack Gilliam who stood in a crouch, legs planted, both arms fully extended, holding a cold and motionless gun.

"You have five seconds," Gilliam said.

The kid turned and raced off into the night, along with his buddy. The one I'd slugged was curled up on the pavement, fetal position, eyes still bugged as though I'd decompressed him and they'd stay that way forever. Gilliam straightened from his crouch and put the gun back in his concealed shoulder holster.

"What's with the gun?" I said.

"You rather I didn't have it?"

I didn't have an answer to that. Gilliam nodded at the kid I'd stretched out. "Where'd you learn that?"

"I work out."

Gilliam gave me a hard, suspicious look. Reevaluating who the hell I might be. Then he turned and motioned for me to follow. Together we ducked around the corner, into the night. Toward Hemming's empty house.

25

I T WAS ALMOST MIDNIGHT. Kate had gone to bed, and I had stalked the television long enough. The cassette was in, the power was on, but three quick shots of tequila had not yet given me the strength to push the button, sit down, watch . . .

It probably wasn't the cassette at all. The whole notion of a videotape was crazy. Erik was right that very first morning. So the numbers read 9963. So what? There must be dozens of explanations.

When Jack Gilliam had sprung the lock in Hemming's darkened study and I'd slid open the panel beneath the VCR, not a single cassette was to be found. Frantically I'd gone through the drawers and closets, but that was it. None.

"Okay," I'd heard Gilliam say. "Time."

I'd started to follow, empty handed, then something

had come to me. I looked at the VCR. Turned it on and pushed the EJECT button. Internal whirring, and a black, unlabeled cassette rose out of the machine. Here I am, it said. Drink me. I grabbed it and left.

I took a deep breath and walked away from the tequila bottle. If three didn't do it, a fourth wouldn't make any difference. I pushed the PLAY button, sat, and watched. . . .

Nothing for a while. My heart slammed around in my chest. Then a pop. Jolt.

My hands unclenched. I fast-forwarded, stopped, played it again. Again.

I rewound the tape, pushed the counter to zero, and ejected it. The bedroom door opened and Kate ventured out. She was pale and apprehensive.

"Well?" she said.

"Jerry Lewis," I said. *"The Disorderly Orderly."*

"Really?"

"Really."

Her body slumped like dead weight against the wall. "I don't know whether to be relieved or disappointed."

"The Disorderly Orderly," I mumbled to myself. I sat down on the couch. Kate wandered toward the tequila, thought about it, then left it alone.

"Now what?" she said.

"Now I don't know what." I linked my hands behind my head. "I was stupid to ever think I could get it."

I wasn't in the mood to talk. Kate nodded to herself, and wandered back down the hall toward the bedroom.

I sat in the darkened living room for a while. Then I roused myself, threw on the Windbreaker, and went out for a walk. Clear the brain. Defunk myself.

I headed east, up and over my corner of Russian Hill, then down into North Beach. A thin fog covered San

Francisco. A city wrapped in gauze, muted lights flickering from the clusters of warm homes. I felt alone. Brutally alone.

I crossed through North Beach and up Union to Montgomery, and from there wound past the Shadows restaurant toward the cozy houses clinging to the woodsy side of Telegraph Hill. Little gardens and picket fences. Streets dead-end everywhere on Telegraph Hill, so no traffic.

I climbed steep steps to the base of Coit Tower. Back in civilization. High school kids lounging around parked cars swigged from beer cans and listened to loud music. I walked to the far end of the parking area and sat on the cold pavement barrier facing the city.

The walk had given me time to come to my senses. Follow Erik's advice. Go to Lt. Mannion's office first thing in the morning and spill it all. Get the wheels going to have Jimmy Hennessy come up and identify Hemming. Start hammering away at Professor Morse's wobbly-legged alibi and keep Hemming under close scrutiny. Follow procedure. Wait for the elusive hair follicle. The damning fingerprint. Exhibit A.

I put the problem aside and walked down the slope of Telegraph Hill and cut across Washington Square. Urban parks lose their charm at one in the morning, so I kept up my pace. The church dominating the north end of the park was well lighted. Joe DiMaggio married Marilyn Monroe in that church. At least, that's what I'd always thought. Then somebody said no, they didn't. No matter. I pictured how it would have been, had it been. A black-and-white world of rice throwing and newspaper men in hats taking flash pictures and Joltin' Joe smiling bashfully at the swarms of well-wishers. Poor Marilyn. Poor Sonia. Two women cut from the same cloth—sexy, vulnerable, doomed . . .

By the time I hit 1464A Union Street I had worked up a good sweat. But my soul was not defunked, and I was in no mood for what greeted me out on the street. The complex I live in has a small garage. It can hold four cars, period. There are twelve tenants in the building and, as per the American way of life, twelve cars. Parking in the city is miserable, so we all wanted the four spots. A tenant meeting solved the dilemma, with each of us allowed to use the garage four months a year, in two two-month increments. My two-month cycle started in July, and I coveted those sixty days and nights with an almost mystical reverence.

A car was parked in the entrance to the garage, right in front of the glaringly obvious sign that all but threatened disembowelment for anybody who dared park there. The urban rationalization is that anything's fair game after midnight on a weekday, since nobody's going in or out anyway.

I scribbled out a firm but emphatic note and tucked it under the windshield wiper and started to turn away when something caught my eye. I looked closer. There was a bright yellow sticker at the lower left corner of the windshield. A parking sticker for San Francisco State University. Faculty.

I have no memory of my feet touching ground. I fought with the front door, jamming the key in wrong three times before getting it right, then took the fifty-four steps three at a time, whirling myself around at the landing and pushing open the bedroom door. Kate was in bed, a book in her lap, and she jolted at my entrance.

"What are you doing?!"

"Are you okay?"

"Of course I'm okay!" Kate curled farther up toward the pillow, eyes wide with alarm. "Why wouldn't I be?"

I didn't answer. I went from room to room, down the hall, into the living room and back, heart slamming in my chest, throat tight.

"Did you hear anything while I was gone?" I said.

"No. Nothing. Please, Quinn. You're scaring me."

I stood in the middle of the room, hands on hips, and let my pulse slow to normal.

"I'm sorry, Kate. I thought—"

A car door slammed outside. I moved quickly to the bay window and looked down. The car with my note was backing out at tire-screeching speed. As it lurched into Union Street I had a split second of clear vision through the windshield. The driver shot a glance up at the window and our eyes locked. It was Professor Ronald Hemming, his face pale and terrified. Then the car jerked into first gear and rocked off into the night at tremendous speed.

I dialed Mannion's home phone number. He answered midway through the second ring in an alarmed voice, thick with interrupted sleep.

"Yeah? What?"

"Mannion, this is Quinn Parker."

Pause. "Parker, I'm going to have your ass—"

"Shut up and listen to me."

That got the sleep out of his eyes. "What did you say?"

"I've got two ID's that link Professor Hemming to another murder. He knows I'm onto him and just now he came to my apartment. Raced off when I spotted him. The woman who's with me now is one of the people who can identify him. She might be in danger."

"Hold on."

Mannion said something to somebody. A minute passed and his voice came back on the line. "Go ahead, honey."

An extension rattled clumsily onto its cradle.

"Okay," Mannion said. "Start from the beginning."

I did. All of it. Woodside, the client records and the missing John Doe, the twisted childhood in Virginia. I didn't say anything about the medieval business. It would keep. I told Mannion how I'd broken into Hemming's house earlier in the evening but hadn't found anything except the Jerry Lewis cassette.

"That was stupid," Mannion said. "He'll see the cassette is missing and trash the other one, assuming there is another one."

"There is."

Silence for a while. Mannion was thinking. "Okay," he said at last. "First thing tomorrow I'll get somebody to keep a watch on Hemming. You and your ladyfriend sit tight. I'll have the city police stake somebody out in front of your apartment for the night. Don't go anywhere. Come by my office at nine sharp tomorrow."

He hung up. Then I called Erik, woke him up. He was pissed that I had gone through with the break-in. From now on I was to do every single thing Mannion told me to do. No ad-libbing at all. Zilch. I told him about my appointment with Mannion at nine, and Erik said to come by his office first, around eight, and he'd try to counsel me through what I could expect with the lieutenant.

I hung up and sat there in the dark. Kate had been listening to my conversations, and she turned from me without a word and went back into the bedroom. The door closed, the light under the crack of the door went out.

I went into the guest bedroom, but sleep was impossible. Things that go bump in the night . . . things that go bump in the street . . .

I went into the office and parted the curtains. Down

below Union Street was quiet. Oscar looked at me curiously. I pulled up a chair and put my feet on the windowsill and took a deep breath. Oscar had his perch, and I had mine. Together we sat in the dark and monitored the uneasy night.

26

I T WAS A CAUTIOUS RIDE to Erik's office. I didn't see any officer guarding the apartment, and Kate would be there alone. She double-bolted everything and I told her I'd give a call as soon as I could.

Erik was exhausted. He sat in his chair like he'd been tumbled into it from a laundry chute. Eyes bloodshot and artificially alert. He hadn't come up with anything better than Mannion's strategy—to keep an eye on Hemming and try to find some trivial pretext under which to arrest him.

There was a knock on the door and Hank peeked his head in.

"What are you doing here?" Erik said.

Hank walked into the office and plunked himself down on the couch. His eyes were on me the whole way. "Called your apartment this morning and Kate told me what was going on. I thought I'd better come by for moral support."

The three of us sat silently for a moment. Then the phone rang. Erik answered and handed the receiver to me. He silently mouthed the word "Mannion."

"Where's the girl?" Mannion said. He was agitated. Curt.

"What girl?"

"What's-her-name. The girl in your apartment who can identify Hemming."

"Kate?"

"Right," Mannion said. "Where is she?"

"Still at my apartment. What's going on?"

"Hemming's disappeared," Mannion said. "He never came back to his house last night and didn't show for his morning class. Son of a *bitch* that he got away!" Mannion said. "He could be anywhere by now." There was a long pause at the other end. Then Mannion said, "Don't bother to come by. No point right now. We've got the grounds-keeper in Woodside on hold, in case Hemming turns up. In the meantime, you and your ladyfriend keep low. No walks in the park."

"Don't worry."

Mannion hung up, and I handed the dead receiver back to Erik.

"Hemming's vanished," I said.

"Great," Hank said. "Perfect."

We sat in silence a long time. "Mannion thinks Kate might be in danger," I said.

Hank rose from the couch and moved toward the desk. "Bring her over to the house for the time being. She can stay in the guest room."

"Hank . . . "

"I mean it. Hemming'd never find her there, assuming he's looking for her at all."

"Appreciate your offer," I said. "But if it's all the same

to you I'm going to salt her away in a house without children."

"Hold on a second." Hank picked up the desk phone, dialed, turned away from me and had a murmured two-minute conversation. Then he turned back. "Done."

"What's done?"

"Kids are on their way for a fun-filled week with grandma and grandpa. Tell Kate to pack her things."

It was a long morning and a longer afternoon. At three o'clock my resistance caved in and I gave Lt. Mannion a call. A thorough search of Hemming's apartment had turned up no incriminating videotapes. It was Mannion's opinion that Professor Hemming was thousands of miles away. Lost in Mexico City's seventeen million. Holed up in a shack in rural Burma. But he wanted me to maintain a low profile, just in case.

I didn't agree with the strategy. That evening I decided to make myself visible. Go out, walk around, see what might get flushed out of the dark. Hemming was either stalking me, or he wasn't.

I walked up and over Russian Hill and down into North Beach. Had a drink at the Washington Square Bar and Grill, sitting alone in the roar of everybody telling each other their important stories. I scanned the sea of heads. No Hemming. I left it at one drink and went next door to the Beethoven restaurant for dinner and sat alone at a table for two. The restaurant—usually packed—was practically empty. Like when the café owner is tipped off about a gangland slaying about to happen and suddenly you're sitting there alone. Guido, the owner, came out and sat with me. The salmon was overcooked, he said. I hadn't noticed, but assured Guido that overcooked salmon ranked real low on my current list of priorities. Guido didn't care. You do something, you do it well. No excuses. Our conversation drifted to recent newspaper reports about barrels of radioactive waste that had been dumped in San Francisco Bay years ago. Now they'd ruptured and the fish hauled in by local fishermen had phenomenal levels of radioactive contamination. Guido joined me for a glass of wine and refused to let me pay for the salmon. Wasn't his night, he said. Something in the air.

I strolled North Beach, Chinatown, and Upper Grant. Passed the Hot Pink Theater and could hear the Jimi Hendrix tape going. Resisted the urge to poke in and see if Michelle was working. The last person I felt like running into tonight was Jack Gilliam. Check that. Next to last person.

I made my way home about ten o'clock. I couldn't have made myself more vulnerable if I'd painted an orange Day-Glo bull's-eye on the middle of my forehead. Mannion was right. Hemming was in Rarotonga, picking mangoes.

There was a message waiting for me on the answering machine. It was from Mannion, and he wanted me to call him at his home. I did.

"Where've you been?" he said.

"Went to North Beach for a drink and dinner."

"You got a peculiar idea about what laying low is."

"I'd had enough," I said. "And nothing happened anyway. I think you're right about Hemming being on the other side of the world."

"He's on the other side, all right," Mannion said.

"What do you mean?"

"Hemming's dead."

I rose out of my chair. "What?"

"Our boy committed suicide late last night. Three in the morning. Swan dive off the Golden Gate."

I couldn't respond. Mannion let me absorb it awhile, work through the shock.

I fumbled around. "But . . . are you sure?"

"Drove his car to the North Tower and apparently went right over the side. A lot of bridge suicides are like that." Mannion paused. "And you were right about the video-tape, Parker. He left it there for us, on the seat."

I felt darkness crowd the edges of my eyes. "The videocassette?"

Mannion exhaled loudly and cleared his throat. "I just finished watching it. You'd better come in to my office tomorrow."

It was a small room several doors down from Mannion's office. A half-dozen cheap plastic chairs faced a fold-out white screen. Two small round tables were stuck in the midst of the chairs, littered with almost-empty Styrofoam coffee cups and granules of salt and crinkled-up sugar packets and coffee-stained wooden stir sticks.

"Have a seat," Mannion said.

I sat. Mannion pushed the white screen to the side of the wall, unlocked a storage closet, and wheeled out a television set and a video recorder. Then he took a cassette from a large manila envelope, pushed it in, and leaned to study the switches as if he'd never run the machine before in his life. He pushed a couple of buttons and eased down into a chair near the television.

"You still don't have to do this," he said.

I took a steadying breath. "I want to," I said. "I need to."

Mannion looked at me a long, long time. Finally he

nodded, pursed his lips, and stood up. "Okay," he said. "If you have to, you have to. I'll be in the next room."

He moved to the machine, hesitated over the PLAY button, then pushed it and quickly moved out of the room.

I went to the window, leaned my forehead against the cold, dark glass, felt the noise of the city hum at the edges of my consciousness. Tears only come with normal tragedies. What I'd just seen was impossible to assimilate. Normal grief had been scorched away by something tight, coiled, unnameable.

I looked at the cassette, now sitting atop the television. I hated the plastic, the black paint, the high-tech logo, the whole goddamn streamlined package. I hated the reel of tape for having continued to record an event so monstrous I almost became sick watching it, and I felt a crazed urge to destroy the material, punish it for being indiscriminate, and to pretend that it felt pain.

The tape had begun with Sonia already unconscious. Dead, perhaps. She was on the bed, nude. At that point I'd turned the tape off, pulse slamming in my body, eyes scanning for something to focus on. I'd hit the STOP button and held it down for five seconds . . . ten . . . fifteen. Drowning the image, making sure it was dead, really dead, and would never resurface.

Yet I had to watch it. I had to know that the murderer himself was there. I had to see Hemming move into the picture, face hidden behind a ski mask, holding a long, thin, surgical knife. I had to see him set it on the dusky, vulnerable flesh, coax the first bite of rich, red, still-warm blood, and then lean all his weight into the stroking blade . . .

I heard something. Mannion was back in the room, tucking in his tucked-in shirt, having trouble keeping eye contact with me.

"Well?" he said.

"The bastard really did it."

Mannion nodded. "Looks that way. The man must have had ice in his veins. I'd've laid down a month's salary all he cared about was tenure and chasing coeds."

"I think maybe that was the point."

Mannion cleared his throat and took a piece of paper from his shirt pocket. "This is a copy of the suicide note. It was in the car next to the tape. Handwriting checked out. They say he was under a lot of stress when he wrote it. Most suicides are."

He handed me the paper and I read.

I swear to you by the grotesque roots
of this tangled tree,
that never did I break faith with him,
my worthy lord and emperor.

"We're checking out this 'grotesque roots of tangled tree' thing," Mannion said. "Guy was an English professor so it's probably—"

"It's from Dante," I said.

Mannion blinked. "Dante?"

"*The Divine Comedy.* It's the—I don't know—sixth or seventh circle of hell. It's where the suicides go and grow into trees and get tortured by strange birds called Harpies."

Mannion stared at me for a while. "This information just sort of on the tip of your tongue, or have you been boning up on your Dante lately?"

"I had my suspicions."

Mannion continued to peer at me. I ran my hands through my hair and frowned. "Why do you suppose Hemming wore a ski mask in the film?"

Mannion shrugged. "So no one would recognize him."

"But who did he think was going to see it? Nobody was going to see it."

"The guy was a head case. Maybe he wanted to watch it but pretend that it wasn't him doing it."

"Did they recover Hemming's body?"

Mannion shook his head. "Went out to sea. Shark food."

I kept pulling at my lower lip and said nothing.

"Look, Parker," Mannion said. "If you're thinking that he really didn't kill himself, the same thing occurred to me. I don't like deaths without corpses, and the case isn't closed yet. But the fact remains that most suicides off the bridge are gone, and we have to be prepared to leave it at that, unsatisfactory as it is."

I didn't push it. My original suspicion of Hemming had legitimized me somewhat in the eyes of Mannion, and he was making an effort to explain himself. Still, I could sense him easing off the case. Why risk making captain? Hemming had given him a nice, videotaped package. Use it. The lieutenant had a lot to lose and not much to win by continuing to spend money and manpower on Ronald Hemming. But once the shock of the videotape had worn off I could feel the vivid pain once again, like novocaine receding from a particularly deep cavity. And the pain only intensified the unresolved nature of everything. A killer with a ski mask. A suicide without a body. Hemming gone and not gone at the same time. Diaries in code and false names on client lists and Sonia refusing to look Ludmila in the eyes about something bad in her life.

Mannion spoke comforting words while walking me to

the car. Put his hand on my shoulder. It was over. I should be relieved.

To celebrate our end of quarantine Kate and I packed a picnic and headed north to Muir Woods. Got out on the Dipsea Trail and traversed sloping hills of swaying grass with the ocean glinting sunlight in the distance.

But Kate sensed my distraction and hiked on ahead of me a hundred yards. The majority stockholders in Quinn Parker, Inc., were convening. There was conflict in the body corporate. I couldn't shake the feeling that I'd been cheated. That justice, somehow, hadn't been served. I'd traveled thousands of miles, had taken a blunt instrument to the head, a pool stick across the back, had logged eye-straining hours sifting through medieval symbolism. I'd dealt with Darlene and Walt and had gazed into the rotten teeth of Mark McCumber. For what? For Hemming to slip out the back door? Th-th-th-th-th-th-that's all, folks! And over the bridge to an exhilarating exit?

No. Things should end like they do in the movies, where you walk out into the darkened parking lot with popcorn on your breath and tranquillity in your heart, where screenwriters tie up all the loose ends to tap into both the universal need for revenge and the universal willingness to pay six bucks a pop to see life as it should be, not as it is.

I watched Kate hiking up ahead. A hundred yards was a good distance to keep from me. I wasn't quite finished. There was still something I could do.

Meeting adjourned. The gavel fell and the majority stockholders went back to their places. A few dissenting voices, but tough luck. Majority rules.

27

THE SAN FRANCISCO BAY–DELTA TIDAL HYDRAULIC MODEL is a very imposing name for what is, essentially, a child's ultimate bathtub fantasy. Built in Sausalito by the Army Corps of Engineers, it is a living, moving, football-field-sized mock-up of the Bay Area's waterways. It can tell you about salination and irrigation and tidal changes and the directions of currents and anything else you might want to know. There was something else I wanted to know.

Kate couldn't conceal her indifference, and elected instead to tool downtown in pursuit of baubles, bangles, and crab Louis that would meet her exacting standards. I wished her luck, watched the white Honda zip away, and headed by myself through the glass doors of the bay model.

There were no more than a dozen people milling around

when I entered, and the model had the echoey, expansive quiet of a large museum.

There was no sense trying to be subtle with what I was going to do, so I walked straight over to the eighteen-inch-long replica of the Golden Gate Bridge and did it. Took a piece of piece of paper from my wallet, crumpled it, and dropped it off the bridge. The little ball of paper inched out to sea, then began to sink. I plucked it out before it went under.

"Gonna jump?"

The voice startled me. It belonged to an old man standing alongside me, smiling. He wore a green military-type uniform and the name tag on his shirt said KERMIT MANSFIELD. He looked about ninety-five years old, face as tough and leathery and heavily lined as a baseball mitt. He didn't wear glasses, and his eyes were a distant, faded blue.

"Just checking on something," I said. "Do you work here?"

"Part-time. They catch you throwing stuff in the water, they'll kick you out, so better not do it."

"Sorry." I stood, hands on hips. "If you work here you must know the waters pretty well."

Kermit shrugged. "I do all right. Me and the wife sail down to Tahiti every spring. Been doing it forty years, just the two of us. Hell, there's parts of the ocean I recognize just like we were sailing through mountains and one is different from the rest. People who say the ocean's the same all over plain don't know the ocean. Course, I'm talking Pacific. Atlantic, I don't know the Atlantic at all."

I waved my hand at the bay mock-up. "Who uses this thing?"

"Technical people mostly. Bureau of Reclamation. Any dredging work, they come by here to figure out the sediment problems. This is all computerized, you know. Push a few buttons and you can recreate almost any tidal situation."

"What about Coast Guard work?" I said.

"What about it?"

"Let's say somebody jumps off the bridge, a suicide. . . . Does the Coast Guard use this to figure out where the body might've gone?"

Kermit had begun nodding his head midway through my question. "They sure do. Not always, but now and then. Three things practically always happen to bridge jumpers, anyway. Either they fish the guy out right away, or the currents'll take him out to Stinson, or the sharks get him. Course, the Coast Guard isn't all that concerned with dead people who wanted to be dead in the first place. They come by here mostly if they think contraband got dumped on a flotation device."

"So if the Coast Guard doesn't find a body it goes out to Stinson?"

Kermit nodded. "All things being equal. Sometimes a strange current'll suck 'em out past the Farrolones, then it's *adios*. You heard of Hurricane Alley? The Florida Keys and up where all the hurricanes go?"

"Yes."

"Well, over to Stinson where all the jumpers go, I heard Coast Guard people call that Suicide Alley."

The mock-up didn't extend past the Marin Headlands, but Kermit pointed a bony finger at the Golden Gate Bridge and traced a slow, graceful curve out to sea, then a sharp tilt north as if following the parabola of a bending interstate highway. Suicide Alley.

"How long does it take a body to wash up at Stinson?" I asked as Kermit and I walked toward the exit.

"Well, depends. Don't really know about bodies, but a boat, just drifting, not a lot of wind . . . two days. Around that."

We stood at the door and Kermit told me about how flying was his true love. He seemed a lonely old guy who felt like shooting the breeze, so I stuck around awhile. He told me he was one of the first pilots to get a license back in the twenties. Didn't fly anymore, though. Hadn't for years. Switch-flippers was all pilots were now. All the fun went out of it. The ocean was better. Man was still pretty much alone out there on the ocean.

"Thanks for the talk, Kermit."

"My pleasure." Kermit squinted out at the sunlit harbor. "Naw, it's a different ball game now. A fellow can still have a little adventure in life, but you got to look harder. Lots harder. Everybody says how you young folks got it so much easier, but I don't envy your generation for peanuts. Not for peanuts, and that's a fact." He shivered as though he'd seen the ghosts of Christmases future, and they were all eating tofu at Jacuzzi-side.

I shook Kermit's hand and left, thinking as I walked back into Sausalito proper about him and his wife out on their boat beneath Polynesian skies, navigating by the stars, recognizing patches of blank ocean as though they were stretches of terrain, unique and complete.

For the entirety of the next day I made a genuine pain in the ass out of myself. Nobody wanted to hear about how the suicide might have been faked. Erik rolled his eyes. Mannion hung up on me. Hank remembered something he suddenly had to do, and Kate got in her car and drove away.

I took my indignation down to the Bus Stop and ran it past Roger. I mean, Christ! Nobody actually saw Hemming go over. The Coast Guard didn't find anything. And what about Suicide Alley? What about the bodies that always wash ashore at Stinson? Hunh? What about that?

Roger nodded through all of it, leaning on the bar, and said that I had a legitimate gripe and why the hell were people being so impatient with me.

Having a bartender agree with you is about as rewarding as striking out the pitcher, but I needed the strikeout. Roger excused himself and went to take care of a large, boisterous group at the other end of the bar. I sighed and looked down into my beer and felt foolish. You're talking to yourself, Parker. Go home and live your life.

Kate hadn't returned from wherever she'd driven off to. No calls on the answering machine. I went out into the kitchen and started preparing another batch of seed mixture for Oscar.

The phone jarred me. It was Irma. She made a big procedure of how she was going to put me through to Lt. Mannion.

"Parker?" he said. "I've got good news for you."

"What?"

"Hemming's body washed ashore at Stinson Beach this afternoon."

I sat down.

"You still there?" Mannion said.

"I'm here."

"Happened a couple hours ago. I'd like you and Paige to come by my office at ten tomorrow. Wrap this up." Mannion hesitated. "Another thing. You wouldn't know about a little accident in the vicinity of Hemming's house a few nights ago?"

I couldn't clear my head. "What?"

"Guy got thrown headfirst into a car window?"

"Oh," I rubbed my eyes. "That. Is he okay?"

Mannion chuckled. "You *do* get around, Parker. Yeah, he's okay. We'll hash it out tomorrow at ten."

Erik and Mannion were already waiting for me at the office next morning. Post mortem. Last chapter. Tying it all up in very official way, like now we can relax and be like normal people with each other. Mannion sat on his desk, pants hiked up to show two inches of white calf.

"Lady thought it was a dead seal at first," Mannion said. "Walked up to it and about keeled over."

"No doubt it was Hemming?" Erik asked.

Mannion shrugged his shoulders. "Body was chewed-up pretty good by sharks. But, yeah. It's Hemming. Male Caucasian, Hemming's height—or at least was before it got trash-compacted from the jump. Same clothes. Blood type. All of it. It's him."

Erik asked how all of this was going to affect McCumber. Mannion gave him his theory and they talked back and forth in that peculiar dialogue known only to cops and criminal lawyers. They had a laugh over what this was going to do to Bill Jameson, The Echo.

"What about the dental plates?" I said.

Mannion gave me a funny look. "The what?"

"Dental plates. I know my frame of reference is merely television, but isn't that the only way to positively identify someone?"

Erik and Mannion smiled at each other, then Mannion turned toward me. "By television standards, yes. But it doesn't matter anyway. Whatever dental plates the body had were eaten up by sharks."

"Convenient."

Erik shifted in his chair and looked pained. "Quinn, you're grasping at straws."

"Wait a minute," I said. "Let me just innocently speculate on something, okay?"

"Fine," Mannion said. "Speculate."

"What's to prevent Hemming from murdering somebody who looked like him—wait a minute, let me finish——murdering somebody like him, taking out his trusty little hammer, bashing away the teeth and tossing the guy over the bridge?"

Mannion chuckled and his tone grew instructional. "What's to prevent him is the fact that forensics would know in about one minute that the teeth were bashed out with a trusty little hammer. These guys are professionals. They *know* it was a shark. They know the bite radius. They know how big the teeth were. They could probably tell you where it was swimming on its last birthday." Mannion paused, took a breath. "It was him, Quinn. It was him."

A week passed. The body that washed ashore at Stinson Beach was boxed, labeled, and dispensed with. The newspapers milked it for all it was worth. Rampaging psychotic professor. Somehow the medieval angle got leaked, and there were silly drawings on the back page of the *Chronicle* showing the circles of hell with arrows going out to photos of real-life victims.

Lt. Mannion made the local news, microphones shoved in his face. There was a lot of public curiosity about the tape of Sonia's murder, and the nightly radio talk shows were filled with editorial comment on the people's right to know. Their right to see. Their right to thrill vicariously at another's tragedy.

It was all pretty sick-making, and I reverted into hermit Quinn, not venturing from the apartment unless I really had to, crawling back into the prevideo world of books and candles and silent evenings in front of the fireplace.

Kate had gone back to Carmel to wrap things up. She hadn't decided for sure what she was doing or where she was going, but either way she was finished with her apartment, and there was packing to be done. Hank quit coming by altogether, and Erik was barricaded in his office, catching up on all the business he'd put on hold to help me pursue the ghost of Ronald Hemming.

I broke my self-imposed exile only occasionally—to see a film or to take a walk down on the Marina Green, eyes watering from the cold Pacific wind. One afternoon I kept walking all the way down to Fort Point, directly under the south end of the Golden Gate Bridge. I stood there and looked up at the span. A long way up. Would Professor Hemming have done such thing? I turned from the bridge and walked home.

Two calls had come in on my answering machine. The first was from Kate.

"Hank's right," she said. "Your machine has to go. I'm sitting here in Carmel making my last official call before this phone gets disconnected. I just wanted to say I'm sorry about the way things have been going with us lately. I don't know . . . the Ulrich radar senses distance. If you feel like coming down for a couple days I'd really like it, and I'm not just saying that. Rent's paid through the weekend, so we might as well—"

The timer clicked her off. Her voice was immediately back.

"Two long-distance phone calls," she said. "But I'll be damned if I'll let that machine chop off my good-bye kiss. Good-bye. Come down. Help me pack. You'll be rewarded with dinner, my last bottle of wine, and maybe sexual favors." Then the sound of an exaggerated kiss; well-puckered, wet, heavy-on-the-suction. I smiled, felt for my car keys, and headed out the door.

28

I STOOD BEFORE THE MOUNTAIN of junk piled high in Kate's living room. I was amazed, as I always am, at the sheer volume of accumulated garbage that comes from the woodwork of a well-kept apartment when it's time to move.

But Kate would have none of my whining. She was full of energy and optimism, and had no doubt we could stuff the thirty boxes of knickknacks into twenty boxes of space. Kate attacked the project with a vengeance. For six months she'd silently tolerated all of Devonwood's constipated rules, and now that it was over there was a gleam in her eye.

We finished up around sunset, took a couple of long, hot showers, then headed into Monterey so she could treat me to the dinner I'd been promised. It was Chinese, down in the cleaned-up Cannery Row section. Steinbeck's Monterey looked just like D'Joint's Carmel, which in turn looked just like Sausalito, and so on and so on and so on. The designerization of America. Ye Olde This and Ye Olde That.

We ate and talked about the food and compared it to Chinese restaurants we both knew in San Francisco. Boring. The dinner was an attempt to be celebratory, to mark the end of something, but I was too distracted.

I kept seeing something. I saw Hemming driving onto the Golden Gate Bridge at three in the morning. I saw him stopping right at the North Tower, the one spot where a leap over the bridge would be sheltered. I saw him dragging a body out of the car, tossing it quickly over the side, then running like hell back in the direction of the Marin Headlands. The way he ran you had a feeling he would run forever. Up, around, and down. Maybe all the way back down to Monterey.

After dinner we went to Carmel Beach and strolled the dark shore, hand-in-hand. Kate was trying gently to nudge us into some privacy, but I was reluctant. Whenever another couple appeared, I gravitated toward them. Finally Kate stopped and turned to face me.

"You're doing it again," she said.

"Doing what?"

"Lost in space. Just like the night in Front Royal." She put both hands on my face and kissed me on the lips. Not softly, not passionately. More of a wake-up call. "What's going on?"

"I don't want to talk about it."

"Why not?"

"Every time I open my mouth on the subject I lose a friend."

Kate stared up at me. "You think Professor Hemming's still alive, don't you?"

"Yes."

"Why?"

"The suicide rings false. It feels prepackaged. Three o'clock in the morning, and right at the North Tower . . . the one time and the one place where witnesses would be least likely to see what was going over the bridge. Then the videocassette right there in the front seat with the quote from Dante. I don't know, Kate. It's too orderly. Too thought-out. Like he was careful to tie up all the loose ends." I took a deep breath and looked at her. "Can't you see it?"

"I guess I'd see it if I looked," Kate said. "But I've chosen not to look anymore."

"What if Professor Hemming were right behind that clump of trees?" I said. "Then would you look?"

Kate turned toward the group of trees, took my hand, and led me there. "Let's sit down and see what comes out of the forest."

We sat on a log that had fallen at the base of the trees and spent a moment or two in silence, watching the ocean.

"See?" Kate said. "Nothing."

More silence. I could feel Kate's eyes on the side of my face, then she reached into her purse. "I've got a present for you," she said.

"A what?"

"Here." She handed me an envelope. "Open it."

I looked at it questioningly, then at her.

"Go on," she said. "Just open it."

I opened the envelope and withdrew a colorful, glossy travel agency folder. Inside was a round-trip air ticket. I held the ticket closer so I could read in the pale moonlight. San Francisco to Detroit, Michigan.

"Maybe this'll take your mind off Professor Hemming for a while," she said. "It's the newest thing in good-bye presents. Makes a good-bye maybe not a good-bye at all."

"Good-bye?"

She was talking quickly now, heading me off. "Critical thing here, you'll notice, is the part about it being round-trip. Risk-free relationship. Detroit flops, you get a window seat back home."

I put the ticket and folder back in the envelope. "When did you decide?"

"Couple of days ago."

"Decision is final?"

"Uh-huh. Even called my old boss. A job's waiting. They never should have let me slip away in the first place, blah blah blah." Kate smiled nervously. Her eyes lowered to the envelope. "You aren't going to come, are you?"

"I've got a better idea."

"What's that?"

I pointed out at the ocean. "Tahiti."

"Tahiti?"

"Why not? I know an old man who can sail us there. He's got the Pacific memorized."

Kate smiled and put her hand softly on my leg. "No," she said. "Tahiti would just be Carmel all over again, only in French and with fewer clothes. You have to know what you're good at and do it. Hard to launch a marketing research career in Polynesia."

"Jesus, Kate . . . Detroit?"

"What's to lose?" Kate shrugged. "Give it a try."

I thought about it a moment. Tried to place myself in Detroit. It was vague. I saw snow, soot, sports pages full of Tigers games. What would I look forward to? Vacations in Florida? Gator World? I didn't see Hank or Carol or Erik or Vapor Trial or Roscoe or the bathroom nymphs or Leon's BBQ. I didn't see billowy white fog drifting through Golden Gate, with only the red towers of the bridge peeking through at the top. I didn't see Quinn Parker. I didn't see much of anything.

The silence went on, and the ocean washed ashore, and finally Kate shook her head.

"Let me make it easy for you," she said, reaching over and plucking the envelope from my lap.

"Can't I have some time to think about it?"

"Would it make any difference?" she said.

"No. Probably not."

"Some things don't need to be thought about, Quinn. They're just done. I don't want to live in San Francisco and you don't want to live in Michigan."

"I thought with true love those things weren't supposed to matter."

Kate attempted a smile, bit her lower lip, and looked away. "With true love they don't."

We stood and walked back to the car and drove the fifteen miles to Devonwood in relative silence. At the apartment we packed the final odds and ends, talked about our lives, and even managed to joke a bit. Somehow the thirty boxes of junk fit into the twenty boxes with a little room left over. We laughed about maybe unbolting the bolted-in sunset painting and stealing it. Devonwood expected the worst from its tenants. Why disappoint them?

When it was all over I stretched out on the living room floor while Kate futzed around with last-minute things in the kitchen.

"Did you pack the broken wine glass?" I said.

"Absolutely!" Kate called from the kitchen.

"What's going to go on your bookshelf in Detroit to remind you of me?"

Kate appeared at the kitchen doorway, smiling.

"Hadn't thought about it. Maybe the Luray Caverns back scratcher."

"Great."

"Do I detect a hint of jealousy, Quinn?"

"Better believe it."

"Listen," she said. "Don't blame me. It's not my fault that we made love so carefully."

"It's a flaw in my character," I said. "I almost never destroy dining utensils during sex."

Kate smiled and came into the room and sat next to me. "Want to see a photograph of the prince?"

"What if I said no?"

"I'd show you anyway."

Kate reached over and slid a box to her side. It was full of loose photographs. As she shuffled through them I caught glimpses of her evolution. The high school cheerleader, the headband-wearing flower child, the career woman. There were travel shots, with backdrops of national parks and European monuments.

"Here he is." Kate selected an oversized photo from the pile and showed me. Kate and the prince were sitting on a grassy knoll in a park, smiling at the camera. The smiles looked forced. He was a handsome guy. Dark, pleasant, athletic.

"Central Park," Kate said. "This was right about the time everything was starting to go poof."

I nodded and kept looking at the photo and then Kate took it away. It was like she was suddenly embarrassed by her need to share this with me. She went into the kitchen to pop the final bottle of wine and I stayed stretched out on the rug, going through the photos. There were a few more pictures of Kate and the prince. The earlier the snapshots, the happier they looked. Eastman Kodak presents, in gradually fading color, the slow and sad winding down of a once-joyous romance. I wondered if my photos would one day find their way into this stack. If they'd be spread in a distant living room for other strange eyes.

Kate came back into the room carrying two glasses of wine. "The last Pinot Noir in the joint."

I took the glass of wine and picked up a photograph from the pile and looked at it. Kate and another woman. They were leaning against the guardrail of what looked like a ferry boat, laughing, arms thrown around each other. The Golden Gate Bridge showed in the background. I started to put it down, but something made me look closer. Then closer still. I felt my blood turn a few degrees cooler.

"What's the matter?" Kate said.

I concentrated on the woman standing next to Kate on the ferry boat. "Who's this?"

Kate looked at the picture, then her eyes came up to meet mine. "That was Sherri," Kate said softly. "That was Sherri Kaline."

When I played college baseball a foul once nailed me right in the catcher's mask. Wedged there. Knocked me down. A blinding combination of impact, disorientation, yet lack of pain. It was the way I felt now.

Because Sherri Kaline was somebody else. I had seen her before. She was a beacon of light, a flesh-and-blood outpost of sanity in a world that was unraveling faster than anyone suspected. Sherri Kaline was not only a woman who had died by pitchfork in a Woodside barn. She was also Brigid O'Malley, the fresh-faced Irish woman who once stood in front of a blustery Donegal castle with Erik Paige.

. . .

I looked up and down the streetlit expanse of Market Street. It was two o'clock in the morning, and the city was quiet. Only an occasional trolley car rattled by, manned by a sleepy driver, nobody riding.

I could smell Ludmila's bath oil on my shirt. I smelled it because she had hugged me. She had hugged me because she was frightened. She was frightened because I had woken her up in the middle of the night at her apartment in Sausalito to get the keys to Erik's office.

Kate had pleaded with me not to go. She swore I was mistaken. Sherri Kaline had never left the United States. Never. She didn't even have a passport. Kate knew it for a fact. The woman in the photo on Erik's desk had to be someone else. Someone who looked like Sherri. That was the only possible explanation.

A trolley car rumbled past and then I walked out into the street and looked up at Erik's office window. Dark. All the windows in the building were dark. I took the key to the building and let myself in.

The lobby was quiet and dimly lighted. In the corner a janitor's mop sat propped in a bucket of murky water. I went to the elevator and took the long ride up to the fifth floor. The cables rattled and the engines whirred, and I cringed against the noise. Razor blades across nerve endings.

The elevator doors at last slid open to the quiet fifth-floor hallway. I turned right and went to the end of the corridor and unlocked the door to Suite 503. Ludmila's reception area was pitch black. I groped for a light on the wall, found it, and waited for a moment while my eyes adjusted to the sudden brightness. Then I moved into Erik's office, shutting the door gently behind me.

I kept lights off. There was enough off-lighting from Ludmila's reception room to illuminate Erik's office. My heart was beating like crazy, and I paused for a moment so it could have a chance to return to normal. Office buildings only look right during the day, with people bustling and phones ringing. At night there's something wrong. Nothing legitimate happens in an office at night. Ex-cons cleaning up. Illicit boss-secretary love affairs. The embezzler hard at work altering files.

The room seemed to react to my entrance. I'd woken everybody up . . . the chairs, the photos on the wall, the Venetian blinds on the yellowed windows.

I pulled a chair up to the desk, turned on the lamp, and took the photo of Kate and Sherri from my coat pocket. I set it next to Erik's framed photo. There wasn't a doubt in the world. Brigid O'Malley and Sherri Kaline were the same person.

For a moment I sat in the office, in Erik's chair, thinking it out. How could it be? Obviously Kate had been wrong about Sherri never leaving the United States. Or had Kate just said that to keep me from rushing headlong into the night? Or had Sherri lied to Kate for some reason? I looked at the framed photo. At Erik's face. At Brigid's.

I took my Swiss army knife and cracked the frame apart and withdrew Erik's photograph from its mounting. Something was wrong. The coloration wasn't consistent. I turned the photo over and ran my finger along the back. There was a thin, almost indiscernible ridge running through the middle of the snapshot. I held it closer beneath the desk lamp and my body went cold. The photo was actually two photos, spliced together. Erik had doctored the photograph to make it appear that he and Sherri were standing before the same Irish castle, smiling at the same camera. There was no Brigid O'Malley. There was no loving mayor's daughter steadfastly·awaiting his return. Erik's outpost of sanity had been built with glue and paste and scissors. . . .

I lifted my eyes and tried to absorb the shock. The furniture surrounded me in the grayish dark. The eyes from the wall portraits looked down at me.

Then I heard something. A creak of floorboards in Ludmila's reception area. I sat very still. Imagination. No! It creaked again. I looked down at the crack of the door and could see a shadow passing by the dim light.

There was no place to hide. A weapon. I needed a weapon. My eyes fell on the letter opener sitting on the desk. It was long and sharp, like a stiletto. Feeble against a gun, but it was all I had.

I rose and gently pushed away the chair with the backs of my legs. Then it happened. The door burst open and I could see somebody silhouetted against the light and I lunged for the letter opener, falling away from the desk in the same motion.

"Freeze!"

A uniformed policeman stood in a crouch, arms extended, gun leveled at my chest. "Don't move an inch!"

I stayed where I was, and the cop moved toward me with cautious, jerky steps. "Drop the weapon!" he shouted. I dropped it. "Face down on the floor, hands on your head. Now!"

I did what he wanted. Then two more men came into the room. Another cop and a young, scared-looking black guy in a beige uniform. Building security. The second cop frisked me and then roughly handcuffed my hands behind my back.

"I didn't break in," I said. "I've got a key."

They didn't say anything. I was hauled up off my stomach and led toward the door. "You've got to listen to me,"

I said. "I'm a friend of Erik Paige. This is his office. He might be in trouble."

The police ignored me. I'd just uttered the third most common excuse a criminal utters when apprehended in the act. I was led with more force than necessary out of the office. The last thing I saw was the disassembled photograph still spread out on the desk, resting next to the snapshot of Kate and Sherri. Then the door closed and the security man locked the office with his master key and the lights went out.

29

I SAT ON THE BENCH in the cell and pulled my legs up around my chest and read the graffiti on the wall. It was three o'clock in the morning, and I was alone. No sound. Just the distant, echoey clacking of a single typewriter down the hall. Forms in triplicate on the graveyard shift.

I was exhausted. Worn out. Until thirty minutes ago I had still been thinking in terms of preventing things, of altering events. I was still functioning under the notion that with enough urgency I could make a difference. Paul Revere with a jailhouse dime. I dialed numbers that reached nobody. Kate was disconnected. Hank and Carol somehow slept through eight nerve-shattering rings. I asked the guard to call Lt. Mannion. He smiled and shook his head. Prisoners always wanted booking sergeants to call important people at three in the morning.

So now I read the graffiti. Scrawled insinuations of

what Rita would do to a variety of appendages, no matter what the shape, no matter what the color. There was a number to call. Then a plug for Jesus. Then a listing of zoo animals that the jailkeeper's mother had slept with. Then an incongruous quote by Nietzsche—"Is not life a hundred times too short for us to bore ourselves?" Below the Nietzsche somebody had drawn a long, snaking arrow up to the information on Rita.

I don't know why I kept reading them, but I did. It was a way of clearing the brain. A neutralizing of the palate, as one sips water to prepare for the heady and dangerous taste of dark wine. But then the graffiti came to an end and I was left with no choice but to taste the wine. To take a leap.

Erik had done it.

Somehow, someway, he had done it. All of it. Killed Sherri, killed Sonia, killed Professor Hemming. I didn't know why. There were no "whys" in the leap I'd taken. Only "hows."

How Sonia would have trusted him, unlocking the apartment door without a struggle. For him she might've slipped on a nightgown. Familiar, but not intimate. How Erik had plucked Sherri Kaline's murder out of thin air as one that might be related to Sonia's. How distracted he had been that first morning in his office. His concern with the switched pictures—Mannion's handiwork—rather than the numbers on the video machine. His own. I saw suddenly how deftly Erik had manipulated things. The basketball game, and how he'd steered our gazes directly to Hemming under the guise of seeking out better seats . . .

In the locked-up silence of three A.M. I had time to remember things. I thought of Sherri's diary. School was in session. Good morning, class. Today we are going to practice learning to recognize patterns. Please open Sherri Kaline's diary to page ten. Now . . . if D stands for Doctor, and P stands for Professor, then what might L stand for? I raise my hand, straining the shoulder sockets. Yes, Quinn? How about Lawyer? The teacher smiles. Very good, Quinn. A little late, but the right answer.

And what about Harv Danson, the second missing John Doe from Sherri's client records? I had been so enamored with how beautifully Jeff Moss fit Hemming's profile that I ignored the similarities between Harv Danson and Erik Paige. The words came back to me now in the early-morning stillness. The overburdened professional casting out his line in the hopes of finding a bit of sanity somewhere. A mild-mannered fellow trailing his fishhook through the waters of madness, hoping to snag up from the bottom any old shoe or tin can or lost fish that would help him make sense of the world. In the absence of a lost fish a castle would do. Exotic shores.

And Ludmila's unfocused intuition had been right. Sonia *had* sensed something bad about to happen. But it wasn't Mark McCumber. It was something that had caused Sonia not to be able to look Ludmila in the eyes. Why such sudden awkwardness from a woman who had looked Ludmila straight in the eyes about every other shared intimacy? Unless the trouble Sonia sensed brewing was a little too close to home. Maybe the "something bad" was emanating from Erik Paige, Ludmila's boss, and it was this that had caused Sonia to look away . . . to not share all with her share-all friend.

I thought of how startled he had been on coming back from the visit with McCumber to see Kate sitting in his waiting room. How he had ducked quickly into his office, and had reemerged just as quickly. Kate was the only person who might recognize Brigid as Sherri. That was why the photo was dumped hastily into the third drawer down, in with the paper clips.

I remembered a thought I'd had, thirty thousand feet above the Nevada desert. Perplexed at the depth of Hemming's anger in the library, it had seemed to me more than just mere overreaction. He had looked at me as though I had killed Sherri and Sonia myself. Somebody had been tormenting him. I was the logical choice.

I sat up on the bench and rubbed my face. Never mind all that. What was going to happen *now*? Erik had probably already been called by the police. He would go to his office to see if anything had been taken. Erik would find the evidence spread out all over his desk. He would know who did it. He would get rid of the incriminating debris and come after the two people who could blow the whistle on him.

I was so deep in thought I didn't hear the desk sergeant walk down the hall and open my cell.

"Come on," he said. "Up."

I stood, looked around. "What's happening?"

The sergeant didn't answer. He just waddled down the hallway, stretching and yawning. I followed. He climbed behind his desk, mounted his rump on the stool, and shoved a piece of paper at me.

"Sign here and you're free to go," he said.

"Free?"

"That's right. Charges are dropped. No charges, no crime. Here. Next to the X."

I stood there a moment, disoriented by the sudden turn of events. Then the sergeant nodded toward the corner of the room. "Friend's over there."

I turned. Standing next to the door, hands in pockets,

was Erik Paige. When our eyes locked he broke out of his pose and walked briskly toward me, hand out, shaking his head, smiling.

"Jesus, Quinn!" he said. "I should have told you about the motion alarm in the office. Just had it installed last week and forgot all about the damn thing."

I froze, turned back to the desk sergeant. He looked at me. My eyes weren't the eyes of somebody who'd just gotten sprung from jail. It got his attention.

"Sign right there," he said. Then, quieter. "Everything okay?"

Erik was quickly between us. "Kate is worried sick about you," he said. "I just saw her. She's . . . beside herself. Come on. I brought my car."

The desk sergeant continued to look at me. I hesitated. "Where is she, Erik?"

"She's fine. No problem. Let's get out of here."

I felt the sergeant's gaze still on me, but I kept from making direct eye contact. I was afraid he'd see the fear, that he might keep me from getting to Kate. I picked up the pen, signed my name as best I could, and went out into the parking lot with Erik Paige.

He handed me the keys. "You drive."

"I mean it, Erik. Where is she?" It was hard to say his name. My lips did not want to form the syllables. Erik was a friend of mine. A fellow I knew and trusted. This person with me now was a stranger.

The smile left Erik's face. "There's nothing to worry about. Let's go to your place."

We drove through the early-morning streets. It was drizzling, no traffic, like a science-fiction movie about the last two people on earth. Erik sat next to me in total silence, slouched against the passenger door. The index finger of his right hand kept tracing a design on his forehead, over and over and over, the way a mother will lull a small child off to sleep with a soothing tickle. His other hand was in his pants pocket. The outlines of the knuckles showed through the fabric. The hand was fisted into a tight ball. Whether he was just attempting to disguise his tension, or whether the hand was clenched around a weapon, I couldn't tell.

My body was in worse shape than I thought. Driving was difficult. Twice I put both wheels on the curb while turning. I found myself coming to hesitant stops at green lights. It took great concentration for me to gather enough saliva in my throat to be able to swallow. I had the sensation of choking.

"Tell me you haven't harmed Kate," I said at last.

Erik didn't look at me. He watched the road before us, trailing the series of delicate figure eights across his forehead with his index finger. "I haven't harmed Kate."

The voice was dull and without inflection. He told me what I had asked him to tell me, no more. The words did not convey a hint of reassurance or truth.

I caught an incomprehensibly long red light at the corner of Hyde and California. Dead of night, streets utterly empty, a sheen of bright rain covering the cable-car tracks. I looked at Erik. He didn't even look like himself. The profile had changed. There had been some genetic restructuring since I'd last seen him. It was impossible that this person could have ever been my friend, someone I drank with, went to ball games with, someone whose office I'd go to now and then for no other reason than to put the feet up and shoot the bull about life's possibilities.

"Why are we going to my apartment?" I said.

"Light changed," Erik said.

I glanced up. The red had finally turned to green. Nothing was automatic anymore. I had to think for a moment that green meant go, then I accelerated into the intersection.

"Why are we going to my apartment?" I repeated. "Is Kate there?"

Some anger came to Erik's face. "Would you please just forget about Kate and drive!"

At last we reached the corner of Van Ness and Union. I parked in a red zone and cut the engine. Soft rain fell against the metal roof.

Erik nodded toward the apartment. "You first."

We walked across the street and I got out my keys, trying to find the right one. My heart was going like crazy. Was Kate up there? Was she alive? Erik stood behind me, shifting his body weight from one foot to the next with rapid, jerky motions. Finally I found the key and let us in.

Fifty-four steps, me in the lead. At the landing Oscar heard us and let out a screech. Lola came out to greet me and, when she saw Erik, bolted back into the room. The only witness to Sonia's murder, and she remembered well.

In the living room Erik motioned me to sit on the couch, and he reached over to turn on the lamp on the end table. Then he dropped into the armchair. In the silence Erik began rubbing his left hand over his face, again and again, stretching his features like something in a funhouse mirror. With the other hand he absent-mindedly reached into his pants pocket and withdrew a gun. He held it carelessly, unthinkingly, as if it was a handful of forgotten junk mail.

"Kate is fine," he said. "I haven't seen her for a week. But I needed something that would get you to leave the police station and come with me. I'm sorry if you were worried."

"Thank God." I closed my eyes and kept them closed for a few seconds. On the entire drive back I had been picturing Kate in every other way but alive and well. I'd seen her savaged, gutted, drained of blood. Now I saw her as she truly was, sleeping peacefully on the floor of her Carmel apartment. I leaned down through the fantasy and kissed her softly on the cheek, unnaturally warm with sleep. Tucked her in. Good-bye. When I opened my eyes Erik was still there before me.

"Why did you do it, Erik?"

"I've done many things, Quinn." Erik kept rubbing his face. "Why did I do what?"

"Kill Sherri Kaline."

For a long time he didn't answer. Then he quit rubbing his face and sighed. "It was the only thing that could be done. It wasn't a matter of choosing from a range of options."

"Don't play games with me, Erik. I need to understand."

Erik paused a moment. He bit his lower lip so hard I thought it might bring blood. Then he pushed himself abruptly out of the armchair and walked to the dining room window. "I watched my father die of cancer," he said. "Swore all his life he wouldn't die in a hospital, with tubes and cords and machines. So when he got sick we kept him at home, took care of him there."

I scanned the area for a weapon. Nothing. Not even an ashtray to throw. Not that I could have thrown one anyway. I had no feeling in my arms. They were just two dead things attached to my body.

"What does your father have to do with Sherri?" I said.

"You wanted an explanation. I'm giving you one."

A tense silence filled the room, then Erik continued. "Toward the end my father and I would sit up in bed and watch television together. He'd talk about his pain. After a while that was *all* he could talk about. How he always figured there was a ceiling to pain. You know, it hits a certain point and then levels off. But the cancer taught him differently. There was no end to pain. It simply got worse and worse and worse. Only death released you. Death was inevitable because it was the only release."

"Erik—"

"You're not seeing it, are you?" he said. There were tears in his eyes, but he was smiling. "Then let me be mundane and literal for a second. I went to Sherri for therapy, okay? Just like I went to Ireland for therapy. We fell in love. I hate to say love, because nobody knows what love is anymore. Give your kids lemonade. They'll *love* you for it. Your engine *loves* high octane gas." He began speaking rapidly, as if the quickness of his speech would keep something terrible at bay. "We loved each other. But she was the therapist, I was the patient. That's a no-no." Erik wagged his finger back and forth. "You can't do that. Ethics. Standards. Sherri couldn't do that. She was too fucking noble for that. Until she met Ronald Hemming, of course." Erik stopped. He took a deep breath, tilted his head back, and stared at the ceiling. His eyes shone in the off-light, brimmed with tears.

I looked at his face, and my mind went back two years. It went back to a small town near the Oregon border, in the dead of winter. Erik needed a signature on a legal document and I joined him for the trip. That afternoon a very important football game was on television, and it was all Erik could talk about. We were hunkered into our hotel room with chips and beer, going over last-minute strategy, when a drunk cowboy ran his pickup truck into a telephone pole and knocked out the town's electricity. Erik was frantic, but when the shock wore off he snapped his fingers and announced his solution. Lugging the television out into the parking lot, he set it on the hood of his car and proceeded to wire it up to the automobile's cigarette lighter. In a few minutes we had half the town gathered round the car. "All right," Erik had said. "This is it!" And he'd turned on the engine. The television flickered briefly to life, wavered, and then died on the hood in a cloud of smoke, steam, and scalded wiring. We'd stared open-mouthed at what had happened, and then Jesus did we laugh. The townspeople shook their heads and walked away, and we laughed and laughed and laughed. That was Erik. That was my friend. His eyes were brimming with tears then, too. But they were tears of laughter, not pain.

"Screw it," Erik murmured at last. "It was doomed from the start. Inevitable, just like my father's cancer."

His voice was soft, but the temples were throbbing and his face was suddenly flushed and alive.

I cleared my throat. "Then you couldn't—"

"Wait a minute!" Erik interrupted. "I know what you're thinking. I'm not stupid. Guy has a problem, therapist lends a loving ear at two hundred bucks a pop, and the guy thinks she's the only person in the world who truly understands him. Am I right?"

I nodded. Erik was suddenly a long ways off. He was stepping back through the smoking rubble, scanning the blackened floor of consciousness for the bits of evidence that made Sherri's murder both necessary and inevitable. It was important to keep him wandering. We could be Hansel and Gretel together. Take his hand and lead him far, far away to forests dark and deep, then leave him there, lost and alone. It was the only chance I had.

"So what happened?" I said.

"I'll tell you what happened. What happened was Sherri's code of ethics turned into a tower of Jell-O when she met Ronald Hemming. *That's* what happened!"

Erik put the gun on the coffee table in front of him.

"Sherri and Ronald Hemming had an affair?" I said.

Erik made a face. "Affair. I love the words we use to describe tawdry, back-room fucking. Yes, they had an affair. Funny what happens to ethics when the right buttons get pushed. I bet the two of them had some real laughs over Erik Paige. Laughed their asses off."

"So that was it," I said. "You killed her because she betrayed you."

Erik focused on me for the first time. "Of course. You act like betrayal isn't a perfectly good reason for killing someone. It is. Because it doesn't just stop with betrayal. That kind of hypocrisy, that willingness to turn your back on something true and good and real and go instead for . . . for garbage! That sort of thing cannot be allowed to exist. It breeds. Proliferates." Erik paused, smiled to himself. There was no remorse here. He felt good about his revenge.

"Why are you telling me this?" I said.

"Because I don't want you to think that I just went bursting in like some overheated jilted lover. I don't want people to cheapen what I did. It was brilliant. I followed them around, saw where they went—what hotels—out-of-town spots. I found out Hemming was a professor. Even sat in on some of his classes." Erik smiled. "Can you picture that?"

I looked at the fire poker, hanging on its rack to the left of the fireplace. I imagined what it would take to reach it. Three steps, minimum. The armchair would be between us once I got there, screening me. Erik wouldn't be able to get off a clean shot without moving all the way to a point behind the couch. It was a chance. Remote, but a chance.

"Let me finish it for you," I said. "You killed Sherri so that Hemming would know that a message was being sent to him. You took the method right from his own textbook. Dante. Bertrand de Born. The person who split people up in life, divided himself in death."

Erik nodded. "I'm still amazed how you caught on to that. But yes. That was it. The last thing I wanted was for the police to arrest Hemming. I wanted him to suffer. I wanted him to regret every morning he woke up to find himself still alive."

"He was there the night you killed Sonia, wasn't he?" I said softly.

Erik nodded. His eyes lowered. "He came after you. They made love and he left. I was watching from across the street."

"Then you killed her?"

Erik nodded.

"And that's why there were no fingerprints," I said. "You wanted to erase Hemming's presence in the apartment."

Erik nodded again. He was somber, looking down at his shoes. His neck was so rigid the tendons stretched against the flesh. "I'm sorry for what happened with Sonia, Quinn. I really am. I know that you two had some history together. But she was giving pleasure to Ronald Hemming, and when I tried to talk to her about it, to make her stop, she got distant and strange and paid no attention. You either take something all the way or you don't take it at all. Love, pain, doesn't matter. Sonia was giving Hemming something that he had to be denied."

"But why did you bring me into it?" I said.

Erik looked directly at me. "You brought yourself in. You were the one who talked to Ludmila and Hemming and went off into the Haight. So I helped you along a little. Why not? More salt in Hemming's wound, and you could feel like you were doing something for Sonia. But I never intended for you to get caught up in this. I really didn't. When Mark McCumber came along I hoped that would end it. End your involvement in it. I warned you in Carmel to lay low. Remember? Then later I tried to stop you from breaking into Hemming's house. I watched out for you, Quinn. You don't realize it, but I did. You're my friend."

He nodded to himself, scratched his chin, and gazed out at the dark bay in the distance. In the course of his speech he had picked his gun up from the coffee table and now it dangled loosely in his hand. I glanced again at the fire poker, at the stretch of floor I would have to cover to reach it.

Erik said, "I had to kill Hemming earlier than intended."

"You made him write the suicide note?"

Erik nodded. "You were in danger. I lost track of how all this would look through *his* eyes. Of course he would suspect you. Of course he would think that you were me, and a cornered animal is liable to do anything. When he came over to your house that night, parked out front . . . that's when I knew it was over. After you called me I went over and killed him. He went into the water that same night. Too bad. It was perfect. Sherri was gone. Hemming was over the side of the bridge. Mannion was happy. You had Kate. I had Ireland . . . " Erik blinked away a sudden tear. "You shouldn't have taken the photograph apart like that," he said. "You really shouldn't have done that. It was a terrible thing to do."

"I needed to know, Erik. I'm sorry."

"It was a terrible thing to do."

I couldn't answer. I couldn't fill up the silence.

Erik was really working his jaw. His eyes shot up at me, alert and combative. "You think I'm crazy, don't you? I don't have the green drool or the rolling eyes, but you think I'm nuts."

"No," I said. "I don't."

He shook his head and looked away, and the tears welled again in his eyes. "The hell with it. Who cares? Hemming got what he deserved, and so did she . . . "

A single tear streaked his cheek, and he reached up to wipe it away. My decision was instantaneous. I lunged for the fireplace, rolling along the floor to avoid gunshots. I went hard into the wall and yanked the poker from its stand and scrambled behind the armchair. My body cringed against the hail of bullets. Nothing. When I looked up Erik was still standing at the window, gazing at me with utter calm.

"What are you doing, Quinn?"

"Put the gun down, Erik."

"Are you going to hit me with that thing?"

"Put it down!"

Erik brought the gun up and gazed at it. It was like he was trying to understand the small piece of forged metal. A strange communion.

"I was foolish to have thought we could do this," Erik said. "But you'll know what I'm talking about one day, Quinn. You'll know, and you'll remember this night."

He raised the gun. I instinctively ducked, but the gun was not aimed at me. Erik put it against his temple and closed his eyes.

"Erik!"

I rushed him with the fire poker and tried to knock the gun from his hands. But I missed and the two of us fell back hard against the dining room table and up against the window. It cracked, I felt it start to give, and for one sickening moment there was the sensation of a four-story freefall. But the window held. We bounced back against the table, and then there was a small, percussive clap like the slamming of a cupboard door and something hit me hard in the chest. I grabbed onto Erik's coat and went down. Going down was the easiest thing in the world.

Erik stood over me, encased in silence, face warped with horror. My shirt was streaming red. Insides strange. Cold and hot, like I'd swallowed an enormous ice cube.

Erik dropped to his knees, put his hand on my chest, and stood back up. The hand was wet with bright red blood. Then he was gone, and I could hear the telephone being dialed. In a moment he was back, down on all fours, his face close to mine. I felt him stroking my arm, soothing the shock from my body.

"Help is coming," he said. "I called the ambulance. Christ, Quinn! Why did you have to do that? Shit!"

I tried to speak, but words wouldn't come. Then Erik's expression changed. He stood, took a deep breath, and looked out the window. "I'm sorry, Quinn. I meant what I said about taking something all the way. Please forgive me."

He raised the gun and pulled the trigger. Glass shattered. Blinking wildly, still alive, he backpedaled, fleeing from himself. Then he pitched forward, toward me, the remains of his face gaping at the impossibility of its own death. He made one last guttural noise, gazed at me questioningly, and crumpled to the floor.

The silence throbbed. Erik lay three feet away, on his stomach, the shredded face angled toward me. I held my own wound with my right hand. Blood leaked through the fingers. My breath was sounding stranger. Full of air pockets. Like sucking the last drops of a milkshake through a straw.

The pain was more than pain. It sent the needle whanging off the machine. Bright light slammed in my eye sockets. I pushed but couldn't move. Arms of foam rubber.

The phone rang. My eyes jolted open, and I realized they'd been closing. Erik's wide dead eyes rested on me. Fluid gargled out of the back of his head, and a liquid the color of engine oil trickled from his mouth. I couldn't move my head. I couldn't move anything. The ice had melted and spread but now it was freezing again, tightening me up. The answering machine automatically clicked on, and Hank's voice filled the room.

"Hello, answering machine. It's just you and me, kid. Pull up a chair, fix a drink for yourself. Your master is down in Carmel stacking boxes and getting laid." Hank sounded a little drunk. "Just got back from San Jose. Carol's over at the grandparents with the kids. Nobody to tell my triumph to except you, so blow the dust off your microphone and listen up."

I tried to move to the phone. Managed to roll on my side and that was it. Hank's voice went on.

"I will now try to re-create, to the best of my substantial abilities, the comedy routine that has the name Hank Wilkie tripping across thousands of South Bay tongues. Well, hundreds. Okay, a lucky couple dozen."

The machine cut him off. Moments later the phone rang again. The message played. Then Hank's voice was right back on. "I've got nothing but time, answering machine. I can do this all night. Okay. Where was I? Oh, yeah. Thought of this a few weeks ago when I was listening to the radio and the test of the Emergency Broadcast System came on. You know, that obnoxious shrill thing they blast in your ear. Anyway, I got to wondering what a disc jockey on the Emergency Broadcast System would sound like."

The machine cut him off. Ten seconds. Erik's dead eyes gazed through me. Then the phone rang again. Hank's voice was back and he hadn't missed a beat.

"The Emergency Broadcast Station deejay. Because I figured it would all be business as usual—you know, the morning commute, except there are nuclear bombs hailing down from all over. Would they have music? Weather? Sports? Imagine what the traffic report would be like." Hank started imitating the sound of helicopter blades, then the tinny voice of a man talking into a microphone. "This is Live Chopper Two over the Bayshore Freeway. Not a good commute today, Harry. The left two lanes have melted, and the Army Street on ramp is glowing red. Highway Patrol on the scene, but rubberneckers have things backed up to the Candlestick Park interchange, and—"

Dead. Then his voice was back. "Never mind. Tell your master to call me when he gets home, and have him give you more than thirty seconds a shot. This time *I'm* hanging up on you. May your microchips be eaten away by futuristic termites."

My breathing was worse. Hurt to inhale. Really hurt. This was death. The hurt gets so bad that one time you decide it would be better not to breathe and that's it.

There was movement near my head. I looked as best I could. Lola. Eyes wide, ready to bolt. I opened my mouth to call her and only a thick gurgling sound came out.

I closed my eyes. Better like that. No Erik. No cat. No dead eyes to usher me along.

I gave up the struggle. Rested against the pain and felt my body stretch and grab, ebbing into nothing.

30

S EE AGAIN?"
I rolled over onto my back and Cort and Matty crouched down and peered at the fresh scar on my stomach. It had replaced the floating thumb trick as the most fascinating thing about Uncle Quinn.

The hot, dry Mexican sun was already tanning the scar away. Hank and Carol were farther down the beach, hand-in-hand. We were about six hundred miles south of carpeted dog kennels, day-care car pools, and "Dumbo's Circus."

"Where's the bullet?" Matty said.

"They took it out."

Cort, the three-year-old, poked a finger at my leg. "Bullet there?"

Matty made a face. "No it isn't."

"They took it out, boys."

Matty and Cort thought about it for a while. "Where did they put it?"

"Probably in the garbage. Bullets are very bad things."

The boys nodded gravely at what bad things they were, but you could see they would've given every toy in the toy box to hold a bullet in their hands.

Then Matty said, "I know where starfish are. Gold ones."

"Really?"

He nodded hard. "Want to see?"

"Why don't you bring me one first?"

"After that you'll come see?"

"Yes."

"It's a deal?"

"Yes. But first bring me one."

The two boys jumped up and raced off down the beach, Matty in the lead, Cort toddling after. I rolled over onto my stomach and looked out at the chalk-white mountains in the distance. We were a hundred miles south of Tijuana, on the Baja Peninsula. Everybody likes jungle with their coastline except me. I like my beach life simple. White sand, white mountains, blue sky, blue sea.

I took a deep breath and reveled in the hopelessly exotic experience of actually being out in the sun again. It had been a five-week kaleidoscope of day and night, night and day, bottles and tubes and doctors staring down at me, trying to look brave and optimistic.

I remembered some of it. Kate. She had come, then left, crying. Lots of visitors. Ludmila, Carol, Mannion, friends I'd forgotten I had. One morning Roscoe showed up at my bedside, a Band-Aid over his eyebrow. He gripped my arm with a powerful hand. "What happened with the giant?" I'd asked.

Roscoe smiled gently, his voice almost a whisper.

"Small ax always chop down the biggest tree, y'know."

One afternoon after it had been determined that I was definitely going to make it, Hank came in and sat at the edge of my bed and filled me in.

Erik's apartment had yielded the evidence of his obsession with Sherri Kaline. More doctored photographs, imaginary letters written to himself in his own hand from her. He had even gone to a hobby store and bought a pile of Irish stamps so that the envelopes would look authentic. It was a love so strong that it deviated into madness. When she started her affair with Hemming it was too much for Erik to handle. So he killed her, re-created her as Brigid O'Malley, and began the delicious, deliberate process of driving the interloper, Professor Hemming, mad. The process was uncompromising. When Sonia did not heed Erik's warnings, even she had to die. She was the true victim in all of this. A free-spirited girl who happened to get involved with the wrong man at the wrong time. The world is full innocent bystanders.

And when it came time for Hemming to die, Erik had abducted him, killed him, and then tossed him over the bridge, leaving the tidy package in the front seat so that Mannion could wrap up his investigation. My paranoid vision over Chinese food in Monterey had been true. Somebody *had* run from the hastily parked car. I just saw the wrong person running.

Professor Hemming was, in the end, what he appeared to be from the start . . . an academic who cared very much about securing tenure and rising in the university world. Someone who had found in Dante an explanation for the evil he had been exposed to as a boy, and who had moved far away from the child-sized caskets of Luray, Virginia, only to encounter evil of another sort. Hemming must have known in his final minutes that the book never closes on tragedy. All ends are open ends. Like Walt's story of the drought, how the memories of long-buried sorrows slowly came to the surface, snagged in the limbs of submerged trees.

After I was released from the hospital I tried to dig back into Erik's past, to flesh out some telling detail of mental illness that would make it all understandable, the way I had with Hemming. After all, Erik had been my friend. I trusted him, and was shaken on more fronts than one. We live in a cause-and-effect world, and I needed a cause. But Erik Paige, knowing all the bureaucratic buttons to push, had managed to erase his past with an efficiency that made Hemming's pale by comparison. I found nothing. Perhaps the "cause" was something I would not have recognized if I had seen it, anyway. Few are as vivid as child-sized coffins. Maybe Erik saw something the rest of us couldn't. Maybe, finally, he had recognized the bent elbow of the traveling projectionist.

Carol's laughter snapped me back to the present. I sat up and watched her as she threw a well-directed clump of sand in Hank's direction. They headed off a little farther down the beach, stopped, and embraced each other.

I reached into my duffel bag and pulled out the shabby letter and unfolded it for the fifteenth time. It was moist, and starting to tear in the crease marks. I put on sunglasses and read.

Dear Quinn:

I hope you understand why I had to leave the way I did. I was at the hospital thirty-one days in a row (I counted) for ten-hour stretches. My diligence was exceeded only by Hank's, who sat in front of your room like some mythological guard, armed with his *Merck Manual* and screening all the medication the nurses were bringing in. The doctors were furious, but he didn't care. You have a great friend there, even though he will probably deny that he spent any time worrying about you at all.

I couldn't take it, though, and when they finally told me you were going to make it, I decided it was time for me to leave. Last thing a recuperating outdoor psychologist needs to come home to is a woman pressuring him for answers.

I'm doing fine. Many friends still here. I live in a funky little fixer-upper three-room house near the river. No bolted-in sunset paintings, but my old armchair would be comfortable here.

By the way, I hereby bequeath that armchair to you, should you care to have it. It's in a friend's garage in Pacific Grove, 184 Lighthouse Avenue. Funny, but remember that broken wine glass? A friend of mine here thought it was damaged in the move and threw it in the garbage. An understandable mistake, and the more I thought about it, the right thing to have happened. Broken is broken.

Was it presumptuous of me to think that you would want to share a life with me? Perhaps. I'm a great one for presuming things. Sometimes it gets me in trouble, sometimes it serves me well. I presumed, after all, that you would want me to invite you to my apartment that first night in Carmel, and look what came of it. But I suspect you are more like Sonia than you think. I often recall the story you told me of how you looked through the kaleidoscope and wanted one of the nine, and she said you could have eight. No matter what, I'm afraid that I would never have more than 8/9 of Quinn Parker, and I want it all. Naive or greedy? Probably both.

Anyway, let the girl have her illusions, so when the sleet is blowing off Lake Michigan I can get indulgent and melancholy and think of what might have been. Kisses for Lola.

Love, Kate

P.S.   I'm not really so glib. This is
       the third draft. It took that long
       to pretend that walking away wasn't a
       kind of small death for each of us.

I folded the letter back up and put it away. Off in the distance a half-dozen seagulls circled the white mountains, and then were gone. I was grateful for the knot in my throat, the slightly blurred vision. We need all the small affirmations of our humanity we can get in an era that increasingly has made our personalities airtight; spot-checked daily, guaranteed to resist heat, cold, and exposure. A slip of paper tucked next to the heart. Inspected by number five.

The beer was getting warm despite the best efforts of the ice cooler. Time for a *tienda* run. Some chips, *cerveza,* maybe stock up on the Cure while I had the chance. I saw a few hangovers coming up in my immediate future.

I sat up and put my shirt on and looked south down the length of cove. I'd been to this beach once before, with Sonia, not long after the Scandinavian Club thing in Berkeley. We'd hopped in the van and logged a long afternoon and evening in Mexico. Slept on the beach, watched the stars. Made love. Her skin had tasted like sea spray.

"It scares me to think we'll be gone someday," she'd whispered that night while the stars blazed over the Sea of Cortez. "A blip of a blip of a blip, that's all it is, and if you waste any of it you're crazy. Let's not waste it."

And she'd drawn me closer, down to the warm sand, and I'd turned my back to the stars.

I smiled, remembering. Rules change, but this doesn't. Plug in Castro or Bush or the Ayatollah—the anthill shifts, different people get rich, different people get shot, the ants scurry to the books and type in new rules and call it history.

Matty was suddenly standing in front of me, Cort huffing along behind.

"Here." Matty held out his open palm. It held a small gold starfish. The two kids were beaming.

"That's a nice one," I said.

"Come on," Matty said, turning to go back down the beach. "Now you come and see. It's a deal, remember? You said."

I stood and brushed the sand from my swimsuit. Goodbye, Sonia. Sleep well. A blip of a blip of a blip. Your blip was briefer than most, but maybe you suspected as much. See you ten thousand nights from tonight, give or take some, depending on my luck.

I followed as Cort and Matty ran down the long sweep of beach. A deal is a deal. And besides, they know where the gold starfish are.